THE CROSSROADS

BY RALPH RYAN

WILDFIRE: Memories of a Wildland Firefighter

THE CROSSROADS

A Journey of Discovery

RALPH RYAN

THE CROSSROADS: A Journey of Discovery

www.RalphRyan.com

Printed in the United States
First Printing 2016

ISBN-13: 978-1537724300
ISBN-10: 1537724304

This book is dedicated to all who have lost loved ones.
Love never dies!

BROKEN SPIRIT

CHAPTER 1

Cedar wood crackling in the fireplace saturated the home with a warm, sweet scent that normally put Rose and Jason at ease. Flames flickered on the knotty pine ceiling and bare walls as if they'd laid claim to their home. Jason sprawled out on the futon in front of the fireplace, took the pills the doctor said would stop the voices and downed another swig of whisky. Rose's voice echoed from the kitchen. He cried out, "Come in here babe; sit with me for a while." He waited like he'd done many times before, but she didn't appear. "If you don't come out here, I'll down all these pills and come to you!"

'Oh, this again,' he heard her say. 'Pills won't bring you home. We'll meet again, but only when it's your time.'

"My time," he shouted before gulping down the last of the whisky. As he did, his eyes scanned the ceiling until they settled on a pine knot that resembled a Martian's face. He laughed remembering how Rose had discovered it while they made love in front of the fireplace one evening. It freaked her out. She felt uncomfortable having those big eyes staring down on her. Jason yelled at the Martian, "What the hell are you looking at?"

'A pitiful man,' the Martian said with a laugh. 'She's gone...not coming back...so why don't you get on with living or get on with dying!'

"Why?" Jason cried, "Why her? She didn't deserve to die; she spent her life saving people. Who would do this to such a beautiful person?"

'Maybe the devil wanted her soul and now he's coming for yours!' The Martian teased.

"Screw you and the devil," he shouted struggling to his feet. "He doesn't have her soul and he's not getting mine without a fight." He stumbled down the hallway into the baby's room and fell to his knees. A torrent of tears splattered the carpet. The love, hope and promise that once filled the house was gone, now only a hollow shell of a home and a man remained. He returned to the living room; slumped onto the futon and the haunting vision returned.

****

He was fixing dinner to coincide with Rose getting home after her shift at the hospital when the phone rang. Her voice was filled with concern over a patient that was in a life or death situation and needed to be flown to the UC Davis Medical Center immediately. He pleaded with her to come home, but her shift change hadn't happened yet and she was still the flight nurse. She consoled him by saying she'd be home in a couple of hours and to go ahead and eat. He hated these situations where she was about to be off shift and had to stay. It didn't happen often, but she was able to ease his worry. Her last words of, "I love you so much, sweetie," rang in his head. An hour later, another call came. He was expecting it to be her saying that they were leaving UC Davis and she'd be home soon, but it wasn't. The shaky voice of a hospital official informed him that the life flight helicopter had gone down and rescue personnel were on the way to the crash site and that was all they knew at the time. The phone fell from his hand.

He ran around the house in a delirious panic, not knowing what to do, when the phone rang again. He picked it off the floor to hear Scott's voice, his best friend and an EMT on the hospital's ambulance. "Jason, I heard about the crash on the scanner; hang tight, I'll be right there." He continued to pace the house as if in a haunting nightmare. When he heard Scott's truck pull into the driveway, he ran outside yelling, "We have to get to her, Scott, NOW!"

Scott grabbed him forcefully by the shoulders, "I know, I know, but they're not by any roads. All we can do is monitor the scanner."

Their worst fears materialized from a shaky voice on the scanner, "We've reached the crash site; there are no survivors."

The words ripped through him like a lightning bolt forcing him to his knees. He desperately grasped at Scott, but he became a blur slithering out of sight. The ground slammed him into a black hole with no outlet. Days passed before he was able to force his eyes open. He awoke in the hospital with a tube in his arm. He wished he was with his wife, wherever she'd gone, but the smell of life disappointed him.

Scott arranged his release back home with strict orders from the doctor. He was to be monitored closely with no alcohol or drug consumption other than what was prescribed for his severe case of depression.

Scott agreed and after settling him in, he had to get back to work. Even though his family and friends tried to keep him consoled, the nightmares took control: Helicopter blades shearing off tree tops as screams streamed from the cabin filled his reality. When the helicopter disintegrated into a ball of flames, it carried with it his reason for living. At her memorial service, he felt like the waking dead, unable to focus on or understand anything.

****

It tormented him over and over again. He screamed, "WHY, WHY?" He saw Rose's hand stretch out to him, but he was just out of reach. A cold sweat coated his body, the pill bottle cracked under his grip. The Martian giggled, 'Go on man, do it!'

He fumbled with the cap when 'NO!' echoed off the bare walls. Rose came back into view. She grabbed his hand and forced him to the fireplace. The bottles flew into the flames against his resistance, melting into a fiery array of colors. He stared at the dancing flames and cried, "Baby, if I can't be with you, I don't want to live. I have no hope, honey, I'm broken down."

She led him back to the futon and lay with him whispering softly, 'We'll get through this together, my love.'

With those words his nightmares turned to dreams. Their life together flashed before him like an old reel film flickering one cherished moment after another. Meeting Rose at a Blues festival on the slopes of Mt. Shasta was the turning point of a confused life. After dating and driving back and forth to the Bay area for months where Rose lived, he realized he couldn't live without her. When she accepted his proposal of marriage, his life had finally found true meaning. They rented an apartment and being a carpenter, he designed their dream home and together, they built it. When she announced she was pregnant he became the happiest man in the world. Having been adopted, he always wondered about his linage. Now he could concentrate on his own family. They were so happy with a promising future. He passed out with her cradled in his arms.

CHAPTER 2

He woke before the sun crested the mountains and sat on the porch torn by uncertainty. What he was about to do would surely bring grief to his parents, siblings, and friends, but he couldn't bring himself to tell them in person. Riddled with guilt, he began writing his parents a letter instead:

Mom and Dad, I have to get away. I've lost everything and my world is crumbling in front of me. Please don't worry about me for I will carry with me all the love you have shown me throughout my life. I need to find answers and even though you are my parents, I still have issues about my adoption and need to find closure.

He read it over and said, "Crap." It crunched in his hand. He tried again:

Dear Mom and Dad, Please forgive me for not discussing this with you in person. I know you've told me over and over again that things would get better with time, but they haven't. With Rose gone and my job and house, I've lost my identity. I need to get away for a little while. You've been the best parents in the world and I love you all very much. Please try to understand. I'll be back soon. Your loving son Jason.

He put in in an envelope and sealed it. The Harley motorcycle Rose had bought him for his birthday was packed and ready to go in the garage. He had no agenda, no direction known, only the knowledge that he had to get away. When the sun broke over the mountains, he heard Scott's pickup rumbling up the driveway. Scott was like a brother to him. They grew up together, did everything side by side. They were the best man at each other's weddings, the best of friends. Scott got out of his truck with Sarah, another lifelong friend. Sarah was once a flame of Jason's and when he married Rose, she decided to pursue her career and didn't date anyone, which puzzled him. She hung onto their time together even though Jason insisted she move on with her life. Scott eyed the bike in the garage, "Going for a ride?" he asked.

Through clouded eyes he said, "Yes."

"Where are you going?" Sarah asked.

"Don't know," he mumbled.

Scott stared at Jason, overwhelmed with pity. He had difficulty comprehending all the misfortune his best friend had endured in the past year and even more difficulty talking about it. Jason had the look of a man who'd lost all hope. Scott eyed Sarah with concern before probing, "Do you want some company, bro?"

"You've done enough for me already, Scott. Thanks for storing my stuff. You can have whatever is left in the house. I don't plan on ever coming back here. I left a message with the bank that the keys will be in the door." He pulled the letter out of his pocket and handed it to him, "Could you please drop this off at my parents' house."

Scott took the letter, his voice trembled, "Where are you going? You can't just run away. I know you've been hurting, but let the people who care about you help you through this. You should go talk to your parent's; they've always been there for you, just like we have. Don't just write them a letter, that's not fair."

Jason muttered, "Nothing seems to be fair anymore."

Scott raised his voice, "Running won't solve a damn thing; besides, Rose would've wanted you to stay and work it out."

Jason looked at his friends. "I need to do this. I don't have anything left. I can't live in my own mind anymore. I need to find answers or it'll drive me insane, if it hasn't already."

"Answers?" Scott answered quietly, but firm. "Answers to what? She's dead. You can't bring her back, Jason!"

Sarah kicked his shin, eyeing him sternly. "Back off, Scott, he doesn't need this."

"He needs to get it together...before it's too late," he whispered to her as Jason straddled his bike. He caressed the medicine pouch strapped to his handlebars and said, "She's coming with me!" Then he fired up the bike.

Sarah cuddled into him, squeezing tight. "I know you have to do this, Jason. I'll be waiting for you when you get back. Please take care of yourself." She kissed him and whispered, "I love you," and backed away.

In a battle of wills, Scott stood in front of the bike staring his friend down. Jason stared back until Scott gave in and approached him. "I think you should reconsider this, Jason. You can stay at my place; we'll find you another job, get your house back. What do you say?"

Jason hugged him saying, "Not this time, bro," and revved the engine. Scott backed off and cringed when the shifter settled into first gear. Jason nodded to them and slowly glided down the driveway.

Scott kicked at the ground, "I wish there was something we could do."

Sarah sighed, "By letting him go, we are. He needs this more than we need him."

TESTING THE WATER

CHAPTER 3

The frigid morning air stung Jason's face. His nostrils quivered and became numb. Fluid slithered down his lip. A quick backhand swipe added yet another layer to his stained gloves. His cheekbones tingled as tears welled in his eyes. It was damned cold.

The winding tree-lined road that took him from his mountaintop home had an agenda of its own. It splintered into a maze of quiet suburban streets. The deep rumble of his motorcycle faded in and out, echoing off parked cars and homes; homes placed side by side gazing at one another in a mirrored reflection of suburbia with the only form of individuality being their color scheme.

The freedom he enjoyed while riding his bike was gone. Sadness had shackled him to a dark and frightening place. Order and consistency were no longer a part of his life. As he wrestled with his emotions, an ear-splitting blast from an air horn jolted him. In his rear-view mirror he saw the front of a semi-truck bearing down on him. Every muscle tensed as he yanked the throttle wide open catapulting him into the morning rush hour traffic. Gas and diesel fumes assaulted his lungs and the sobering slap of fear forced him to concentrate on the road.

He turned off Interstate-5 onto Highway 44 heading east. Valley oaks gradually gave way to stands of pines and firs. Their shadows streaked by him like a strobe light. The air became cooler as he gained altitude. Volcanic rocks appeared to grow out of the landscape. Coming out of a sweeping turn, the dome of Mount Lassen appeared before him. He felt arms squeezing his waist in acknowledgment. He went to touch them, but they weren't there. A chill rippled through his body.

He turned into the park and stopped at the fee station by Manzanita Lake. Mount Lassen reflected off the glass-like water. It was so clear he thought he was looking into a mirror. He didn't recognize the reflection that was looking back at him. The image scared him; piercing blue eyes stinging through him; no longer his eyes, no longer his life. He jumped on his bike and drove on. Passing the lake, the landscape transformed from mixed conifers to a forest of stubby Lodge Pole pines that grew out of a solid layer of volcanic debris. Boulders of every size and shape studded the ground. The landscape again transformed at Emigrant Pass where the Devastated Area revealed the destruction caused by the volcano's eruption and the resulting mudslide. Beyond, healthy forests reappeared. He passed Summit Lake and more memories. He held back the tears and wondered; *'has my life been reduced to memories?'*

The parking lot for the trailhead to the summit of the volcano came into view. What lie ahead had his body trembling. A few steep, twisting turns later the sparkling water of Lake Helen filled his vision. He pulled into the picnic area and stared at the water remembering Rose's exact words, "This is where I'd want my ashes to be scattered when my time comes, babe. I can't think of a more peaceful place to rest."

His response had been forceful, "Don't say that sweetie, you're not going anywhere. We have a long life ahead of us."

The water sparkled like her eyes. He removed his boots, rolled up his pants and cradled the pouch with her remains. On wobbly legs he entered the frigid water. Tears streamed down his cheeks as he kissed the pouch before opening it. From his hand her ashes entered the water. They shimmered through the water brushing against his legs. The urge to join her was overwhelming. He walked deeper until a stern, 'JASON!' boiled up from her ashes.

"Why?" He screamed, "Why you, Rose?" as he struggled back to shore and fell to the ground. He strapped his boots on, attached the pouch to his bike and while the bike warmed, he looked at the stunning aqua green water proclaiming, "You're where you wanted to be, Rose. I love you, baby."

He left the park trying to stave off the pain. Glimpses of Mount Shasta reminded him of happier times. He merged onto highway 89 and headed for those days. Coming out of a sweeping turn onto a long straight stretch of highway, Mount Shasta punctured the sky above the streaming forest. Granite ridges seemed to grow out of the glaciers and the Red Banks looked out of place from the rest of the mountain. Jason knew the ridge well; he'd rested there often during his many treks to the summit.

****

The mountain beckoned him on, causing him to twist the throttle wide open. Trees streamed by creating a steady blur that hypnotized him. The mountain grew rapidly. He felt strongly connected to it and wondered if his ancestors had originated from there. It was a holy place, not only to the local Indian tribes, but also to the Spiritual pilgrims of the world who ordained the mountain a chakra of the earth. He laughed at how Rose's expression resembled that of a young child; filled with awe when he told her about the Modoc Indians, the Mount Shasta Grizzly Legend, and the Klamath Indian's legend of chief Llao of Mount Shasta and chief Skell of Mount Mazama, and how they fought each other with fire balls from atop their mountains. Her expression rapidly changed from awe to fear when he gave a history of Mount Shasta's UFO sightings, the obscure existence of the mountain dwelling Lemurians, and the Big Foot legends.

As he was about to crest a hill, a blinding object filled his vision. As he closed in on it, he had to blink a few times to make sure he wasn't day dreaming. A metal dragon glistening in the sunlight on a trailer parked on the side of the road with the hood of the truck open forced him to throttle down. Passing the truck, he saw a man with half his body bent inside the engine compartment. The sound of his bike shifting gears caused the man to poke his head out. He watched as Jason did a U-turn. He pulled in front of the truck as the man turned. He had a long, well-groomed beard that tapered to a point obscuring part of his Green Bay Packer football jersey. His bright blue eyes gleamed as he yelled out, "Hi there, thanks for stopping," as Jason approached the truck.

Jason's voice boomed, "I had to," pointing to the dragon.

"Oh, that's my burner bro, Gabe's, creation," radiated from him with admiration. "Had a friend in Mt. Shasta help out with the hydraulic system, I'm heading home, but my truck seems to have other plans."

"Well, let's take a look at it," Jason said as he offered his hand, "I'm Jason."

"Dave, nice to meet you."

"So, what's the problem?"

Dave tugged at his beard, "It started miss-firing coming up the hill and then it just died."

As Jason traced the battery cable connections, he had to ask, "What's with the dragon?"

Fire jumped from Dave's eyes as he paced around Jason proclaiming his alliance, "I'm a burner."

Curiosity spiked Jason's words, "A burner?"

Dave's brows rose, "You've never heard of the Burning Man Festival?"

"Been caught up in other things," echoed Jason's existence. "I've heard of it, but don't know much else."

Positive energy poured from Dave's body and words. "Well let me clue you in. Every year during the last week of August, tens of thousands of people gather in Nevada's Black Rock Desert." He pointed to the east, "It's just over that mountain range there. We create a temporary metropolis in the middle of the desert and call it Black Rock City. It's dedicated to community, art, self-expression, self-reliance, and fire."

"Really," Jason said as he ruled out the battery cables and began tracing the spark plug wires. "Sounds like a commune to me."

Dave threw his arms up in the air, "Oh, it's much more than that; it's about spiritual enlightenment, inspiration, self-confidence, and the art work," he pointed to the dragon, "is out of this world. People come from all over the world to experience its radical form of individuality. It's the biggest support group in the world where the human spirit can be lifted to unparalleled heights."

Jason's body tensed, the tightening around his mouth didn't go unnoticed. Dave earnestly remarked, "If a person is in need of some fulfillment...some inspiration...a reason to anticipate again, then Burning Man is the place that can provide that."

The shrug of Jason's shoulders caused Dave to dig deeper. "I've been a burner for decades, and I've seen people arrive there looking for answers and by the end of the week, they're a totally different person than when they arrived. They found answers to the most secret questions. Everyone seems to benefit from the experience, maybe you could too."

Jason lifted his head from the engine, "Spark plug wires are good." He returned to the engine and examined the coil as he softly said, "What makes you think I'm in need of answers?"

Dave pulled at his beard again, "Because I can see it in your face and eyes. Since being a burner, I've learned to read people and that's the vibe I'm getting from you. Am I wrong?"

Was it that obvious, Jason wondered? "Okay," he confessed, "maybe I'm in a bad spot right now, and maybe I'm looking for answers...aren't we all?"

Dave touched his shoulder compassionately, "What's the question?"

Jason muffled in response, "Good question!" Then excitement took control, "Ah, ha," he said. "I found the problem, look here; the coil wire snap is loose and broken. That's what caused the miss-firing. Do you have any foil?"

Dave opened the cab door and rummaged around. He returned with a piece of foil. Jason crammed some into the plug cap and like a doctor in the operating room asked with his hand out, "Do you have any tape?"

"Yeah, I have some duct tape."

Jason taped the coil wire to the coil body and ordered, "Give it a try."

The engine rumbled to life. Dave let it idle for a while before turning it off. He jumped out of the truck and grabbed Jason's hand vigorously, "Thank you, thank you. You saved my butt." He reached into his pocket and pulled out some cash.

Jason laughed, "It was nothing; put that back in your pocket." He looked at the dragon, "Can I check it out?"

Dave's nervous energy topped out. He pushed Jason toward the dragon detailing its creation, "Like I said earlier, this is my bro, Gabe's, creation. He was a garbage man for some time and spent years collecting scrap metal and trinkets and then he spent more years welding it all together."

Upon closer inspection, Jason's jaw dropped. It must have been thirty-feet long, ten-feet tall, and its tail curled like a scorpion's. Its breast plate was crafted from rusted round point shove heads. The legs were made from old driftwood pieces, and the body sprouted thousands of horse shoes, gun parts, swords, chains, door knobs, kitchen utensils, tools, car emblems, wire insulators, pad locks, antlers, wood stove doors; you name it, it had it.

Dave crawled onto the trailer and opened a door to the dragon's belly. He crawled in and sang out, "Watch this!" The head swung back and forth, its mouth opened and closed. He handed Jason a stick with a wick at the end and lit it. He ordered, "Hold this up by its nostrils." Jason carefully lifted the flame and suddenly a whoosh of fire shot out of its nostrils. The head swung around spewing fire, causing the passing motorists to stop and glare.

Dave shut it down and excitedly said, "Hell of a creation, isn't it?"

Jason gawked, "Never seen anything like it."

"Well, at Burning Man," his voice sailed, "there's plenty of out of this world wood and metal sculptures, not to mention people, and at the end of the festival, the wooded effigies' are burned. That's why it's called Burning Man. You got to check it out man." He stroked his beard while looking at his new friend. He rushed to the cab and returned with a note pad, and then words as sincere as Jason has ever heard came at him, "Tell you what, since you won't take payment for saving me here, I'm going to leave you a ticket at the will call booth at the entrance of our festival. Just tell them who you are and they'll steer you to our theme camp. Don't worry about a thing; I'll have food, drink, and shelter for you. I guarantee you right now that you'll have the experience of a lifetime. What do you say?"

Jason thought a moment, "Okay, if I'm in the area, I'll definitely check it out."

Dave's look mirrored suspicion, "And if by chance you can't make it, I'll give you my contact information and I'd be honored if you come by and check out my shop."

"What kind of shop?"

"I own Autoshield Automotive Services. I do windshield repairs and replacement, and clear bra coating. I have a warehouse in Rancho Cordova. I also have parties there for my burner friends. Now, I'm proud to say I can buy you a beer because a guy bought the warehouse next to mine and with lots of help, he built a craft beer joint called Claimstake Brewery. Best damn beer I've ever tasted."

Jason took his information with the desire to spend more time with the man and his Burning Man adventure. He reached out, "Thanks for the invite."

Dave bypassed his hand with a genuine hug. "Thank you bro; I'll plan on seeing you in the fall."

"Yeah," Jason said. "I think I'd like that. Drive safe and don't forget to get a coil cable as soon as possible."

****

Dave watched as Jason motored away. He got up to speed and was so absorbed by the Burning Man narrative that the road that split to the ski resort came up suddenly. A quick U-turn had him heading for the ski resort nestled at the base of the mountain. If any place felt like sanctuary this was it. He'd met Rose there during a Blues concert, proposed to her further up the mountain, and married her on the lawn where they'd met.

He entered the ski resort's parking lot. The mountain loomed large before him. At the top, a lone Cirrus cloud stretched from the summit as though the peak had a hold on it. He parked and sat on the bike while scanning the Alpine forest below the summit. He located the canyon where he'd proposed to Rose and decided it was a fitting place to spend the night. He headed across the meadow, stopping at the exact spot where his world had changed forever. The meadow came to life. Children ran past him laughing while he zigzagged around older couples nestled in lawn chairs and young lovers sprawled out on cozy blankets. Little Charles and the Nightcats ripped out their jump style Blues from a large stage. Crisp piano notes spurred on a booming bass, as frisky guitar notes accented the ensemble.

His heart pounded recalling the moment he'd first saw Rose. She was sitting next to his chair when he returned from a beer run. He believed her to be the most beautiful girl he'd ever seen. Her tanned legs, petite body, and big green eyes froze him in his tracks. He knew at that instant he had to talk to her. Luckily, he managed to start a conversation with her, which let to dancing and more conversation until the last note rang out. When she agreed to give him her phone number, he realized he was on a mission and became focused on keeping their feelings alive.

****

The wind rustled the hardwood leaves and whistled through the pines. Birds added an endless melody. He hiked for an hour before coming to their sacred spring. Water gurgled out of the ground nourishing a huge fir. He sat at its base and looked out over the Sacramento River Canyon. To the north, the sparkling water of Siskiyou Lake shimmered from a light breeze. To the south, the polished granite spires of Castle Crags rose out of a lush green forest. Rose said of the Crags, "They look so out of place, standing all alone, shinning above everything else. It feels like I'm looking back in time." Jason realized he was now looking back in time.

He fought off the tears while remembering how he had rolled onto his knees in front of her from that very tree with an engagement ring clasped in his hand. He said to her, "I can't begin to tell you how much you mean to me. I've never been so happy in my life. You're an angel. I want to spend the rest of my life with you. Will you marry me?"

When she heard his words and saw the ring, her breath escaped her. She cried, "Oh my God Jason, you took me off guard. Yes baby, I'd love to be your wife."

Smiling at the memory, he took a beer out of his pack and raised it to the sky, "Rose baby, I miss you. I brought you a beer, come on down and join me." The gurgling creek and the wind singing through the trees gave him peace. He finished the beers and fell asleep in her arms once again.

CHAPTER 4

In the morning, a bone chilling cold drove him from his sleeping bag and a dream where he felt like he was falling through the air. It was a peaceful fall, not like previous dreams where he felt helpless and feared how it would end. It drove him to his feet. He packed the beer cans away and headed down the mountain. To his delight, nobody had messed with his bike overnight. While it warmed up, he noticed a halo-like cloud sitting on the summit of the mountain and felt it was a sign from his lost love.

At the crossroad of Highway 89 and I-5, he looked down both directions. "Which way?" he asked looking at the pouch hoping Rose would give him some direction. After some indecision he said, "Well, baby, we came from the east, no use going back there. We could head north to Yreka and take Highway 3 over to Weaverville, then to the ocean." After thinking about it, he yelled above the rumble of the motorcycle, "No, baby, how about we go up to Grants Pass and head over to Crescent City? Yeah, that sounds better."

He topped off the fuel tank and bought three breakfast burritos in the city of Mt. Shasta before heading north on Interstate 5. Outside the city, Cinder Cone loomed large. A high desert plateau opened up sporting ranches with lush green trees and cattle roamed the range. A barn by the freeway had a sign painted on it declaring, 'The State of Jefferson.' The air became cooler as he approached the Siskiyou Mountains.

He moved his arm to rest it on her knee, but found nothing. Not fearing for his safety, he twisted the throttle wide open until the vibration rattled his helmet. He didn't let up until the plateau merged with the mountains and the highway twisted up the grade through sharp sweeping turns. At the summit, a sign welcomed him to the state of Oregon.

The descent was steeper than coming up. His hands tightened on the handlebars as he took the turns faster than he should have. Adrenalin shook him out of his state of reflection. The freeway leveled out at Ashland and he set the cruise control until the traffic through Medford demanded his attention. Once outside of town he settled back into cruise mode. At Grants Pass, he turned west onto highway 199 toward Crescent City and the ocean. Another high desert opened up and the afternoon heat forced him to shed his riding jacket. When he reached Gasquet, the cooling coastal influence brought him comfort. Smelling the salty air he knew the ocean was near.

****

Crescent City was clear and warm. He stopped to fuel up and had lunch at the Lighthouse Restaurant. It overlooked the dock where fishing boats of all sizes bobbed in the light swell. After eating a sourdough bowl of clam chowder and fish and chips, he strolled along the pier to settle his food and watched the boats trickle in with the day's catch of crab, salmon, and rockfish. He looked up at the sun and a sense of urgency forced him back to his bike. He figured he had a few hours of riding time left before the sun set. Highway 101 took him along the coast and within an hour he was back in Oregon. Riding through the coastal town of Brookings, the main street overflowed with people exploring the flea marts, souvenir shops, and restaurants.

An hour later he was in Gold Beach, which looked like Brookings, with the same small town feel. "This wouldn't be a bad place to live," he said to the pouch, "maybe someday we'll check it out more thoroughly." Leaving Gold Beach, the highway paralleled the coast. Large rocks rose out of the ocean with many of the tops splattered white from the birds that roosted on them. Small beaches dotted the coast. He stopped and walked along the surf feeling peaceful, so peaceful; guilt riddled him. Why couldn't Rose be here to feel this? He kicked the sand yelling against the stiff onshore breeze, "Rose, baby, I'm going to put a little of you in the ocean so that you can travel the world."

Her ashes warmed his palm. He touched his tongue to her as he waded into the freezing water. Before releasing her, he said, "You're in me too, baby. Here you go, take the current; I'll see you on the other side." She disappeared into the water. With reluctance he waded back to shore and walked in the sand until his feet dried. He didn't want to leave, but the sun signaled it was time to press on.

Within half an hour, a steep downgrade brought him into the little town of Port Orford. Tired from the day's ride he pulled into a motel at the edge of town. It offered a view of the ocean and across the street a sign read, *Battle Rock Monument*. He checked into the motel and ran across the street to check it out before nightfall. A historical plaque detailed the struggles between a local native tribe and a group of settlers that had also laid claim to the area. A huge rock outcropping punctured the shore, close enough to access at low tide. A trail snaked through the brush and trees to the top of the rock. It was on this rock where the settlers fended off the Indians until help arrived. Jason shook his head in disgust predicting the outcome of that battle.

Hunger pains forced his attention to the street. He noticed a few restaurants as well as gift shops lining the highway, but their lights were off and no cars were in the parking lots. Weekday, he thought. They must roll up the sidewalks before sunset.

A lone sign across the street flickered with life. He saw two cars in front of the place and closed in on it. The sign read, *Paula's Bistro*, and he rushed in the door fearing they would lock him out. The wooden floor creaked under his weight and the first thing that caught his attention was an oil painting on the wall. He locked into the girl's eyes. They were as blue as his and as life-like as any he'd ever seen in a painting. They followed him to the bar where a bartender, sprouting a full beard, was wiping down the counter and talking with his lone customer. The bartender greeted him. Jason noticed more paintings on the walls and asked the bartender, "Who painted all these pictures?"

The bartender pointed toward the kitchen saying, "Paula, the owner and cook."

"Is she Irish?"

"Actually, she's German," he said. "Why do you ask?"

"I just noticed the blue eyes, freckles, and red hair in the paintings. They look Irish, very captivating."

"If you're interested, she does sell her art," he added.

"I'm riding a motorcycle; no room for a painting."

"She'll ship them anywhere, does it all the time for people who stumble onto the place."

"She's very good."

"Wait until you taste her cooking," he said with a smile. "Can

I get you a drink?"

"Do you have any micro-brews?"

"Ever tried Moose Drool Ale?" he asked.

The words swirled in his head. Who would want to drink moose drool? He laughed at the name and ordered one up. "What's good on the menu?" he asked.

"Whatever Paula cooks is good, but the seafood platter is her specialty. Fresh from the ocean today, you should give it a try."

"Thanks, I think I will," Jason nodded.

"One sea food platter coming up," the bartender said as Jason took a long swig of the beer. It tasted good and he finished it quickly.

"And I'll have another drool," he said with a laugh.

The patron at the bar had been listening and noticing Jason's riding leathers asked, "Where you heading?"

Jason didn't rightly know and answered, "North."

"Better check the weather report," he added, "there's a cold front moving through tomorrow. That's why we had such a colorful sunset tonight."

Jason raised his beer in acknowledgement and said, "I'll do that, thanks for the heads up."

A woman came out of the kitchen with a large steaming bowl. She placed it on the counter in front of Jason and said, "You looked hungry, so I made it special for you. No skimping on anything here."

The aroma rising from the bowl made Jason's stomach growl. He grabbed a fork and said, "Thank you," before digging into the crab, salmon, clams, and rockfish.

Paula watched him work on the bowl and laughed, "Hungry as a moose, huh?"

Between a mouthful, he added, "Haven't been eating very well lately. This is the payoff, though." He soaked up the last drop of sauce with sourdough bread and rubbed his stomach. He had to sip his last beer because his stomach was so full. He thanked the bartender and Paula, and then walked along the beach beside Battle Rock to settle the food. Once in the motel room, he turned on the news. The man at the bar was right; a cold front was moving in and expected to hit land fall by morning.

The thought of being stuck in a motel room for a day was

more than he could bear. He pulled his rain gear out in preparation. In the morning, the sky sprouted a blanket of fast moving clouds as he headed north out of Port Orford. They streamed in not delivering the punch the news had predicted. A light drizzle pestered him all the way into Washington State.

The drizzle turned into a light rain, then a heavy downpour. It was coming in sideways off the ocean, splattering on the inside of his riding glasses. The cold and wetness numbed him. He squinted through the lenses to find the fog line and followed it until a rest stop sign came into view. He slowed and took the off-ramp. It twisted toward the coast where a patch of blue sky appeared. Within minutes the storm passed inland basking him in sunlight. He set his rain gear and leathers on a rock to dry. As they steamed under the sun he walked along the beach. In the distance, he noticed a silver beam of light emanating above the ridgeline. It drew on him and he decided to seek it out.

CHAPTER 5

When he returned to the parking lot, his leathers had dried and the beam still lingered. He suited up and rode toward it. Clearing a ridge he found the source. A tall church steeple reached for the heavens and at the very top, sunlight reflected off a cross. Below the church, a harbor revealed fishing boats bobbing in the surf like sea gulls.

He rode to the pier protected from the wind by an oblong inlet with moss covered cliffs on both sides. A rustic restaurant overlooked the harbor. He stretched his sore muscles while walking down the timber planked pier. The smell of seaweed and salt kissed his lungs. He watched an angler slowly steer a small boat into the harbor. The captain, and only occupant, docked his sea battered boat close to where Jason was leaning on the rail. A burly statue of a man with a thick gray beard began off-loading his boat. His skin appeared like leather with deeply etched wrinkles lining his forehead. He squinted up to Jason and in a deep, crusty voice, said, "Afternoon mate. Beautiful day wouldn't you say?"

"Yes it is," Jason answered back.

He climbed up a creaky ladder, stood before Jason and declared, "I'm Richard Cain, my grandfather fished these waters, and my father did too, and now I'm fishing 'em." He cocked his head at Jason, "You fish, lad?"

Jason laughed. "I fish lakes and rivers; never been on the ocean." He offered his hand saying, "I'm Jason McPherson." The man's grip cracked his knuckles.

"Never been on the ocean?" he mused with suspicion. "Where're you from, lad?"

"I live by Shasta Lake in Northern California," then mumbled to himself, "Or did."

"You're a long way from home, what brings you to our small inlet?"

Jason thought a moment and lied, "I'm on vacation."

The man repeated, "On vacation, huh? I was born and raised

in this town, never been on a vacation, never needed one for that matter." He lifted a crate filled with crabs saying, "Here, give me a hand with this, will ya?"

Jason didn't mind helping Captain Cain unload and secure the boat. He stacked the crates onto a cart and pushed it alongside the Captain while he explained, "We have bottom feeders like cod and halibut. I troll for salmon, perch, flounder, sole, and pot crabs. There's a bounty out there; I rarely come in empty-handed." Before reaching the restaurant, Richard stopped in his tracks and said, "I've been thinking about what you said back there, you know, about never fishing the ocean."

"Never," Jason confirmed.

"Well, being since you're on vacation, how about we go out tomorrow, I'll show you my way of life," and with a chuckle added, "at no charge."

Jason thought about catching something bigger than a trout and answered, "If you're serious, I'd love to."

Richard laughed. "When it comes to fishing lad, I'm always serious. Tomorrow it is, be here at 6:00 AM sharp."

Excitement filled Jason for the first time in a long while. He pushed the cart with a renewed sense of vigor. A cook met them at the service entry and grabbed a crate. Jason grabbed one and followed the cook, while Captain Cain joked with the staff, "That pesky sea lion followed me the whole day. You'd think she liked me or something. I know she wasn't hungry, because I fed her before setting out."

*****

When Jason came out of the kitchen, he faced a tall girl with an apron wrapped around her waist. Her turquoise eyes stunned him. She looked him up and down with her hands on her hips and broke into a smile. He returned the gesture. Captain Cain noticed and said to her, "Kristy, give this lad a meal of my catch, he was very helpful to me today."

Kristy broke Jason's stare by saying, "Follow me." She led Jason to a window table overlooking the bay. "I'm Kristy and you are?"

"Uh," he mumbled, "I'm Jason."

"Welcome to our town, Jason. I noticed you ride in. Richard is quite the character. He's been supplying us with fish and crab for as far back as I can remember. My parents own this restaurant and I work here during my summer breaks from college."

"Which college," he asked.

"The University of Washington in Seattle"

"What are you majoring in?"

"Promise not to laugh?" she said with a giggle.

"I promise," Jason said wondering why he might laugh.

"Believe it or not," she said, "I'm a psychology major." Jason didn't respond immediately and she went on, "I think the mind is a fascinating thing, as well as the people who try to manage it."

"It sounds challenging," Jason said remembering his junior college days.

She added, "I like the challenges. How long do you plan on staying here?"

"I don't have any immediate plans, but I do need a motel room, any suggestions?"

She looked out the window and pointed. "Follow that road to Richard's house, the blue one up there on the corner, and turn left. There's a motel about two hundred yards up the road with a covered parking area. The fog in the morning puts a layer of saltwater dew on everything. Your bike will be somewhat protected there. Now, what part of Richard's catch do you want?"

"I had a seafood platter in Port Orford last night, how about some salmon."

She nodded, "Paula's place, right?"

"Yeah, how'd you know?"

"Only bistro in town, she's quite the cook; love her artwork too. Fresh salmon it is." She scurried away shadowed by his stare. Her friendliness put him at ease. She returned with a filet of salmon that covered most of the plate. Spices rising off the plate made his mouth water.

"Here you go, Mr. Jason, can I get you anything else?"

"Do you have Moose Drool Ale?"

She laughed; then in a provocative tone said, "Sounds kind of slippery to me, but there's nothing wrong with that."

"Then I'll have one," he said wondering about her comment.

She returned with the beer, touched his shoulder softly and said, "Enjoy your meal."

Looking at the plate, he said, "Thanks, how could I not!"

The soft pink flesh peeled easily from the skin. He closed his eyes while chewing, savoring it as if it were his last meal. He finished the whole plate. When Kristy returned, she looked at it and said, "You have a hearty appetite. I was betting you wouldn't be able to finish it all."

"I've been in the saddle all day, didn't stop to eat until now. That was the best salmon I've ever tasted, my compliments to the chef."

"You're going to have to do that yourself," she said clearing the table.

"I will. How much do I owe?"

She stopped cleaning giving him an unsettling stare. "What," he said in defense.

"You heard Richard; the meal is on the house." She paused and then said, "With one condition."

"What's that?" he asked.

"You have to stop by and see me tomorrow."

Jason smiled at her, "I think I can do that." He put a ten-dollar bill on the table as he stood up. "I've had a long day and need to get some rest. Thanks, Kristy."

He walked into the kitchen and thanked the chef. As he headed for the door, she reiterated, "See you tomorrow, Jason?"

He nodded with a smile.

*****

Captain Cain was in his yard and signaled Jason to pull over as he approached the house. When the motorcycle went silent, Cain said, "Jason, my lad, we still on for tomorrow?"

"Aye Captain, we shove off at six," he said in a pirates tone.

Richard laughed and put his arm around Jason's shoulder and guided him toward the house. It was a modest home with uniquely shaped pieces of driftwood placed around the yard. A small plump woman with a broad smile came onto the porch. She greeted him with a Scandinavian accent. "I saw you two getting along down by the dock and from what Richard was saying about your love for fishing and knowing him as I do, I expected him to invite you for a trip." She smiled at her husband with great affection and pointed to two weathered wicker rocking chairs on the porch and said, "Please sit." She scurried into the house before Jason could decline the offer. She returned with two cups of coffee. They sipped coffee while rocking to their own rhythm.

After a short silence, Richard said, "You know, I miss having young people around. Most of the kids around here end up leaving for more exciting places. Kristy always comes back, though. She's a good girl. I noticed she has eyes for you," jabbing Jason's arm.

Jason reflected a moment; then said, "She does seem like a nice girl."

"Too bad she's a girl," Richard added.

Jason tilted his head quizzically and asked, "Why do you say that, Captain?"

"Well, if she were a boy, I think I'd have a better chance at keeping my boat in the water when I get too old to fish alone." With a barrel laugh, he added, "Which was probably yesterday. I don't have anyone to carry on, now."

Jason sensed sadness in his voice. Mrs. Cain came out of the house and asked Jason, "Do you want more coffee?"

"Oh no, thank you," Jason graciously replied. "I've had a very long day riding. I should get some rest for tomorrow."

She took his cup, "Richard is excited that you want to go fishing. He doesn't get much company on the water these days. It should be fun for the both of you."

Standing up, Jason added, "I'm looking forward to it and thanks for the coffee." He shook Richard's hand, "See you tomorrow, Captain." The last rays of sunlight streaked through the clouds in an array of soothing colors as he pulled into the motel lot. At the desk, he requested a wakeup call for before dawn.

CHAPTER 6

Reaching for the phone in the morning, he realized how sore his body was. The previous day's ride was over six-hundred miles and he felt it in every muscle. A long, hot shower gave him comfort. He craved coffee and rode through the morning fog to the pier. The restaurant lights were on and the smell of coffee drifted across the parking lot. Kristy greeted him at the door and escorted him to the same table where a steaming cup of coffee awaited him. "I'm surprised you beat Richard here, he's usually the first one to show up," she said. "Did you sleep well?"

"Like a rock."

"Do you get seasick?" she asked.

"I don't know, never been on the ocean."

She handed him two pills. "You'd better take these just in case. The sea can be very unforgiving."

From outside the restaurant, a crusty voice sang out, "Oh, what do you do with a drunken sailor, what do you do with a drunken sailor, what do you do with a drunken sailor, early in the morning."

Kristy laughed, "Your Captain has arrived."

She poured Richard a cup of coffee and he quickly drank it. "Not going to catch any fish sitting around drinking coffee," he said pounding the empty cup on the table. Kristy shrugged her shoulders and pushed Jason out the door behind him.

Jason followed Richard's instructions. "Check the oil, lad. The dipstick is on the right side of the motor. Then see how much fuel is in the tank." Jason checked the oil and told Richard the fuel level was at half a tank. The motor rumbled to life, sputtering and misfiring until it warmed up. When all four cylinders were firing smoothly, he ordered Jason to release the tie downs. The old boat creaked on the swell to open water. Jason felt the rhythm of the swells course through his body. A salty spray gently kissed his skin. Sunlight burned patchy holes in the fog as the pier disappeared. Captain Cain was at the wheel singing.

Jason yelled into the cabin, "Captain, I have a question for you."

"Shoot, lad."

"What do you do with a drunken sailor?"

A loud belly laugh erupted from the cabin, followed by, "Well lad, you lock him in the cabin with the Captain's daughter, of course." His laughter rode on the wind. The boat broke through the fog bank to warm sunlight. The motor fell to an idle. Captain Cain moved to the gunwale, bent over, and raised a crab pot from the depths. He emptied the scurrying critters into a crate and released the pot back to the sea. Jason positioned himself over the rail and grabbed the next buoy. They worked as a team until the last pot filled the second crate.

"A bountiful harvest today, wouldn't you say, lad? Now it's time for you to catch some ocean fish." He set up a couple trolling poles off the sides of the boat and while explaining to Jason how his homemade cruise control device worked, one of the poles bent sharply toward the water. Jason rushed to the pole and gave it a yank. The salmon dove and Jason let out a yell as he fought the fish. The fight was nothing like a river trout. He wished Scott could be there with him to feel the power of an ocean fish and to relive the times they'd spent together without a care in the world. He felt like a kid again.

Richard shut the motor off and worked his way to the back of the boat to get the net. In passing, he said, "You remind me of my son." Jason glanced at Richard and noticed his eyes tearing up. As he fought the fish, he wondered about the comment. This was the first time he had mentioned anything about having a son. Richard netted the fish and said, "You're going to have some fresh salmon again for dinner, son."

Jason was stuck on his comment and said, "You have a son?"

"Oh, I didn't think I said it loud enough for you to hear. I was just remembering better times. You're a lot like our Thor."

Jason debated inquiring further, but still asked, "So where is he now?"

A quiet, "He's dead," trembled from the captain's mouth.

The swell picked up causing Jason to feel sick to his stomach. He leaned over the gunwale and puked. When he was purged, he said, "I'm sorry, Richard."

"Don't be, son, most people get sea sick the first time out."

Jason's voice quivered, "I mean about your son."

"Oh," Richard said, "it happened many years ago, but I still miss him dearly. We fished all the time. Most of the pain is gone now. I've come to accept it as God's will."

"What happened to him, if it's alright to ask?"

Tears formed in Richard's eyes as he said, "He'd just graduated from high school and instead of partying with his friends, he did his usual routine after school; he took his kayak out for a ride." He choked while saying, "He never returned." After a deafening silence, he continued, "When his kayak washed up on shore, everyone with a boat went out searching for him, but we never found him."

Jason's heart pounded. He wanted to consul the old man, but his own pain grew and clouded his thinking. "Fucking ocean," he yelled.

Richard seemed annoyed by his comment, "I blamed the ocean, I blamed myself, I even blamed God, but none of that brought my son back."

"To hell with God, then," Jason said, remembering saying those exact words during Rose's service after the pastor said it was God's will that took his wife and unborn son.

Now Richard seemed insulted and demanded, "Why would you say such a thing? What do you know of God?"

Jason response was furious, "If he is so damn righteous, why did he take your son and my wife and unborn child? Where's the righteous in that?"

Richard slumped in his seat. "You lost your wife and child?"

"Yes, Richard, I lost my family and if it was God's will, then to hell with this God. He might as well be the devil."

Richard sat up; his eyes bulged, jaw muscles tensed. Jason feared he'd gone too far but after a moment of awkward silence, Richard acknowledged, "I felt the same way for years. I hated God, until I realized that that way of thinking was destroying my life, my marriage, and turning me into a bitter old man. I needed help, so I embraced God instead. He saved me from certain doom. Look around you Jason. In the big picture, we all came from him. Where did this ocean come from, the fish that sustain us, the sun, the clouds? Everything comes from God and if you believe in him, you don't need to ask WHY. It's asking for answers that diverts our attention from the ultimate truth. My only goal in life now is to serve him."

"You put a lot of blind faith in him," Jason said standing up. "He took your son and my family and now you don't want me to ask why, just accept it as God's will?"

"He wanted my son and your family to do his work, not ours. One day, we will be with our loved ones. I was blind before I put my faith in him. At least now, I have peace. I can see by what you're saying that you don't have peace or faith in your life. If you want to see what real misery is, read the book of Job in the bible, then you'll see what I'm talking about. You do know the bible, don't you?"

"Yeah," Jason said with distain. "I was brought up a Catholic; was even an altar boy." He paused and then added with more distain, "Unmolested!"

Richard shook his head, and Jason continued, "I felt the spirit when I was young, but as I got older the commercialized and political aspect of religion turned me away."

Richard mused, "It could save your life."

"Life?" Jason yelled, "What life? I don't have a life, just misery."

Richard paced the deck, stopped in front of Jason and demanded, "Who? Who worries about you riding that motorcycle to wherever you're going? You should confide in them, allow them to give you support, to give you comfort. There has to be someone!"

That someone was Rose and after serious thought, Jason said, "I guess my folks and my siblings worry about me, but sometimes I'm not sure."

"What do you mean by that, lad?"

Another demon surfaced in Jason. He looked Richard hard in the eyes and said, "I was adopted. I've never met my real parents. It's all a damn mystery."

Richard eyed him sternly, "We're all children of God."

Jason mumbled, "To hell with God. Why did he put me on this earth without parents to care for me? Where's the righteous in that?"

"You just said your folks; I'm guessing you meant parents,

didn't you?"

"Yeah, they raised me, but our blood is different. Look at me; I'm a blue-eyed half-breed. Do I look like a McPherson to you? Wouldn't you want to know your heritage if you looked like me?"

"Blood is a fluid, it sustains our bodies; it doesn't necessarily sustain our mind or soul. Why torture yourself about it?" Richard demanded.

"If you didn't know your blood line," Jason scoffed, "you might think differently."

Richard took a deep breath. "Have you ever asked your parents about it? You seem to be reaching out blindly." When Jason didn't answer, Richard added. "That's the recourse of a desperate soul. In due time, your desperation will transition into emotional hibernation and your relentless hunger will be sated only by you feasting on your own soul."

"Who gives a fuck about my soul?" Jason shouted. "The only love I've ever known to be all mine died in a helicopter crash. One love was real, the other wasn't born yet. My child would've been the answer to my hunger. Now the devil is the only one who cares about my soul."

"It's good to let it out, son, just between you, me, and God."

Jason turned to him, "Really, Richard? It's the pressure from the outside that's causing the pressure inside. I'm having a hell of a time dealing with it."

"Then get it out, lad. Give it back to the outside."

Jason sighed deeply, "I wish it was that easy, Captain."

"All you can do is to keep trying. Keep searching for your peace of mind and remember, sometimes it doesn't matter what you believe in, just as long as you believe. Look at me, I found peace. It's out there for you too; go find it and then go home. I fear where the ripples of your decisions might take you. Don't let the devil know your weaknesses or he will get your soul."

Jason mulled over his words, "I don't have much use of my soul anymore." They rode the waves back in silence. Approaching the dock Richard said, "Easy now lad, keep the bow away from the dock. Let the swell push us in."

When the boat was close enough, Richard hopped onto the dock and secured it. Kristy's silhouette could be seen from the restaurant's window. Jason's slow movements and unsteadiness was a sign of seasickness. When they were within hearing range, Kristy came out all excited, "How was the sea out there today? Did you get sick, Jason? Were the salmon running?"

Richard reined her in, "As you can see young lady, the fishing was good today and my first mate rode the swells like a true sailor. He only puked once."

Kristy giggled, "You men look tired and hungry." She looked at Jason and asked in a sultry tone, "What's your pleasure tonight?" After a pause, she added, "fresh salmon or crab?"

"Let's have both," Richard interjected. "How about we gather in a few hours? It looks like my first mate here could use a nap. Why don't you join us tonight Kristy."

She laughed, "I'll have to check with my boss." Glancing at Jason, she added, "You look pale, I'm going to fix you my secret tonic. It'll instantly settle your stomach and give you your color back."

Jason gulped it down and within minutes, his stomach settled and he felt much better. "Thanks for the cure, I needed it," he said with a forced smile.

"I should patent it," she said with pride. "You can't imagine how many times I've offered it to flatlanders. Go get your nap and I'll see you later."

*****

Riding to the motel, the Captain's words swirled in his head. He remembered seeing a Gideon bible in the drawer by the bed in his motel room. After a long shower, he settled on the bed and grabbed the Bible. He opened it to the book of Job and read until he fell asleep. In his darkness, a verse swirled in his thoughts until the alarm sounded:

"Have I sinned?
What have I done to you, O watcher of men?
Why have You set me as Your target, So that I am a burden to myself?
Why then do You not pardon my transgressions,
And take away my inequity?
For now I will lie down in the dust,
And You will seek me diligently,
But I will no longer be."

On the ride to the restaurant, Jason questioned his very

existence and the inequalities in his life and still could not accept losing the love of his life to God's will. He parked and sat on his bike for a while filled with more questions than answers.

Kristy saw him from inside the restaurant and knocked on the window waving him in. She looked happy as she seated him. Richard and his wife entered shortly thereafter and Kristy scurried back and forth from the servers station bringing them coffee and preparing the table. Richard caught her hand and sternly said, "You're supposed to be joining us. Please take a seat."

She resisted a moment and then plopped down. "I don't get to do this very often. I'm here to work."

"Relax," Richard ordered. "You work too much. It's time for you to enjoy a good meal with good company."

She signaled her counterpart to the table. "We're ready to order."

Richard interjected, "I've already done that."

Plates of salmon, crab, fresh vegetables, salad, and bread adorned the table like Christmas decorations. Richard took his wife's hand and Kristy's. Kristy raised an eyebrow to Jason and bumped his leg. He took her hand and Mrs. Cain's. Richard bowed his head and said, "Lord, thank you for your plentiful bounty and especially for the company of such wonderful people. May your kindness be rewarded."

Kristy and Richard's wife said, "Amen."

Jason looked up to see Richard's eyes on him; he said, "Amen."

Richard nodded and said, "Let's eat."

During the course of their meal, every local that entered the restaurant instantly gravitated to the table to greet Richard and his wife. Jason met the Sheriff, the Mayor, fellow anglers, and the Pastor, who especially showed an interest in him. "What brings you to our little hamlet?" he asked Jason.

Jason didn't know why he was there and instead of sounding aimless, said, "I'm on vacation and just happened to have been drawn here."

The Pastor's quizzical look fell on Richard. He then asked Jason, "How so?"

"I was riding through the storm and saw a break in the clouds down by the ocean, so I followed the sun to a rest stop. While I warmed my bones and dried my leathers, I saw a beam of light being reflected off what I now know to be the church's steeple. I followed it to your town."

With a surprised expression the Pastor said, "I haven't heard that one before. Maybe we'll see you at the source of your draw come Sunday?"

Jason saw Kristy smile, he said, "Maybe."

The Pastor turned to Richard, "Give me a call later," before taking his leave. He shook Jason's hand again and said, "It was nice meeting you, Jason. You all have a pleasant meal."

Richard watched him walk away. With admiration, he said, "Now, that's a fine man there. We are blessed to have him."

Richard's wife and Kristy nodded their heads. Jason figured the man played a large role in helping Richard and his wife get through the loss of their son. After a delicious meal, Richard and his wife took their leave. Jason watched them leave and said to Kristy, "That's quite a couple there! They seem so at peace, considering what's happened to them."

"It didn't come easy," Kristy said. "When they lost their only son to that damn ocean, their lives unraveled. I remember hearing him talk about joining his son. If it weren't for those of us who loved him, which is the whole community, he probably would've never come back from the ocean. Pastor Michael checked on them every day; prayed with them, and gave them strength to accept the passing of their son."

"Do you believe it was God's will that took their son?" he asked.

She appeared confused. "Let's just say I believe it was love that saved their lives. As to how he deals with the loss everyday, that's his conviction. I don't think I could rely so strongly on faith, so I can't answer that. If it was God's will, then I guess I do have a problem with that!" After a pause, she asked, "Do you believe in God, Jason?"

Talking religion made him uneasy. With trepidation he said, "I accused Richard of having too much blind faith. He didn't like that very much. He went on about how I was being selfish and that I was more concerned with my own flesh and mind. He said that by God's grace alone, I will be saved."

Kristy leaned toward him softly saying, "Why would he say

that to you?"

Jason swallowed hard. He didn't want to go through the pain of detailing his loss again. He lied, "I don't know, we talked about many things. I think I challenged his faith too much."

"Yeah," she nodded, "that's one thing you don't want to do with him."

Jason turned the conversation to her, "So, how do you like college and living in a dorm?"

"It's okay, I'm learning a lot and meeting fascinating people, but the thing is; I miss my family and these people."

"I'm beginning to see why," Jason admitted, "this sure seems like a nice place to be from."

Kristy looked at her watch. Surprised, she said, "It's getting late. I need to help clean up. How about if I bring a bottle of wine to your room when I'm done?"

A physical twinge for her surfaced, but his mind scolded him to the point he could only say, "Thanks for the offer, Kristy, but I'm really tired tonight."

"Oh, that's okay," she said with a hint of disappointment. "I do have tomorrow off. Could you take me for a ride on your bike? There's an old coastal road near here I know you'll like."

The idea seemed refreshing. Jason stood, "Sounds like a good plan, how about meeting here after the fog burns off?"

She beamed, "That's around 10 o'clock." She saw him to the door and gave him a quick, unexpected hug and a peck on the cheek. "See you tomorrow, Jason, sweet dreams."

His dreams were far from sweet. His physical attraction to Kristy tormented him. Could Rose ever forgive him for thinking of another woman? Could he forgive himself? Guilt flashed through him like a lightning bolt. He pulled her picture out of his wallet and pleaded, 'Please forgive me, baby, you're the only one for me.'

Her voice startled him, 'Jason, my love, I don't expect you to stop living. You gave me the best life anyone could ask for. You need to move on, baby. I want you to feel again, to be yourself again. It torments me that you can't let go of your pain.'

A tear splattered on her picture. He quickly wiped it off. "But I can't, baby!"

'You must!'

"But how?" he pleaded.

'Maybe God can help you.'

"God," he shouted. "It was God that took you from me. How can I trust in him?"

'I can't find your answers for you, honey. You have to put your faith in something other than me. I'm only a memory now.'

"You aren't a memory. You're here, we're talking."

'Are you sure it's me talking, or is it you?'

"Don't do this to me, Rose. I need you. I'll do whatever you say, just don't ever leave me out here alone, please!"

'I'll promise to stay only if you promise to move forward without me holding you back anymore. That's the deal. Can you do it?'

He caressed her picture. "I'll do whatever you say, baby, whatever you say."

'Then get on with living.'

CHAPTER 7

Pulling into the parking lot, he noticed Kristy pacing in front of the restaurant. She seemed excited and when he turned the motor off, she asked, "Do you want some coffee first?"

"No thanks, I had some at the motel. You look ready, let's hit the road." She settled onto the passenger seat and wrapped her arms around his waist. His gut muscle tightened. Rose had been the only person to ever sit there and feeling someone else's arms around him, a sense of betrayal flooded through him again. He swallowed hard and before starting the bike, he cautioned, "Stay centered on the seat. Don't lead into the turns, let me do that, otherwise it'll affect our balance, okay?"

She gleamed, "Anything you say."

She directed him to an old road where he carefully maneuvered around potholed asphalt. The road led them through stands of spruce and alder, where the scent mixed nicely with the salty air. The trees opened to a sheer cliff that slid hundreds of feet down to the ocean. White crested waves crashed onto the rocks in a steady rhythm. The sight took the breath out of him. Kristy told him to pull over. Not far from shore, a pod of whales broke the surface, spouting water high into the air. Jason had never seen live whales before and the sight transfixed him.

"They're heading north for the summer," she said. "They do this every year at exactly the same time." When the whales went out of sight, she said, "My favorite beach is down the road a ways, let's go check it out." The road gradually lowered to sea level and she tapped his shoulder, "Pull over by that log."

A small cove opened up that stretched a short distance in both directions until the white sand butted up to the cliffs. The winter surf had washed up huge piles of logs. Someone had built a fort with the remnants. As soon as he set the kickstand, Kristy was off the bike and running through the sand. Her shoes flew off, followed by her top. She stopped by the surf and waited for Jason to take his boots off and join her. She yelled, "Come on Jason," like a kid discovering a new source of joy.

He rolled up his pant legs and waded into the frigid water. She seemed unaffected by the coldness and ran through the water like a little child, splashing water at him and laughing. The water numbed his legs and while looking down at the rolling surf, he became so affixed; he almost forgot where he was. Kristy noticed and yelled, "Are you alright?"

"Yeah," he yelled, "the surf has me mesmerized."

"I get dizzy when I look down at it for too long," she said dancing in the surf. "Come on, let's walk the beach." After strolling in silence, she turned to him and asked, "Do you find me attractive?"

Jason stopped, trying not to look at her appealing nakedness. He focused on her eyes and said the only thing he could think of, "Are you kidding?"

She giggled, "I hope my bareness doesn't make you uncomfortable. I spent a summer in Sweden, my ancestral home a couple years ago and nobody wore tops there, so I'm doing what they do back in my parents' homeland."

The word *homeland* stung him. He wished he knew of his homeland. He knew his mother was white and his father was a Native American, but which tribe, where did they conceive him? Kristy interrupted his thoughts. "Well then, why haven't you responded to my advances? I was beginning to think you were gay or something."

He laughed, "Do you always get what you want?"

In a matter of fact tone, she said, "If I want it bad enough, I do."

"You're one lucky girl then, because I've found that you don't always get what you want."

"Yeah?" She said, "then what is it you want, Jason?"

He felt himself breaking down. In a strained voice, he said, "I want what was taken from me."

She grabbed his shoulders, "Someone stole from you?"

"Yes, you could say that."

"Who?" she asked sternly, "Who stole from you? Is that why you're riding all over the place? Are you looking for someone or something? At first, I had this feeling you were running from something, but now I have the feeling you're searching for something."

Jason kicked the sand. He wasn't sure how to answer her questions. If Richard was right, then God took his family and to explain his feelings about that to her would spoil the day. He looked into her sparkling turquoise eyes. They seemed so innocent, empty of life's pain and sadness. He envied her and remembered Richard saying on the boat, "Humanity suffers in life because of the sins we commit." What sin did Rose commit? What possible sin could an unborn child commit? What sin could this young girl commit? Confusion clouded his thinking. If he accepted his loss as Gods will because of man's sins, then why not get on with sinning? He envisioned himself taking this girl and ravaging her on the sand. Why not inhabit the emptiness of her soul and seek no more?

"Jason, are you alright?" He turned and walked away from her. She followed pleading, "Stop, talk to me...please." She stepped in front of him and noticed his eyes filled with tears. "What is wrong, Jason? What did I say to upset you?"

"It's not you," he cried. "It's me. It's every God damn thing. Look Kristy, I'm sorry for putting you through this. My life is one big mess. I lost my wife and unborn child. I lost my job and our home, and I don't know who my real parents are. I feel like I'm being punished, but I don't know what I did. Is God paying me back for my sins or is the devil living through me? I just don't know."

The shock on her face startled him. She backed away without taking her eyes off him. "All I can tell you Jason is that love can conquer all." After a moment of silence, she continued, "There are a lot of people out there that can help you deal with your pain. I could get you in touch with them if you want. My life has been so sheltered compared to yours. If there's anything I can do, please tell me."

"I'll be alright," he shrugged. "But thanks for offering." He walked to his boots and laced them up feeling confused about faith, fate, and her. He could see in her eyes that she wanted him, but this was not the time to rely on someone else. He smiled at her on the way to the bike, hoping she would think everything was okay. He pulled over where they had viewed the whales for one last look, but they were gone. Just outside of town, Kristy tapped his shoulder, "There's a bar within walking distance from your motel, how about we get a drink?

He nodded saying, "Now that sounds like a great idea."

*****

Entering the crowded bar, he noticed fishnets laced with seashells adorning the walls and a large swordfish hung from the ceiling. She looked back at him saying, "Tourists!"

The jukebox sounded out a Credence Clearwater song. They found a small table and when the server arrived, Kristy ordered a margarita and Jason asked for a micro-brew. He powered the first one down, cringing at the carbonation. "Ah," he said returning the empty glass to the table.

Kristy laughed, "You weren't thirsty, were you?"

"Still trying to wash down the road dust," he said signaling the server for another.

Kristy toyed with her straw and asked, "Do you get lonely riding by yourself?"

"Not really, I have so much to think about right now, I don't want to have to entertain someone on top of it all."

"You know," she said leaning toward him, "Just when I thought I had you figured out, I realize you're more complicated than I could ever imagine."

"It comes with the territory," he said. "My life has been a roller coaster, that's for sure."

"I have this feeling," she whispered to him, "Everything will work out for you. If there's anything I can do, and I can do a lot, I'm ready."

That scary feeling about her resurfaced, his words were sincere, "I appreciate that, Kristy. If my life wasn't so messed up, I'd probably take you up on it."

"Tell you what," she said taking a piece of paper from her purse, "I'm going to give you my address and phone number. Keep it safe and if you should ever need to talk or want to see me again, you'll know how to get me."

He put the paper in his wallet, "Thanks, I'll keep it safe, but don't hold your breath."

"I won't," she said unconvincingly. She stood up and said, "What kind of music do you like?"

"Blues, all the way."

"Blues?" she said. "I don't think they have any Blues songs on the jukebox. Let's take a look. My parents listened to Rock 'n' Roll when I was growing up, so that's my favorite."

"Did you know Rock 'n' Roll originated from the Blues?" Jason added.

"Really?" she said, "I would've never guessed. Help me pick out some songs."

At the jukebox, he explained, "Here, Canned Heat, blues based band from the 1960's, and even Aerosmith here has blues roots."

"Aerosmith? No way," She said with a laugh.

"If you don't believe me, check out their *"Honkin' on Bobo"* disc. Just about every rock 'n' roller learned the blues chords before adding their own styles."

"How do you know so much about the Blues?"

He got excited, "I play a couple instruments."

"No way," she said jabbing his arm. "What instruments do you play?"

"Harmonica; blues harp as we call it, and guitar."

"See," she said with admiration, "You're a mystery man, for sure." She blushed as she asked, "Are you any good?"

"There's no mystery in loving music. I love the Blues because it comes from the soul, don't know if I'm good or not, but it works for me."

"So, what else can you do?" She probed while ever so gently brushing up against him.

"I'm a carpenter by trade," he said easing away.

"You're kidding?" she said with a giggle.

"No, I used to build homes for a living, until the economy crashed and I lost my job."

"Let me see your hands," she said reaching for them. She followed his fingers with hers to his palm and then softly stroked his hand. The sensation radiated through him as she said, "Yup, those calluses are working man's hands."

"Told you so," he said.

The jukebox started playing her selections. She swayed in front of him, "Do you dance?"

Jason looked around the room, then at her, and with a laugh said, "Not until I can loosen up my two left feet."

She laughed and led him to their table. Pushing on his shoulder, she said, "Sit down. I want to tell you something."

"What's on your mind?" he asked.

She emptied her glass and gave him a serious look. "What if," she said, "what if I said I wanted to go with you?"

He squirmed in his seat. "You're kidding, Right?"

"No," she said loud enough to attract the attention of the people sitting nearby. She giggled and in a quieter voice said, "I mean, no. I've been thinking about it a lot and why not?"

"First of all," he said pointedly, "I don't know where I'm going next and second of all my bike is loaded, no room for any more stuff. Besides, you have college to go back to."

She leaned close, "Not knowing where a person is going makes it an adventure and I need that in my life. I can travel light and when it's time for school you can drop me off at a bus station."

Jason laughed, "Look Kristy, it's not that I don't like you. In fact, I think it could be fun under different circumstances."

"Different circumstances?" she questioned loudly again. "This would be a perfect opportunity for the both of us; me to move forward in my life, and you to move away from your past." His expression caused her to add, "And another thing, when you go searching for something sometimes you lose sight of exactly what you're looking for. I could help you forget about the bad things that have happened to you."

"I'm sure you could," he whispered. After an unnerving silence, he added. "What would your parents think? What would Richard think? A stranger rolls into town on a motorcycle and takes their little girl away. It wouldn't look good."

"Who cares," she shrugged.

"Well, I do. It's the alcohol talking, you can't be serious."

"I'm talking what's on my mind alcohol or not. It's what I want to do." She signaled the server for another margarita.

"Maybe you should slow down on that."

"You're beginning to sound like my parents!"

He settled back in his chair wondering what was missing in her life. She gulped down the margarita and leaned across the table, "You know something, Jason? Maybe, just maybe, it's better to have loved and lost than to have not loved at all."

She wanted what most people wanted; love. He knew he wasn't the one to give it to her. Finishing his beer, he said, "I'll walk you home."

Her walk showed she'd had too much to drink. At her doorstep, she grabbed him and slurred, "I'm sorry. I don't drink much and when I do, I say stupid things. How about we sleep on it and talk about it after church tomorrow. Will that work? Please say yes."

He whispered, "Okay." She gave him a hug and went inside. He stood at the door thinking, *what have I gotten myself into?* He knew he couldn't be a part of her dream and wished he'd had someone to talk to about it. Consulting Rose was definitely out of the question. Not wanting to go back to an empty motel room, his steps took him back to the bar.

*****

An empty stool at the counter opened up and he took the seat nodding to the young man sitting next to him. He had a pleasant face with few days of growth. After receiving his beer, the man said, "You're not from around here, where're you from?"

Not minding a conversation, Jason replied, "Northern California and you?"

"Right here."

"That's nice," Jason said. "Quite a town you have here."

"Yeah, too small at times, but a hell of a lot cooler than California."

Jason shook his head, "I'm beginning to like the weather here."

Without cause, the man uttered, "It appears you like other things here as well."

His tone sounded offensive. Jason eyed him saying, "I'm not following you."

"The girl you were with, Kristy, I know her. We had a thing in high school."

"So," Jason said, "what's that have to do with me?"

The man looked down as if embarrassed, "I thought we had a good thing going, you know, first love kind of thing, but she didn't want what I did and in the process she took me for a ride, just thought I'd warn you."

Jason heard the hurt in his words. "Thanks for the warning,

but we're not an item and won't be. By the way, what's your name?"

The man perked up. "I'm Stanley, and that's a good thing because I'll tell you a little secret about her."

Jason turned from him saying, "No thanks, I don't need or want to know anyone's secrets."

"Well I'm going to tell you anyway, because I need to. I bet she told you she's on break from college, right?" Jason didn't respond. "After high school she just disappeared, poof, gone, no good-bye, no see you later, just gone from this town in a heartbeat. Her folks said she was off to college, but I think it was for another reason." He slammed his drink down and continued. "I think I got her pregnant and she ran off to get an abortion, that's what I think happened, by God. She doesn't acknowledge me, wouldn't even look at me when you two were in here and that's the way it goes when she comes back. We see each other, but no recognition what so ever and that's been driving me crazy. What if she did kill my child? What would you do if someone did that to you?"

Jason looked at the man firmly saying, "I'm sorry if that's what happened, but it seems like you're not sure about it; maybe you should talk to her and not assume things."

"I've tried, but she won't give me the time of day." He got close to Jason's face and pleaded, "Maybe you could get it out of her."

"No, no, I can't do that," Jason said shaking his head. "I'm just passing through; it's not my business, sorry." He got up from the stool, "I hope you find some peace," and left the bar. Walking to the motel, he thought it ironic that his last remark to the man mirrored what he'd been hearing from a lot of people lately.

He dined at a different restaurant and settled in for the night. The thought of slipping out of town while the town folks were in church crossed his mind, but he wanted to see Captain Cain and his wife again. After a long hot shower, he settled on the bed and flipped through the TV channels. He stopped on the Discovery Channel as it was airing a documentary on wildland firefighters. Being from California, wildfires were as common as snow in the Rockies. His thoughts turned to Scott. When he was a senior, his class went on a field trip to the California Smokejumper base in

Redding and ever since that trip, Scott couldn't get it out of his mind and swore to him that one day he'd be jumping out of a perfectly good airplane with a parachute to fight fire. The videos of the actual jumps with fires raging below put goose bumps on him. What an adrenalin rush it must be to do such work. He knew Scott liked to live on the edge, but this was over the edge. He fell asleep thinking of the people he'd left behind.

*****

Church bells echoing through the hamlet woke him in a panic. He jumped out of bed realizing he'd forgotten to ask for a wakeup call. He dressed quickly and headed to the church. When he noticed a group gathered by the entrance, he let out a sigh and headed straight to where Richard and his wife were. "Good morning, lad," Richard bellowed with a broad smile.

"Morning," Jason answered nodding to them both.

"Almost thought you'd miss the service," Richard joked.

"Forgot to ask for a wakeup call," Jason grumbled.

"Well then," the old man said, "shall we go inside?"

As they entered the large French doors, Kristy slipped in behind Jason nudging him. Turning, he noticed how nicely she looked in her summer dress and hair all done up. He smiled saying, "Good morning, Kristy."

"Great morning, Jason."

They followed Richard and his wife to a pew and seated themselves. Jason noticed the muffled voices of the congregation echo under the vaulted ceiling and the display of stained glass murals adorning each side of the room glistened from filtered sunlight. He felt the holiness. Scanning the pews, he noticed Stanley on the other side of the room. He was nicely dressed and had his head bowed.

Jason remembered the ceremonial aspects of the service from his childhood indoctrination. The standing, sitting, kneeling, fumbling through the bible, the hymn book, and getting stern looks from his mother when he was restless brought back conflicting memories of a young boy who was looking for answers, but to what he often wondered. At least now, he knew what the questions were. The pastor made his way to a nicely constructed pulpit and scanned the pews. He smiled broadly and welcomed the worshipers by outstretching his arms saying, "Come let us rejoice by praising God's name." He led the congregation in prayer and afterwards, "Amen," echoed loudly from the pews.

His smile faded as he looked among his flock. Jason felt his eyes on him when he said, "Today, we shall address the concept of Hope. HOPE," he said loudly, "is a word and expectation that looks forward with anticipation to the future, yet multitudes of people have lost their hope. Some are hopeless about specific areas such as their marriages, children, health, finances, or jobs. But for others, this emotion permeates their entire lives. They exist, but have no hopes, dreams, or goals. This is not the way God intends for us to live. He created us to live with purpose, working toward goals and feeling a sense of anticipation for the future."

With a hollow stare at the pastor, Jason's thoughts took over. This sermon is not for me. I have no expectations looking forward and definitely no anticipation for the future. I'm groping through the darkness for an answer that probably wouldn't matter anymore even if I did find it. Why am I here? Why am I listening to someone preaching hope? He looked toward Stanley and saw a mirrored face; lost to any ray of hope. He looked at Kristy, her expression appeared hopeful, as did Richard's and his wife's. Is it possible for me, is there any hope to be found, he wondered?

When Jason refocused on the pastor, his eyes were still on him as he summarized the sermon about Jesus and a Samaritan woman. "First of all," the pastor said loudly, "she had made wrong choices." He paused a moment to let it absorb, then said, "Secondly, she had repeatedly failed." He looked around the congregation as he said, "Thirdly, she may have felt trapped, and finally," he said with outstretched arms, "She was isolated from her community." He went on to tell how the woman met Jesus at a well and discovered him to be the Messiah, which changed her life forever. She began the day as a rejected and hopeless woman, but found her hope restored in Jesus because he accepted her just the way she was, didn't condemn her, and loved her unconditionally. Nice story, Jason thought, but I don't think it's going to work for me.

The service ended and as the people filed out, the pastor stood by the entrance greeting his congregation. He shook Jason's hand saying, "If you'd like, we could have a talk at your convenience."

Jason felt cornered; he forced a smile saying, "Thanks Pastor, I'll think about it."

Richard noticed Jason's uneasiness. The look in his eyes signaled a fight or flight predicament. When the opportunity opened, he whispered to Jason, "Please say good-bye."

Before he could respond, Kristy nudged him, "I have to go to work. Could we meet up later?"

"Maybe," he said loud enough for Richard to hear. "The Cain's have invited me over." Richard looked sad as he nodded to Jason.

Jason walked to his motel room feeling smothered; he methodically packed his bike longing for solitude. He then walked to the Cain's house, where Richard was waiting for him on the porch swing. Hearing the men greet each other, Mrs. Cain rushed out of the house with two cups of coffee. When each held their steaming cups, she scurried back inside. Richard took a sip and smiled at Jason. "You know Jason; it's been a pleasure meeting you. You remind me so much of Thor. You have filled a void in my life and even though you have suffered greatly, always remember that you are in our prayers and we pray that you will find hope again. Maybe not through my religion, but through the grace of God in whatever form he will present himself to you. Keep the faith as we have and you will find what you're looking for." By now, his eyes were teary. He reached into his pocket and pulled out a small crucifix. After cradling it for some time, he handed it to Jason saying, "Thor didn't take this with him when he went out on the ocean that day. I don't think he'd mind if I gave it to you. He too was somewhat skeptical of the power of religion, probably until now. Please accept this, let it ride with you on your journey and maybe it will come to life for you."

Jason felt its warmth in his hand. He looked at the old man, "Thank you Richard, I will keep it always."

Richard smiled, cleared his throat, and said, "I'm not real good at good-byes. Do you know where you're going next?"

Jason stared out at the ocean, "Not sure, probably going to head east." He looked at the restaurant and thought he saw Kristy's silhouette by the door. "Could you tell Kristy I said good-bye?"

Richard shook his head, "You should tell her yourself, but I understand and I will. She too will miss you."

Mrs. Cain came out and asked if they wanted more coffee. Jason answered, "No thanks, I'm about to leave."

She took his cup and gave him a tight hug whispering in his ear, "It was so nice to have met you. You gave Richard a much needed boost and for that I'm very grateful."

He smiled at her as she pulled away. Richard stood up and they embraced. "Be safe my son," he said, "I'm confident we'll meet again." With that, Jason walked away.

THE OPEN ROAD

CHAPTER 8

Unsettled feelings about Kristy dominated his thoughts as he sped east through Washington State. She was grasping for something that he couldn't give her, just as he was grasping for something that might not be there. He checked his rearview mirror often for fear of seeing her chasing him down, but all he saw in the mirror was his own face and his dilemma. Maybe he was seeing a part of himself in her, and running was all he could do. At any rate, she didn't deserve to be left hanging in that way, but he didn't know how to confront her insecurities or say good-bye. A beam of light had guided him to that small coastal town and yearning hearts had driven him away.

Mile after mile streamed past as a blur. Thoughts of his parents, his siblings, Scott and Sarah, people he'd left behind dominated the miles obscuring the world around him. Should he have left his family and friends back home in the manner he did? Was he so utterly lost that living people didn't matter to him anymore? Was he on the verge of finding nothing? Washington State soon became Idaho. The steep, sweeping decline down the eastern slope of the Bitterroot Mountain Range demanded his attention. To his right, polished glacier peaks rose thousands of feet to the sky. To his left, huge drainages dropped off the side of the road and stretched for miles across the canyons. The glaciers that carved the canyons left behind boulders of all sizes; some poking through solid canopies of forest. He felt like a bird gliding down the mountain.

The momentum of the grade eventually gave way to rolling mountains with solid stands of pines and firs. Sporadic patches of dead trees revealed the damage done by bark beetles. He followed the ever-growing Bitterroot River until it opened up into a large valley and the state of Montana. The city of Missoula soon came into sight. His gas tank was on empty as well as his stomach. He bought a local newspaper and flipped through it as he ate his hamburger and fries. The weather section showed a cold front moving in from the west. He studied his map and decided to head south, away from the storm. The Great Salt Lakes appeared large on the map, so he challenged himself to making it there before dark. He continued to follow the Bitterroot River south. It sandwiched him between the rugged Bitterroot Mountains where jagged peaks adorned the skyline and the Sapphire Mountains until he reached the pass at Sula, which led him back over the Bitterroots into the Salmon River Valley. At times, he was the only one on the highway except for an occasional squirrel darting across the road. The smell of pine rode on the air with a twist of frigidness and the rush of the river seemed to drown out the sound of his bike. At Challis, he turned southeast toward Pocatello.

The mountains slipped into the Snake River Plains and he was able to loosen his grip on the handlebars. He set the cruise control and stretched his legs out across the engine guard. All day long, his eyes followed the sun as it moved slowly across the sky. At Pocatello, he fueled up with a sense of urgency. He was obsessed with making it to the Great Salt Lakes. Back on the road, the feeling of freedom that had eluded him to this point washed over him. He tracked the flight of a hawk, felt the temperature changes in the slightest dips in the road, heard frogs croaking in creeks, smelled the cattle, and crops. Why do I need to get to the lakes by sunset, he wondered? I've been in the saddle all day, seen beautiful country and now I'm racing to a place with no significance. His hand backed off the throttle. Pleasant thoughts consumed him. He saw Rose dancing in front of the fireplace cradling her baby bump. She looked so happy it brought a huge smile to his face and he remembered how she effortlessly was able to comfort a patient after a terrible loss. Every bone in her body was filled with compassion; she was a saint to everyone she came in contact with. He laughed at the little surprises she'd put in his lunchbox like love notes, his favorite candy bar, reservations to a fine restaurant, her own free massage certificates and countless old valentine candy hearts. Those were the days he thought as the lights of a sleepy little town came into view.

A hotel light glared deep red with a flickering bar sign underneath. His bike guided him into the parking lot. Road weary, he took a long hot shower and walked to the only restaurant in town. A big juicy steak with mashed potatoes and mixed vegetables bloated the void in his stomach. To settle his meal, he walked from one end of town to the other. It featured one gas station with two pumps, a small post office, the motel, and an auto repair shop with farming equipment cluttering both sides. A few of the shops that lined the road through town displayed American flags. Outside of town, lights flickered from the many ranches that dotted the valley. The flickering bar sign lured him inside for a quick drink before hitting the sack. It took a moment for his eyes to adjust to the dimly lit room. The smell of alcohol and cigarette smoke distinguished the bar. There was no lively crowd, no displays on the walls, only a few patrons at the bar and country music dominating the conversation. The bearded bartender eyed him as he walked across the room to the bar. The other patrons did the same.

Jason nodded to the bartender and took a stool. He looked to the man on his right and nodded, the man turned his head away. The bartender wiped the spot on the bar in front of him saying in a flat tone, "What can I get you?"

"Do you have any micro-brews?"

The bartender laughed causing the others to look his way, then said, "We have Coors, Bud, and Miller, which will it be?"

Jason shrugged his shoulders, "Bud, I guess."

"Bottle or draft?"

"Draft, please."

The bartender adjusted his ball cap and poured a glass. He placed it in front of Jason, "That'll be two-fifty."

Jason slapped a ten spot on the bar and took a long swig. It didn't have much taste, but the carbonation was refreshing. From the corner of his eye, he noticed the man next to him watching him drink. He set his glass down and nodded at the man again. This time the man nodded back and raised his shot glass. He downed the liquor and signaled the bartender for a refill slurring to Jason, "You're not from around here!"

"No sir, just passing through."

"We don't get many passing through types here," the man slurred.

Jason held his laughter, "I can tell." The bartender snickered while filling the man's shot glass. The patron watched anxiously and as soon as the bartender set it in front of him, he gulped it down and ordered another. Jason felt pity for the man. His grey hair was uncombed, his plaid shirt ripped, and from his bloodshot eyes a certain pain was evident. The man lit a cigarette and offered one to Jason.

"No thanks," Jason said, "I don't smoke."

He slapped the pack on the bar and said, "Well be that way, then."

Jason added, "They're not good for you."

"Oh, what are we, Mr. Goody two shoes, now? Ever taken anything that wasn't good for you?" Jason ignored the question; then the man asked, "You ever been married?" Jason looked at him again without answering. "Well don't do it," he said slamming his fist on the bar. "They'll leave you. You can work your fingers to the bone to make them happy, but in the end, they'll sure as shit leave you." He emptied his beer glass, turned toward Jason and pointed to the shot glass. "This is the love of my life, now, and you know what?" He leaned closer to Jason and whispered, "I like it...no I love it!"

Jason felt the man's pain, "I'm sorry."

The man bolstered himself up in his chair, "I don't need your goddamn sympathy. I need another drink. How about we arm wrestle for the next round?" The man put his muscled arm on the bar waiting for Jason to accept the challenge. Jason turned from him. "Come on," the man slurred.

The bartender leaned toward him, "Take it easy Fred, the man doesn't want to wrestle. Maybe you should go home."

"Go home! Go home to what?" he shouted, "my fucking cattle?"

Jason slid a few dollars to the bartender and left the bar. He saw himself in Fred a year earlier, drinking himself to get away from the misery, which only led to more misery. Jason knew what it was like to have no hope or passion for anything. No real reason to live except for anticipating the next drink. He had a restless night and woke with the thought of the man at the bar. Did he make it home all right? Did he ever contemplate suicide? Did he deserve such a lot in life? There were too many unanswered questions, not only for this man, but for himself also.

*****

After breakfast, he headed south through Utah into New Mexico. Brilliantly colored sandstone spires popped out of the desert as far as the eye could see. Puffy clouds raced above the desert as if being chased until they bottled up to the mountains and spewed lightning and thunder. He was in Sioux country and at one time, it stretched from the border of Mexico all the way up to Canada.

Jason crossed into Arizona toward the Grand Canyon. He measured time by gas stops. Sometimes the world zipped by without much thought, allowing him to absorb the smell of the fields, the cattle, and occasionally, the smell of death stung his nose. He felt every temperature change from the coolness in the canyons to the heat waves shimmering off the pavement on the open plains. Birds soared above him as if leading the way, and sometimes hordes of insects came out of nowhere splattering his face and helmet. He wasn't viewing the world through a window; insulated from the elements; he was the picture.

The looks he noticed from people in the cars he passed varied. Young women flashed big smiles and waved to him and on one occasion, a pretty girl flashed him her breasts. Some of the men had the look of envy, probably wishing they were in his shoes, and wives had fantasies written on their faces as they stole a glance. The stares he related to the most were that of young boys looking at his motorcycle in awe, mirroring his fascination as a kid while traveling in the family car. Eyes that envisioned a sense of freedom.

The further north he drove, the worse the weather became. Ominous black thunder cells flanked him, spewing out solid sheets of rain. It was as if they'd created a gauntlet for him to slip through. He stopped only to refuel. At Flagstaff, he turned off Route 66 and headed for the south rim of the Grand Canyon. The rain was right on his tail as he pulled into a campsite. By the time he set his tent up and covered his bike, rain splattered off the nylon in a musical rhythm that carried his exhausted body into a deep sleep.

He woke to warm sunlight filtering through the tent. The air was crisp from the night's cleansing. His stomach ached from hunger. Before riding to the tourist center for breakfast, he explored the area. Not far from his campsite was the rim of the canyon. He climbed onto a rocky ledge that sheared thousands of feet down to the Colorado River. The vastness and depth of this gap in the earth's surface took the breath out of him. Millions of years of erosion displayed a mosaic pattern of colors, each stratum representing a time frame than no human could possibly conceive. The canyon pulled on him, the urge to jump was overpowering. He wanted to soar with a Condor that rode the thermos in front of him.

After a healthy breakfast of bacon and eggs, the lure of the canyon became overpowering. He wanted to look up from the bottom and started his descent. The trail dropped steeply, leveling out every now and then onto small plateaus. Heat waves shimmered off the colorful stone. A cooling sweat covered his body. With each break, he looked up and felt as though he was going to fall over backwards from the vertical sheerness of the canyon walls. The Colorado River, which gave off a greenish blue hue from the rim, was now silted brown.

The trail leveled out one last time before descending to the river. A strange sensation radiated up his boots. Without conscious thought, he was being lead away from the trail toward a pinnacle of reddish orange sandstone. He climbed through crevasses, around jetting rocks, and up a cliff to an enclave. At one end, the remnants of warming fires had scorched the rock black. It was big enough to shelter a few grown men. The view was spectacular; for miles in either direction the opposing canyon wall danced with color. Scooting to the edge, he looked up to a sheer cliff that climbed out of sight; it made him dizzy.

Below, the Colorado River meandered through the cut in the earth. This is the spot, he thought. This is where the natives took shelter, where they cooked, and where they slept during expeditions. He felt the stone absorbing him, the wind carrying his spirit on her journey through the canyon, a peacefulness so empowering it could be home. A joyous hoot blared from the cave; it echoed down the canyon, across the river, and bounced off a millennium of time. He emptied his mind of all thoughts, creating a state of nothingness within himself allowing things to unfold in their own way, in their own time. Contentment had finally found a place in his heart. The upset and worry that had fueled his journey was being replaced with the wisdom that things will improve. Before leaving the enclave, he found a sharp rock and cut his palm. His blood dripped onto the rock anointing it with his life force. The connection was complete; his territory marked for the rest of time.

*****

He returned to the trail feeling re-energized and happy, even though he knew the mile climb up the canyon would be physically demanding. The rim greeted him after three hours of steady hiking, a small price to pay for the peace it afforded him. He bought some snacks and a six pack of beer and rode back to his campsite. The sweat from the hike had dried to a crust on his clothes and body. He gathered some clean clothes, a towel, and walked to the showers. A few sites down, he noticed an old Triumph motorcycle. It looked well-traveled with aluminum side boxes plastered with decals. Nobody was around, so he took a closer look. Crests from Switzerland, Luxemburg, Austria, Germany, Spain, France, England, Ireland, Scotland and many more had him fixated. A voice from behind blared out, "Top of the day to ya mate."

Jason concealed his laugh at the accent as he turned around to a scruffy red bearded man with pleasant green eyes. He resembled a Leprechaun. Jason answered in jest, "Howdy partner, haven't seen many Triumphs like this in a while."

"If I was to hazard a guess mate, you won't in another great while," the man answered.

"These stickers here," Jason pointed, "You've been to all these places?"

The man laughed, "And many more. The one from hell burned up."

Jason liked his spunky attitude. He offered his hand, "I'm Jason, pleased to meet you."

The grip was crushing. "Shawn McPherson, the pleasure's all mine."

"McPherson?" Jason questioned.

"That's what I said mate, McPherson, a fine Irish name if I may say so me self."

"That's my last name too," Jason said as the man eyed him curiously.

Shawn raised his bushy brows and erupted with a loud belly laugh. With a questioning tone, he declared, "Well then mate, I guess we're related. Have a sit down and we can toast to our blood line." He went to his tent and returned with a bottle of Scotch and two plastic cups. "The best Scotch ever made," he said half-filling the cups. He offered one to Jason and raised his cup, "To the McPherson clan," and downed a gulp. "Ah, now that's fine whisky, my lad."

Jason took a sip; it tasted like the Scotch his father drank. He grimaced and shook his head from the bitterness. Shawn laughed, "Irish men don't make faces like that; let's try it again mate." He raised his cup proclaiming, "May your glass be ever full. May the roof over your head be always strong and may you be in heaven half an hour before the devil knows you're dead."

Jason downed the shot without displaying the sting and asked, "Where are you from?"

Shawn smacked his knee, "I'm an Irishman from England; bloody shame, I'd say. Married into a Brit family and got divorced from a Brit family. She ran up the credit cards, so I took all the savings and 'ere I am...in bloody America." He raised his cup to Jason, "'ere's to our wives and girlfriends, may they never meet," and emptied his cup. "How 'bout you lad? Where you from? Wait," he said quickly. "Let me hazard a guess. You're from," he scratched his head looking at Jason. "I got it, if you're a McPherson; you must be from Ireland." His belly laugh sounded throughout the campground. He filled the cups again, raising his, "Here's to the McPherson clan."

The scotch became mellower with each toast; Jason smacked his lips saying, "I'm from bloody Northern California," and let out a rival burst of laughter. When they settled down, Jason asked, "How much did it cost to ship your bike here?"

Shawn filled the cups, looked Jason dead straight in the eyes and whispering, "I rode it across the bloody ocean." Laughter erupted again. When it trailed off Jason asked, "No, I'm serious. How'd you get it here?"

"Well, after I had it repaired, I shipped it by air freight, me lad."

"Repaired?" Jason said.

"Aye, me had an accident before coming here."

"What kind of accident?"

"A bloody accident," Shawn reflected. "I was speeding down a narrow road when a woman comes hurling around the corner. I swerve to miss her and as she passes, she leans out her window and screams 'Pig' at me. I looked at her and yelled, 'Bitch.' As I reached the bend, I crashed into a bloody pig." He paused for a sip then continued with a laugh. "Messed up me bike, but I had pork chops for dinner."

Jason laughed wondering if the story was true. Shawn became agitated, "Furthermore," he said, "if I knew the bloody faggots at customs was going to dismantle me bike looking for a bomb and taking a full day at it, I would've stayed in Europe. They treated me like a damn terrorist."

"Yeah," Jason agreed, "Times are changing, but at least you're here and seeing America by the best means possible."

"Bloody damn right, my friend, I'll toast to that." He refilled the cups. "Now, my lad, I have a question for you."

"Shoot," Jason said feeling the warmth of the whisky in his stomach.

"Now, I don't mean to be disrespectful," he said with a wink. "But I can't help but notice that you look more like an Indian than an Irishman! Am I missing something here, lad?" Jason downed a shot and laughed. Shawn cocked his head and asked, "What's so funny mate?"

Jason declared, "I'm a blue-eyed, Indian Irishman. Bet you'll never see another one like me."

Shawn scratched his head. "I guess you're right, lad. The world is getting smaller. No need to worry, my friend, you can drink like the best of us Irish." He stared at the whisky bottle as sadness blanketed his face. Jason wondered if he had said something wrong, "Are you okay?"

"Aye, I was just thinking about me best friend, Patrick O'Brian. We grew up together; the best of buds, you know. He got cancer and was dying. While on his deathbed, he called to me and says, 'Shawn, come 'ere, I'ave a request for ye'. I kneeled by his side, 'Shawn ole boy, we've been friends all our lives, and now I'm leaving 'ere. I'ave one last request fir ye to do'.

"The tears were running down me face as I say, 'Anything Patrick, anything ye wish, it's done.' He whispers out, 'Under me bed is a box with a bottle of the finest whisky in all of Ireland. Bottled the year I was born, it was. After I die, and they plant me in the ground, I want ye to pour that fine whisky over me grave so it might soak into me bones and I'll be able to enjoy it for all eternity.' I was overcome by the beauty and the true Irish spirit of the request. 'Aye,' I told him, 'tis a fine thing you ask of me. I will pour the whisky, but might I strain it through me kidney's first?" Jason laughed until his stomach ached. Shawn stood up, "Speaking of which, I need to take a whiz." He returned and raised the bottle to the sky, "Patrick would be honored," and offered to pour another toast.

Jason stopped him, "No thanks, I'm toast. I need to crash."

Shawn slapped him on the back, saying, "It's been me pleasure to meet you, Jason the blue-eyed, Indian Irishman. I'm riding out to California in the morrow. If I don't see you; may your road be filled with whisky, women, and song."

Jason's cheeks ached from all the laughing. "The pleasure has been all mine, my friend; ride safe." He stumbled away from the happy leprechaun, past his tent, and toward the overlook. The last rays of the sun created shadows on the canyon walls. Images of Kachinas filled his vision. They danced along the face of the cliffs raising their spears toward him as if beckoning him to join them. He stood on the sheer ledge wobbling, wondering if they would catch him before hitting the bottom of the canyon. Rose's image appeared from the cliff silencing the warriors. She put her hand out to him saying, 'No, my love, go back to your tent, and Jason,' she whispered with joy, 'I love seeing you laugh again, baby. I want to see more of that, okay?'

He smiled at her saying, "I will try, baby," and made his way back to camp.

He woke to the sun beating down on his tent and a splitting headache. Crawling out, he noticed the Irishman's site was empty. A note with a rock securing it sat on his picnic table. It read, 'T'was a pleasure drinking with you, mate. If you ever cross the pond, look me up. Happy trails.' His address followed. He put the note in his wallet and broke camp.

After breakfast and plenty of coffee refills, he felt ready for the road. He plotted a route from the canyon toward the Painted Desert and New Mexico. With one last look at the grandness of the canyon, he saddled up and headed out.

HOWLING WOLF

CHAPTER 9

Pavement suddenly gave way to gravel, breaking Jason's visual odyssey. He'd been so absorbed by the colliding colors of the sandstone spires that shot up from the desert floor that it stretched his imagination into a world that seemed to have no end. His hands tightened on the handlebars as he eased off the throttle and coasted to a stop. Puffy white clouds moved lazily across the sky and sage brush baking in the afternoon sun saturated the air with a bitter aroma.

Lizards came out of their hiding spots to see the intruder. They climbed onto rocks and did pushups, while eyeing him suspiciously. Jason laughed at the sight and started talking to them. "Hi guys, getting your daily exercise, are you?" He grabbed his canteen and took a drink. Feeling their eyes on him, he said, "I bet you're thirsty," and poured a little water in the cap. As he went to place it on a rock, they scattered. He backed off a short distance and laid down eye level to their world. The lizards reappeared from under their hiding spots and looked at the new object with interest. One of them slowly crawled to the cap and without hesitation started drinking. Another one joined in, then another, until there was no room for any more. They bullied and chased each other from the cap. The dominate lizard spent most of the time chasing the others away. Jason got up saying, "You should share, you're all family." He rummaged through a saddlebag finding an empty water bottle. Cutting the bottom off, he placed it a short distance away. The dominate one scurried across the sand to the bigger gift, leaving the cap to the others.

A screech jolted him from the little world. He looked up to a bald eagle circling overhead. He told the lizards to hide. Curious as to where he was, he studied his map. He'd been avoiding the big highways wanting to experience the less traveled roads thinking they'd be more revealing. The map showed that particular road ending at an Indian Reservation, but it clearly went into the reservation.

Feeling refreshed and ready to move on, he started his bike and headed toward the mountains in the distance. The packed gravel road entered the foothills, where the temperature changed with each dip and rise in the road. He was having fun accelerating on the downhill stretches, feeling the gravitational pull like being on a rollercoaster. Riding up a long hill, he noticed the eagle he'd seen earlier was following him. He was sure of this because there was a noticeable part of its wing span that had feathers missing. He began to wonder - was he following the eagle or was the eagle following him?

As he continued riding the hills, his bike began to sputter as if it was running out of gas. The gas gauge showed half a tank. He stopped at the top of a rise to see if he could find the problem. Double checking the gas tank, he ruled out gas as being the problem and pulled what tools he had out of the saddle bags. He suspected it was a problem with the carburetor and after inspecting it, he found nothing unusual from the outside. He started the bike, revved it a few times, but it continued to run rough and then died. "Damn it!" he yelled. He removed the float bowl from the carburetor. Once exposed, he noticed that one of the arms that held it to the bowl assembly had broken off and was in the bottom of the bowl. There was no way to fix it. He cursed loudly and yelled out, "Now what the hell am I gonna do?" as the eagle screeched from the top of a ponderosa pine not far from him.

He found a tree close to the road with a view of the valley and sat down to collect his thoughts. A gas station or repair shop is what he needed. He weighed his options, wait there with the hope someone would come by, or start walking, which disturbed him, because he didn't want to leave his bike unattended in the middle of nowhere. He retrieved his map and tried to pin point his location by referencing the peaks in the valley to the map. Within the reservation's boundary, there appeared to be a small village. "Should I stay here and hope someone comes by before it gets dark, or start walking toward the town?" he asked the eagle. The eagle took flight, circled over him once and soared down to the valley until it was out of sight, leaving Jason alone to make his own choice.

He sat under a shade tree surrendering to his predicament.

The quietness became deafening and in the shimmering heat, the multicolored spires that stretched across the valley swayed back and forth. The sight blanketed him in a vale of tranquility. He noticed the ponderosa pine where the eagle had roosted was the biggest tree in the area. Its thick bark appeared as large slabs deeply etched into the trunk. A blackened area on one side of the tree gave testament to where lightening had struck the tree and burned around the base. A sweet fragrance that resembled vanilla filtered into his lungs. He sniffed the air around him until he realized that the tree he was leaning against was the source. He turned around and buried his nose into the bark and took a deep breath of the Jeffery pine's sweetness.

He'd become so relaxed he was on the verge of dozing off when he noticed a dust trail in the valley streaming toward him. He jumped up in excitement and watched as the trail slowly snaked toward him. While he waited, he readied his bike and himself, glad that his prayers had been answered; not that he prayed much, but the time spent with Captain Richard made him at least consider prayer. The vehicle was in the roller coaster section of the foothills with sunlight reflecting off the windshield whenever it crested a hill. He stood in the middle of the road ready to flag it down. When it crested the last hill, he noticed it was an old pickup truck with chipped, faded paint, and mismatched front fenders. Despite its outward appearance, it was a beautiful sight to see as it coasted to a stop in front to him.

An old Indian opened the door with a hard shoulder push and soon stood before him. He wore a big rounded cowboy hat with two long gray braids hanging down each side; a plaid shirt and faded blue jeans covered the top of his moccasins. His face was deeply wrinkled. Although Jason could tell he was very old, his dark eyes had a youthful look about them. Glad to see the man, he yelled out, "Thanks for stopping, I was beginning to think I was going to spend the night here."

Looking at Jason, the man smiled, "That would not have been so bad."

Jason responded, "Well, I'm not very prepared for that right now and my bike is in need of repair."

The old man motioned all around him with his hands, "Everything you could possibly need is all around you."

"What I need is a gas station or parts store, is there one near here?"

The Indian chuckled, "There is a gas station in our village."

"Can you help me get my bike there?" Jason asked kindly.

"I don't see how we are going to get your motorcycle in my truck, but I do have some rope, I could tow you there."

"That would be great," Jason said offering his hand. "My name is Jason. I really appreciate your help."

The Indian shook his hand saying, "I am Howling Wolf." Together they rigged the rope to the pickup and Jason's bike and when they had finished Howling Wolf said, "I will travel at the same speed up and down the hills. If the rope becomes slack going downhill, use your brakes to keep it tight. My village is about seven miles away. If you need me to stop, signal with your hand, okay?"

After straddling the bike, Jason yelled out with excitement, "Okay, I'm ready whenever you are."

Before getting in his truck, Jason observed the Indian take a deep breath as he scanned the valley below, then he raised his head and nodded to the bald eagle. Jason hadn't noticed the eagle's return and thought it peculiar that it had been around so much and that the old man had a connection to it. He made a mental note to see if it followed them to the village.

Howling Wolf started the truck and with his left arm out the window, he circled his hand pointing his index finger upward and then forward. He moved slowly until the rope was tight and started up the road. It took a couple of hills for Jason to get the downhill breaking part smoothly. All went well, except for the dust the pickup blanketed him with. Every now and then a cross wind blew the dust away giving him some relief, but that was sporadic at best. After what seemed like an eternity, he eventually made out a building in the distance. The truck slowed and stopped. Jason jumped off his bike and smacked off the dust.

It wasn't much of a service station by city standards; only one gas pump sat under a metal roofed overhang in front of a small store. A two-bay repair shop was connected to the store and vehicles with numerous body parts missing were lined up along the side the building as well as a large stack of lumber, which caught his attention being a carpenter. The wood siding was chipped and peeling and in need of paint. A long wooden bench was by the store entrance, occupied to capacity by older men talking and laughing, while pointing at him.

When Howling Wolf got out of his truck, all the men got up and greeted him with excitement. Jason thought he must be a person of importance judging by their display of respect. For some reason, the sight of this compelled Jason to think of the eagle; he looked around and saw it roosting in a tree. It had followed them to the gas station. Who was this man, Jason wondered, as he entered one of the open bay doors of the garage. Noticing a man around his age working on a truck, he said loudly, "Excuse me, sir." The man stopped what he was doing and looked at Jason. "Do you know where I can get some parts for my Harley?"

The man laughed. "We don't have any Harley parts here, but you probably could find them in Silver City," he replied.

"That would be a big help," Jason sighed.

"Come on in the store, I'll get you the phone book. Do you know what parts you need?"

Jason followed him saying, "I'm sure it's the carb float bracket."

"We send a man to Silver City to get parts every Wednesday. There's a Harley shop there. If you can locate what you need, I'll see to it that you get it," he added.

Jason found a Harley shop and made the call. They had the part in stock and he paid with his credit card. The mechanic was listening and motioned Jason for the phone. He talked to the person and set up a pick up time for his parts runner to get them on Wednesday. It was Friday and Jason was disappointed that it would take so long to get his part. He asked the attendant "Is there any chance of getting it sooner?"

The man said, "Not a lot of traffic comes our way; Wednesday's have always been our parts day and unless you can get a ride to town, you are going to have to wait. Sorry."

"How far is Silver City?" Jason inquired.

"It's about 180 miles away."

Worried about his bike, Jason asked, "Can I park my bike in your garage until then? And is there a motel here?"

The man's laugh was pointed, "There's no problem storing your bike but as far as a motel, now that could be a problem."

"Great," Jason said sarcastically, "now what am I going to do!"

"I will talk to Howling Wolf, he will have an answer," the man said nodding his head.

Since it looked like he was going to be there awhile, he offered his hand saying, "My name is Jason, and yours?"

"I'm Joseph, but the old men call me Running Pony, because I ran everywhere when I was a child."

He looked to be around Jason's age, his hair cut short, not like the older men who had long braids. Jason was not intimidated talking to Joseph as he was with Howling Wolf. He felt like the old man could see inside of him and that made him uneasy. Curiously he asked, "Who is Howling Wolf? Everyone seems to treat him like he's important."

Joseph looked out the window to the old men and said, "He is the oldest member of our tribe, our medicine man, but don't call him that. He claims only to use what our mother earth provides him. Very wise and honored in these parts; many consult him about many things. He's our doctor, psychiatrist, psychologist, history teacher, you name it; he's all of that to us."

"Wow," Jason said, "I sensed he was special, but not to that extent.

"As a matter of fact," Running Pony added," he's chosen me to be his apprentice. I'm in the process of learning as much as I can from him. He's taught me that our Native American culture is the most misunderstood culture in the United States, and that our people have suffered great hardships since the Europeans claimed this country. He says that in spite of these obstacles, or probably because of them, he is teaching me the traditions and ceremonies of our people to keep them alive, being that he will soon travel to the next world." Looking serious for the first time, Running Pony added, "And don't think it was an accident him finding you."

"What do you mean by that?" Jason asked, feeling a little uneasy.

"You will need to consult with him for answers," he said nodding his head.

Jason thought out loud, "But I'm just passing through."

"Where are you going?"

Jason looked away from him not wanting to lie to the man's

face. He didn't know where he was going, but he didn't want to appear as lost either. With trepidation, he said, "Well, I'm looking for someone...something."

"Out here?" Running Pony said eyeing him suspiciously.

Jason wasn't sure how to explain it. He'd been looking for his birth parents all his life, always resulting in dead ends, but that wasn't the reason for his trip. Or was it? Hearing this man's voice while on his Reservation brought hope regardless of how he ended up there. He answered, "I'm riding across the country hoping to find answers."

Joseph looked at him understandably, "Everyone tries to find their place in life. During that journey, hopefully we get to walk the Spirit Road; maybe you're here to walk that road."

Jason's neck tingled. Me, on the spirit road! Then suspicion, "But I'm not of your tribe."

"Jason," he replied, "when we walk the Spirit Road there is no religion, color, or creeds. No your way or my way, only universal love and understanding are found on that road and besides, your blue eyes and native features have captivated Howling Wolf. He looks inside of people like no one else can and I believe he sees in you a channel through which the Great Power can work. Relax, my friend, go with it, it can do you no harm."

Jason muttered anxiously, "Whatever."

"I'll talk to Howling Wolf and find a place for you to stay until your part comes in."

*****

While Joseph went outside, Jason looked around the store noticing artifacts and works of art hanging on the walls. Old pictures of proud, distinguished men gave him a glimpse of the real native people. He felt sad for them, thinking of how their way of life was destroyed by the settlers. A nicely framed diploma from Western New Mexico University with Joseph's name elegantly inscribed on it also hung proudly on the wall. Jason was in a different world, one of simple beauty where everything seemed to have meaning and purpose.

Joseph came in laughing, "You're in luck; we have a tipi in the forest for you." He waited until Jason's face reacted with disbelief then patted him on the shoulder saying, "Just kidding, man."

They both laughed. Jason liked Joseph. He had a sense of

humor, was genuine, and got right to the point when needed. Impressed by the collection of artifacts and art work, Jason commented, "You have an impressive collection of folklore here, Joseph."

"Thanks, we've had offers from museums to display them, but the tribe elders decided to keep them here so our young people can always remember and keep our heritage alive on the reservation."

Curious about a certain piece of art that caught his eye, Jason took a closer look. It was made from an animal hide and secured with leather to a circular frame. Feathers and strings of different colored beads hung around it with two arrows crossing its face. "What is this work?" he asked.

Running Pony ran his hand over it. "That is a spirit wheel. The Ocelot hide and crossed arrows represent the hunters, and the wild turkey and pheasant feathers represent the hunted; a balance of spirits. The medicine bag commits the spirits of the animals so they will bring mystical powers of protection to the wheel."

"What do the different bead groupings represent?"

"The red on black grouping signify the blood of the prey and the remorse of the hunter for taking the prey's life. The green, white, red, and blue beads represent the four directions, which have great significance in our culture; and the red, yellow, black, and white represent the people who inhabit our planet."

"That's amazing," Jason said, "it's so beautiful in itself."

"It's not that amazing to us," he replied, "we've been living off of and cherishing the gifts of Mother Earth for centuries. It's our heritage...our linage."

"Our heritage...our linage!" resounded in Jason's mind. He felt a stabbing in his chest; a sensation he'd felt after searching for his birth parents in the past only to be told by his adoptive parents and the authorities that his adoption was a "closed" one; an adoption that carried no history with it, no paperwork; a dead end. When he'd stopped seeking answers, the stabbing went away, which suited him fine most of the time.

Running Pony suggested they go outside so he could introduce him to the elders. They'd been in the store for quite some time and he didn't want the elders to think Jason was indifferent to them. Running Pony added, "It's a sign of respect to conduct introductions before all else."

Jason felt the eyes on him as Running Pony introduced him to every person there. Howling Wolf told them that Jason would be their guest for a while. Joseph excused himself and went back into the garage. Jason quietly listened to the men talk and only spoke when he was addressed. He noticed their conversations flowed smoothly and Howling Wolf was the one who usually had the last word. After they concluded what seemed like a tribal meeting, Howling Wolf signaled for Jason to follow him. Before they got into his old pick-up, he asked, "Do you need anything from your saddle bags?"

Jason replied, "Oh yeah," and ran to his bike, rolled it into the garage and gathered some things. He said to Running Pony as he was leaving, "Thanks, I appreciate your help."

Running Pony nodded, "No problem, I'll see you later."

*****

Jason jumped into the truck and they headed down the dirt road into the village. He noticed small, simply constructed homes and trailers scattered throughout the area. Children were playing and running around and when they saw the truck, they ran alongside it waving and shouting happily. Jason smiled and waved back to the children. Howling Wolf groaned, "Our future generations." Jason noticed sadness in his voice. He pulled into a driveway and shut off the truck. "Joseph has offered his home to you. He has many things city folks are used to. He felt you'd be more comfortable here. Take a shower if you like and make yourself at home, he will be here after he closes the store."

"Thank you very much, Mister Wolf,"

He smiled at Jason and said, "Drop the Mister part, Lost Spirit."

Jason repeated to himself, 'Lost Spirit,' why's he calling me that? The confused look on his face prompted Howling Wolf to speak, "I am calling you Lost Spirit because the eagle directed me to you. I know you noticed him. The eagle protects one's spirit, and I believe that you are somewhat lost or you would not be here. So the name makes sense to me."

Remembering what Running Pony had told him about Howling Wolf, Jason didn't know whether to argue the point or accept it as what it was; the truth. Was it that obvious, he wondered?

Howling Wolf continued, "I can see in your eyes that you are not walking in balance; not with nature, not with yourself. We all need to walk in beauty and in order to do this we must be in harmony with all things and in order to do that, we must be in harmony with ourselves first. Harmony will help you to become one and in the process it will neutralize your problems. My people take care of things that we are not happy about by honoring it and giving it thanks because it has taught us a lesson, and we replace that negative with a positive, since they cannot be in the same place at the same time. I can feel your struggle, Lost Spirit. There are ways to make it better." Jason listened intently knowing the Shaman was right. Howling Wolf added, "Now that you have arrived, we have much work to do. Enjoy your evening with Joseph, for he is a good man. I will call on you tomorrow."

Getting out of the truck, Jason looked at Howling Wolf. Their eyes spoke to each other. A peaceful feeling blanketed him, one that totally disarmed him and gave him a sense of purpose. He entered Running Pony's house heading straight for the shower. The water drained brown from the dust he'd accumulated from the tow. Tired from the day's ordeal, he plopped on the couch and quickly fell asleep.

CHAPTER 10

The sound of Joseph entering the house stirred him; he swiftly sat up. "Relax," Running Pony said, "you are welcome here." He sat in a chair across from the couch.

Joseph looked tired. Jason asked, "What time is it?"

He replied, "Its 10:30. I wasn't planning on being so late, but Howling Wolf had a lesson for me, so that's where I've been."

"What kind of lesson, if I may ask?"

"Howling Wolf has picked me to carry on our traditional ways. There is much to learn about herbs and chants. It requires much study and dedication. As a tribe in a modern society, we are trying to merge these worlds while keeping the old traditions alive as well."

Jason said, "I noticed your diploma in the store, it looks like they made a good choice, but a B.A. in Business Administration?"

"If you'd met me outside the Res., it probably wouldn't have surprised you, would it?"

Embarrassed, Jason said, "I didn't mean it that way; it just doesn't seem like the kind of degree you would need here."

"Our world is changing fast and we need to keep pace," he said. "Look around the country, Native Americans are assimilating into the white man's way of doing things. We need to be able to handle our affairs within our communities, not from people on the outside."

"It must've been a heavy load for you," Jason said remembering his college days.

"Let's just say there was never a dull moment in the city, but I missed this place knowing that Howling Wolf had chosen me to learn and preserve our traditional ways. It was the proudest day of my life, far more meaningful than that diploma hanging on the wall. He leaned toward Jason and said softly, "Just between you and me, the interest he shows in you is quite an honor."

"I'm still confused about this all, but whatever he has in store for me, I hope I won't disappoint him."

"It's not a matter of that," Joseph explained, "he's going to show you things and what you do with it will be up to you."

"This is all very strange," Jason said shaking his head.

With a comforting smile, Joseph added, "Don't worry, Lost Spirit, you'll be fine."

"Oh great," slipped out of Jason's mouth. He was embarrassed that Running Pony now knew the name Howling Wolf had given him.

"You better get some sleep," Joseph said, "he'll be calling on you at sunrise." He gave Jason a blanket, saying, "Good night."

"See you in the morning," Jason replied, settling back into the couch. He drifted in and out of sleep; his mind wouldn't let him rest. He tried to process the day's events, but nothing made sense. The last dream he remembered disturbed him and to escape it he slowly opened his eyes. When he was able to focus, he saw Howling Wolf sitting in the chair staring at him. He wondered how the old man had gotten there without being heard. Sitting up, he sheepishly said, "Good morning, Mr. Wolf."

"Thanks should be given to the Creator for every morning we are able to rise," he chuckled.

Jason folded the blanket, "Is Joseph up yet?"

"He has been up for quite some time; he's out collecting herbs for me," the old man said pacing anxiously. Jason noticed he was dressed differently; instead of jeans and cowboy boots, he wore moccasins and buck skin pants and shirt. Howling Wolf watched him lace his riding boots. He cleared his throat and said, "We're going for a walk, are you ready?"

"Sure," Jason replied jumping to his feet.

The old man crossed his arms over his stomach and stood motionless while staring at Jason's feet. Uncomfortable by the glare, Jason asked, "What?"

Still looking at his feet, Howling Wolf noted, "How can you feel Mother Earth through a layer of plastic?" He pointed to a pair of moccasins by the couch. "Running Pony has gifted you with an essential tool."

Jason quickly switched footwear as the old man headed out the door. The sun hadn't risen over the mountains yet; Jason took a deep breath of the fresh morning air as Howling Wolf slung a bag over his shoulder. It appeared to be made of buffalo hide with eagle feathers tied to the strap and beads adorning the fringe at the bottom. Howling Wolf headed away from Joseph's house toward the mountains without saying a word. The pace was brisk. Jason tried to make conversation to slow the old man down, but he moved in silence with Jason trailing further behind. Jason watched his silver braids glide back and forth across his back as pangs of hunger ached in his stomach. He became irritated, cursing to himself in the hope the march would soon end.

Howling Wolf crested a hill and waited. Noticing Jason's exhaustion and changing appearance, Howling Wolf removed a bladder from his bag and offered it to him. Jason gulped it down noticing it didn't taste like the water he was used to; it instantly soothed his stomach. Howling Wolf nodded. "It will pass."

Jason looked around and saw how far they'd traveled, the village being barely distinguishable. Shadows slowly slid down the multi-colored spires in the desert, making for a beautiful sunrise. A screech startled him. Looking up, he caught a glimpse of the eagle diving down the ridgeline screaming past them like a missile. Jason responded, "This is an awesome place, Howling Wolf."

"It is where my journeys start as well as yours." Howling Wolf walked to a nearby tree that had a depression around its base and sat down. He fit the depression perfectly. He signaled Jason to a tree next to his. Once seated, the old man said, "We are on the magnetic alignment of north and south, which brings balance. If you look over there, the sun is rising from the east. That is the direction of enlightenment, because the sun represents knowledge. If you should find yourself in a situation where you cannot find answers, face east and explore your dilemma. Eventually an answer will come to you by tapping into your unconscious knowledge, which will then relay the answer to your conscious mind and give you guidance."

Howling Wolf studied Jason's face before continuing, "West is the direction of gratitude; every day at its end, face west and give thanks to the Creator for another day of life, regardless of that day's events for everything happens for a reason. The direction over there, south, stands for the destiny of all mankind. If you desire strength, or know someone who needs strength, remember this direction and ask for help. North is for health;

mental, physical, and emotional, so if you ever need a healing energy, face her and you will be energized. Remember and respect these directions, Lost Spirit, for they are essential to our survival."

Jason listened intently as he fought off his returning hunger pains. He'd never felt this type of need before, and to experience it distracted him. Yet he knew many people in the world felt hunger every day and he had no idea it felt so bad. Howling Wolf pulled out a small leaf from his medicine bag and handed it to him, "Put this under your tongue and your hunger will leave you." Jason did as directed and the distraction slowly quelled. Howling Wolf then said, "Through fasting, which has been taught to us from ancient medicine men, we are able to receive the medicine's ways and guidance. A person comes to know these ways by doing so; you can retain things only when you're not full. It is also a cleansing process that enables us to receive clear visions. Look around you Lost Spirit, you are a part of nature, let her work through you. The Creator will communicate to you through the things that he has created; be aware of this and don't let anything escape you. Know the difference between looking at things and seeing things. Our knowledge started from the world around us; we learned to predict things from careful observation and by using our senses. That tree you are sitting under is living and can teach you many things. Hug it, smell it, talk to it Lost Spirit, become one with it and when I return we will continue."

*****

Howling Wolf got up and walked away. The thought of talking to a tree seemed strange, let alone hugging one, yet he did it and focused on doing just that. Many sounds coming from the woods around him distracted him and he felt vulnerable being alone. His rambling thoughts centered on the saying of not being able to see the forest from the trees. As he communicated with his tree, the sun moved across the sky. When Howling Wolf returned, he went to his tree and sat down. "You are on a learning path, Lost Spirit. The Creator can communicate to you through many different means and your tree here is one of those means. Remember, to experience something is to know something. Running Pony has spent many years at the white man's schools learning many things, but until he experiences these things himself, he is only remembering someone else's words and thoughts. You have experienced the tree and one day when you try to explain to someone that every part of a tree can give us energy, it will come from your heart because you actually felt it."

Jason wasn't sure what he was supposed to feel from the tree, "I can't say for sure what I'm feeling; how am I to know when it happens?"

Smiling brightly, Howling Wolf touched his tree and said, "Many things we learn do not surface until we need that knowledge. It is stored in the sub-mind, available yet not always noticeable, so be careful what you put into your mind. Always try to place positive things in and live hopefully, Lost Spirit."

Jason nodded, "These trees are firmly attached to Mother Earth through veins that reach deep into time."

Howling Wolf smiled in agreement. "When I was a young buck, my parents died from small pox. In our culture children are cared for by all the mothers of the tribe from birth. It was a great loss and I grew up living by what they had taught me. My sense of belonging was to the Creator and Mother Earth, for that is what sustains us in this life. We are brought in on the Red Road, which leads to life and spirituality and to oneness with the Great Being. I can feel it in your heart, Lost Spirit; that you long to be recognized and accepted by those who brought you into this world like the way a wild animal gives birth and nurtures their young unconditionally, but that is not always possible, even with the wild creatures. The Great Eagle brought us together so that you can see and feel your sense of belonging."

Jason's eyes clouded as he listened to Howling Wolf; he said in a shaky voice, "How could I be a lost spirit if the eagle brought us together? Doesn't that mean I have some direction?"

The old man cocked his head, "Life is suffering. Coping with that suffering gives our lives meaning and strength. Accept it; use it as a turning point in life. That is why you are here. It has been your reaction to your life's circumstances that has made you a lost spirit."

"But I have carried these feelings all my life," Jason cried, "Now, I'm finally doing something about it. What can be so wrong with that?"

"There is nothing wrong about it," Howling Wolf replied, "the Creator allows things to happen to us to show us what kind of character we are made of; sometimes he takes us the long way to get there. Even though you may think you are just floating around on a breeze, you are and have been on the spirit road."

Jason's thoughts centered on what Richard had said to him about his belief in God; he noticed a parallel between the two dogmas, yet felt confused and uncomfortable with the thought of being tested by a higher power.

Howling Wolf watched the sun set through ever changing cloud formations. When the brilliant array of colors had given into the evening, another spectacle appeared from the east. The ridge line illuminated; the silhouette of trees standing tall on the mountain top announced the rising of the moon in its full glory. Howling Wolf rose from his beloved spot and said to Jason, "It is time for us to act."

They followed a path that led deeper into the forest. Along the way, Howling Wolf learned about Jason's upbringing. He was raised by two very loving parents, who provided him with all that was needed to become a responsible adult. He also had a younger brother and sister, much to the surprise of his parents, for they thought they were unable to have children, thus resulting in Jason's adoption. All three children were treated equally despite the noticeable physical differences between Jason and the rest of the family. They put him through college and were very proud of his achievements.

Howling Wolf asked, "When was the last time you spoke with your parents?"

"A long time ago," Jason replied.

In a commanding tone, Howling Wolf said, "You should let them know how you are doing. They are probably worried about you."

"I'll call them when we get back to the store," Jason said thinking he should have done it earlier.

*****

They'd been hiking uphill for quite some time. The light of the moon made the hike easy and when they crested the ridge, a small valley appeared below them with a large creek meandering through it. It sparkled in the moonlight, looking like a long silver snake slithering across the valley. Howling Wolf pointed to a cluster of trees nestled by the creek and said with excitement,

"That is my home, down there."

Jason didn't see a house or anything that resembled a home as they made their way down the ridge to the valley and followed the creek toward Howling Wolf's "home." Walking behind the old man with the moon light reflecting off his buckskins made Jason wonder what life must have been like for Howling Wolf in his younger days. To wake up each day and see this valley without any "civilized" interference must have been quite the life.

Making their way toward the stand of trees Howling Wolf had pointed out, Jason noticed the outline of a tipi nestled in the pines. He thought back to when Running Pony had said they'd found him a teepee in the woods. It wasn't a joke after all. Entering the site revealed the teepee and a fire pit. A neat pile of firewood was stacked next to a large log used for sitting. Howling Wolf opened the flap of the tipi and went inside. He came out with two wooden bowls, a grinding stone, and a piece of flint. He motioned Jason to sit on the log as he gathered dry grass and pine needles and placed them gently into the fire pit. Using a knife, he struck the flint a few times and the sparks smoldered in the dry fuel. Blowing on it produced a flicker of flame which grew into a small fire. As he carefully fed the fire, he said to Jason, "Always respect the spirit of fire; it is the sun stored in the wood and when released it gives us warmth and energy. When it is disrespected, it can burn us, our homes, and our land. Treat it with the respect you would a grandfather, because it has been around for a very long time and deserves to be handled gently."

Jason watched as the growing light danced off the surrounding trees and the tipi. The reflections it made on Howling Wolf's face revealed how old he really was; his features deeply etched as if of stone. The flames dancing in the old man's eyes sent shivers down his spine. Howling Wolf must've seen the same in Jason's eyes, because he stirred and said, "You have very powerful eyes Lost Spirit, at times I feel like I am the one being taken on a journey."

The comment surprised Jason and he responded, "I've had people comment about them before, but I am looking out and don't know what it feels like to be looking in."

Howling Wolf thought a moment, "We will both benefit from our seeing."

Jason asked, "Do you come here often?"

"Not as much as I would like to, and less now than when I was younger." Howling Wolf sighed, "I have brought many young braves up here to fast and prepared them to journey into the spirit world, but those days are fewer now since many of our young people tend to move off the reservation and become part of the modern world."

"How do you prepare one for the spirit world?"

Putting sticks on the fire, Howling Wolf said, "Not everyone is allowed to journey into the spirit world. I choose those who show me that they are worthy by their thoughts, actions and deeds. This sometimes takes years, or it might take days depending on the strength of their spirit and their will." He leaned closer to Jason, "I have chosen you to journey that road because the great eagle has brought us together and that in itself is a sign of the strength of your spirit. Now it is up to me to help you see a different world; one that hopefully will guide you the rest of your life. If you look over there," he said pointing to a nearby tree, "you will see the eagle is still with you."

Jason looked at the tree and saw the eagle sitting on a branch. Its continued presence mystified him. He heard the old man's words, but the question of, "why me," kept coming to mind.

Noticing Jason's confusion, Howling Wolf continued, "Once a person is chosen, the next step is to prepare them for the spirit world by fasting. You have begun to experience the effect of that already," he said with a laugh. "When you are not full, you can retain things. You must also become a clear channel in order to receive whatever will be revealed to you.

Jason realized that he'd not eaten in two days, but the hunger pains weren't gnawing at him. The words, *To know hunger, is to know feast,*" came out of his mouth without conscious thought.

A deep laugh echoed across the valley. Howling Wolf slapped his knee, "Not bad, Lost Spirit, I didn't know you were a poet. Try this: *To be the sky, is to feel the wings of the eagle.*"

Jason looked at the eagle and smiled. "That's good, Howling Wolf. *To feel the open road, is to be truly free.*"

"Ha," Howling Wolf said, slapping his knee again. "I got you on this one. You have been riding your iron horse all over the country, but you are not free...are you?"

"At one time," Jason said fighting back emotions, "when riding with my wife, I was truly free."

Empathy laced the old man's words, "Fear not, Lost Spirit, you will be free again." He continued, "*To have heard the buffalo, is to know thunder.*"

Jason gathered himself and fired back, "*To feel the wind, is to be kissed by her.*"

"Now we're getting somewhere," Howling Wolf said. "*To know darkness, is to see the light.*"

Feeling the coldness on his back, and the heat on his front side, Jason acknowledged, "*To know cold, is to know heat.*"

"*To feel the rain, is to feel life,*" Howling Wolf countered as he looked up into the night sky.

Feeling the harmonica in his pocket, Jason said, "*To know the Blues, is to know suffering.*"

Howling Wolf looked stymied. "Can't say I know much about the Blues; only that it is the music of our black brothers who were also exploited by the whites. Do you know their struggles, Lost Spirit?"

"I know their music. It touches my soul in ways nothing else can. The Blues has developed a universal following; a language where all people can express the feeling's that lurk in their souls. At any rate, it gives me an outlet." Jason thought about the Blues legend, Howlin' Wolf, and added, "The Blues also has a master by the name of Howlin' Wolf. He kind of reminds me of you, Howling Wolf!"

The old man smiled and said, "How so?"

"Well, he had a booming voice and a looming presence. Someone once said about his music, 'This is where the soul of man never dies.' Quite a few parallels, I'd say."

Howling Wolf appeared to blush, looked up to the full moon, and said, "And on the subject of feeling life, I am now going to prepare our tonic."

CHAPTER 11

Howling Wolf gathered one of the wooden bowls and headed to the creek. The light of the moon illuminated his body and Jason watched as the silhouette of the old man slowly merged with the creek, up to his waist. Responding to Howling Wolf's movements, the eagle took flight with such force, the concussion of its wings startled Jason. After standing motionless in the creek for quite some time, Howling Wolf submerged the bowl into the water and raised it toward the heavens. Jason heard him chanting; then he took a drink from the bowl, turned around, and carefully made his way back to the fire, still chanting.

He placed the bowl on the ground and retrieved the other one. Taking some herbs from his medicine bag, he placed them in the bowl and using the grinding stone minced and ground them together. Jason watched the ritual intently. Howling Wolf then took some pine needles from a tree and ground them into the mix. When he looked satisfied with the consistency, he reached down and scooped up a little soil and tossed it into the air. The heavy pieces quickly fell to the ground and he swiftly positioned the bowl so the fines fell into it. He explained to Jason, "I am asking the spirits of all that is alive around us to reveal themselves to us through the taking of them into our bodies. There are many different tonics that I can make. I have chosen this one especially for your benefit Lost Spirit, because of your need for a sense of belonging. I feel it is the best place for us to begin."

Howling Wolf poured some water into the dry mix and stirred it with a small twig from the same tree he'd gotten the pine needles from. He set the bowl down, put the twig in his mouth, swirled it around, and smacked his lips. Smiling at Jason, he said, "Ummm, just right!"

Jason laughed at the sight. It reminded him of when his mother used to let him lick the mixing spoon when she made cakes. He was glad to see the little kid in Howling Wolf. A serious expression fell on the old man's face and he looked at Jason,

"When our children are only a few days old, we properly introduce them to the elements asking that they recognize and protect our children. You are not a child, but it is better late than never."

Howling Wolf rose and said, "Come Lost Spirit." He walked into the meadow and directed Jason to stand in a specific spot and then faced each of the four directions saying, "You surround us all of our lives, please protect him and reveal yourself to him when his life is in need of balance." Howling Wolf then slipped off his moccasins and motioned Jason to do the same. Looking down on the ground he said, "Oh great Mother Earth, please continue to support him, for I know he will always respect you."

Howling Wolf walked to the creek and entered it up to his knees, as Jason followed behind. He bent down and splashed Jason with water, "Oh great giver of life, please continue to wash over this spirit and never let him know thirst." He then looked up at the moon and star studded sky, raised his arms, he said, "Great lights in the night sky watch over this soul and guide him through his darkest nights."

He then positioned Jason to feel the breeze in his face and said, "Continue to cover him with your gentle touch, for the journey on his iron horse will be long and in need of your constant presence." He grabbed Jason by the shoulder and escorted him back to the bank of the creek and said, "Today, when we watched the sunset, I asked Grandfather Sun to shine upon you and surround you with its warmth and supply you with its loving energy throughout all of your days."

Tears gathered in Jason's eyes and before he could speak, Howling Wolf walked back to camp. Jason stood there a few moments, absorbing the moment. His body felt weightless, like he was hovering above the ground. He could see his feet moving to camp, but couldn't feel the ground. Howling Wolf was tending the fire when he entered camp. He took a seat next to him, feeling overwhelmed. Howling Wolf gathered some ashes and said, "As I mentioned earlier, fire must be respected as a grandfather. I have asked it to help you to see your path, so that you do not stumble." He rubbed the ash on Jason's arm while explaining what the mix will do to him once his journey into the spirit world began. "I have helped many souls travel the spirit road and have been entrusted with the knowledge of the use of many herbs and prayers. As I said earlier, this tonic was specifically made for your journey and it contains peyote. This is a very important part of our culture and has been used for over two-thousand years. It has many derangement properties and makes one's senses highly sharpened. You will be extremely aware of what's around and inside of you. I will be here to guide you and to keep you safe, along with your spirit protector, the eagle. Do you have any questions before we begin, Lost Spirit?"

Nervousness crept through Jason as he listened to Howling Wolf. He'd never taken a hallucinogenic drug before, only smoked a little pot. The thought of doing it now, under these circumstances, frightened him. He trusted Howling Wolf, which quelled his fear. He joked, "Well, since there aren't any buildings to jump off of or a buses to run in front of, I guess I could try it just once."

Howling Wolf shook his head and laughed, "You listen to too much propaganda, Lost Spirit." He went to his tipi, returning with a drum that had a wolf's head painted on its surface, a cluster of eagle feathers fashioned like a fan, and a bundle of dried vegetation, and sat down. "The tonic will help you to bridge this world into the spirit world. This is a religious ceremony and I guarantee you will not see any buildings or buses." They both laughed and Jason relaxed.

CHAPTER 12

Howling Wolf cradled the drum it in his lap and rubbed it affectionately. "It was made for me by my teacher and one day, I will pass it on to my student, Joseph Running Pony. The drum represents the heartbeat of our Creator. The life-giving energy of our tall standing brothers flows through the wood that makes up the shell, and the skin also had life once. Together they represent life that has gone on and its pulse will keep you in harmony with your own heartbeat as you travel the spirit road."

He took the bundle of vegetation and put the tip of it in the fire. After it burned for a few seconds, he blew it out; it smoldered giving off a bitter-sweet fragrance. The old man grabbed the feather fan and explained to Jason, "This is white sage; we use it to purify people, places, and things. Before you go any further, we must rid you of any bad spirits and christen this holy place. He stood up and while chanting, used the fan to disperse the smoke, first to the four directions, then around the camp, and finally he fanned the smoke on Jason. When he was finished, he smothered the sage bundle in the soil.

Howling Wolf began beating on the drum in a slow rhythmic pattern. After a while, it mimicked Jason's heartbeat and as he closed his eyes and concentrated on the pulse; his body began rocking in cadence with the drum. The drumming suddenly stopped. Howling Wolf took the bowl with the tonic and stirred it again with the twig. He raised the bowl to the heavens and said a prayer in his native tongue. He took a drink and then offered it to Jason with both hands saying, "It is time, Lost Spirit; drink."

Jason accepted the bowl and nodded to Howling Wolf before taking his share. The first taste was so bitter, Jason struggled to swallow it. He looked at Howling Wolf to see how much he should drink. The old man motioned his head upward. Jason finished the tonic shaking his head before putting the empty bowl on the ground.

The old man began beating his drum again while chanting.

The sound was coming at Jason in waves; first strong in his face, then fading away into the valley where the crickets and frogs joined in creating an ensemble that pulsated through his body. It traveled through his arms and legs, then his core. Every nerve in his body sang out while it entered his head. He saw himself on the verge of leaving his body; then suddenly he was viewing himself from above. He was pure consciousness floating above the camp, able to see and hear everything. He looked over to the tree where the eagle sat and noticed it looking at him. He looked at Howling Wolf; without seeing his lips move, he heard the words, "Lets travel!"

Jason's awareness traveled to the tree where Howling Wolf had gotten the pine needles. He entered the tree through its needles. The tree's life force engulfed him into a vibrant channel saturated with nutrients as he moved through the needles to the branches. They splintered out in every direction. He traveled every branch, experiencing live areas and dead spots. Insects chewed on him. He felt the thick, sticky sap slow his movement until he broke out into a bird's nest. The tree's breath nourished his lungs with oxygen. A pinecone sucked him in, exposing tiny seeds waiting for the right time to fall to the earth to start the process anew. He loved being in the branches but just as he became comfortable, he was caught up in a channel that moved him down the trunk of the tree. The nutrients flowing up from the roots tasted sweet, and the thick coat of bark gave him protection from the outside. Darkness fell on him as he was pulled down into a massive root system, where hand-like tentacles grasped the earth and sucked life into itself.

A nudge forced him out of the roots into the surrounding soil. As he looked back to see who or what had done it, all he could make out was the tree's massive tap root and thousands of lateral roots sporting hair like follicles, spreading out in all directions. If it wasn't for that push, he felt he could have spent eternity living inside the tree. He maneuvered through the earth, passing thousands of roots until a giant boulder filled his vision. Willing himself to turn, he narrowly missed flying into it. "This is awesome," he murmured as he traveled under the contour of the earth's surface, passing by ant colonies, rodent burrows, buried prey, sand, pebbles, rocks and huge mountains. He dove deep into the earth, experiencing total darkness where massive slabs of rocks made traveling difficult. The concept of hell popped into his mind and the thought of going there scared him. Fearing he would get lost, or worse yet, stuck in hell, he pointed himself upward and jetted toward the surface.

Nearing the top, he felt water on his body and was instantly swept into the current of the creek. He slowly meandered to another creek, which joined another and before he knew it, he was in a large river carving its way through the earth toward the ocean. He traveled through the mountains, chiseling deep canyons and offering spectacular waterfalls. Passing through the gills of fish and being drawn up by the mouths of many different creatures gave him purpose. Tree roots pulled on him from the banks, keeping the forests alive and teeming with activity. Leaving the forests and mountains, he entered into the valleys and plains. Meandering through the towns that sprung up, he was sucked into large pipes and distributed throughout the homes, factories, and farm lands, only to be spit back out into the river with an awful taste in his mouth and his vision clouded. Sickness racked his body as he passed through man's creations. He swam fiercely to get away from the stench until the smell and taste of salt filtered through him, diluting the toxins. He swam endlessly through the ocean until the warmth of the sun's rays penetrated the water, drawing him to the surface.

Emerging on a wave, he basked in the warm sun looking up at the clouds. Suddenly, he was pulled up into the air and traveled for miles until he joined a caravan of clouds heading back to the mainland. Moving across the ocean more clouds gathered and he felt moisture gathering around him. The land pulled on him, the mountains pulled on him, and when he was able to touch the peaks, he fell from the clouds as snow kissing everything below him. He bounced off trees, landed on the earth, and traveled to the nearest creek. He knew the smell, feel, and texture of this water. It felt like home. He wasn't surprised when he popped his head above the water and saw Howling Wolf's camp.

Suddenly, a tight grip on his shoulders flung him out of the water into the air. He somersaulted and twisted, gaining altitude at a blinding speed. When he'd peaked and was about to fall, he put his arms out and began to fly. He'd dreamed of flying as a kid, but this sensation was far beyond his imagination. Once comfortable with the sensation, he dove straight toward the earth. The gravitational force was unbearable and the piercing noise of him cutting through the air was deafening. As the ground rapidly filled his vision, he panicked and pulled up hard barely missing the ground and swooping past the eagle, almost knocking it off its perch. The bird screeched at him as he whistled by. Looking down, he saw Howling Wolf shaking his finger at him.

As he soared through the night sky, he felt a peeling sensation on his skin, as if he were shedding out of a cocoon and in a split second, he was fractionalized and became part of the wind. He had no control and found himself roaming the surface of the earth, blanketing everything in his path. Sliding through the forests he touched every needle and leaf of every tree. Experiencing the coldness high in the mountains and the gradual warming as he descended into the valleys was breathtaking. Soaring over the oceans, he drove the surf and regulated the tide. He cooled the land and gave life to every lung. He continued to flow through the fur of animals, through caves, up high mountain passes, and rocked the tops of trees. As he floated above the earth, he felt the presence of Howling Wolf beside him. Looking over, he saw him point to the heavens. Jason nodded and before he knew it, they were traveling through a different space. Transparent images of people and animals and of everything that had ever lived passed before his eyes. The sight was frightening. It was very crowded in that sphere. He looked over to Howling Wolf for assurance and the old man whispered, "These are the spirits of those who have passed before us, and this is where we will go one day, but fear not, Lost Spirit, it is not our time yet."

*****

Jason was spellbound. He recognized the faces of many people he had studied in history books as the steady stream of spirits passed them by. Howling Wolf pointed and said, "Look over there, those are my parents," as tears followed the contour of his weathered cheeks and fell toward the earth. Howling Wolf's father sat proudly with his wife by his side draped in a Calvary blanket. The old man looked at Jason and said, "It's difficult looking in from the outside but when we are called to this world, it will appear different than it does now. We will have a purpose inside this world, but only then will we know what it is."

More spirits clouded their space. Suddenly, Rose appeared before Jason. He screamed out to her, only to have Howling Wolf rein him in. "Don't. She is at peace. She's knows you're here, but we must not interfere. We are only observers; to mingle with the spirits can have dire consequences."

Jason reached out to her and yelled anyway, "Rose, baby, I love you. I miss you. I need to be with you." She swooped up to his face and said, "Fear not, my love, we will be together again, but this is not the time. You must be strong and move on. I miss you dearly." She then disappeared into the crowd.

He screamed after her, "Don't go; take me with you, please!"

She looked back at him and said, "Don't mess with the spirits; you don't want to change what will be!"

Howling Wolf knew Jason was entering shaky territory. He released Jason from the heavens onto a lightning bolt. It smashed him into the ground in a blinding flash, knocking the air out of him, pinning him to the earth. He sat up, not knowing where he was. The beat of Howling Wolfs drum grounded him. His arms and legs began to tingle and as if in a vacuum, his consciousness reentered his body.

Howling Wolf cautioned, "Don't fight it; ride it out, you'll be okay."

Jason eased back into himself and sat dumbfounded for what seemed like an eternity. He could see what was happening around him, but he couldn't move. Howling Wolf started chanting and a wave of relaxation spread through his body; he became limp. He was exhausted and confused. The yearning for Rose was unbearable. He felt himself being picked up and carried to the teepee, where he was laid on bear skins. His last memory was seeing Howling Wolf closing the flap of the teepee and disappearing.

CHAPTER 13

Jason awoke disorientated, his head pounding. His body was sore like he'd just played a double overtime football game in the late summer heat. The urge to get up was overruled by his body. He laid there staring out the hole in the top of the teepee. Memories flooded his mind as he tried to distinguish if he'd really gone to the spirit world, or just visualized the events. As he pondered his journey, the spirits of the hides he was laying on seemed to come to life. He quickly forced himself up and went outside. The fire pit was out and Howling Wolf was nowhere in sight. Quickly looking over to the tree where the eagle had kept its vigil, he saw no eagle. By the position of the sun, he'd realized he'd slept late into the afternoon. A chill blanketed him; he decided to rekindle the fire, remembering Howling Wolf's words about respecting fire as he would an elder.

Warming himself by the flames, he noticed when fixating his eyes on an object it moved away from him, swaying from side to side. He fought to keep control of his senses. He focused on the old man following the creek toward him, and the eagle flying above gave him renewed energy. Not wanting to appear exhausted or freaked out over the intensity of his experience, he jumped up and headed out to greet him. He raised his arm saying, "Good morning, Howling Wolf."

The old man looked at Jason and then to the sun and replied, "Good afternoon, Wandering Spirit."

Jason noticed "Lost" had been replaced by, "Wandering." He felt like he'd graduated to a more respectable level. With newfound confidence he said in a strong voice, "Yeah, that's what I meant, but I have been on a very long journey and the face of time has concealed nothing."

Howling Wolf cocked his head, "So then," he demanded, spreading his arms toward heaven, "what did time show you, Wandering Spirit?"

"First, Howling Wolf, I want to thank you for choosing me to enter your world. I had no idea! What time showed me last night was that life can be found everywhere and in everything and when it leaves the world that we know, it doesn't die. It changes form and continues to live on. Last night, I also saw myself leaving my home looking for a sense of belonging, for answers, and today, I realize that I belong to Mother Earth, yet I still have a longing that needs to be understood."

Howling Wolf smiled, "You are learning quickly, Wandering Spirit. You have emptied yourself of everything you carried here and became a vessel to receive the blessings of the Great Spirit; now you are a channel for those blessing to flow into the lives of others. This is the real reason for us finding each other; you have the gift of becoming a medicine man, if you should so choose."

The words burned into Jason; he felt confused and not worthy to be accepted into such a group of people. Not wanting to disappoint his teacher after such a revealing statement, he expressed his uneasiness, "You have no idea how honored I am; your open faith and confidence in me exceeds my own. The problem is, I question myself as to who I am. I wouldn't know how to use what I am learning."

Howling Wolf listened intently and when Jason went silent, the old man calmly said, "Your words do not surprise me, in fact, I expected you to respond in such a way. You saw the power of the spirit world. It is not the place you would want to journey to often, for it could sweep you away. That world which lives outside of you, you have seen its vastness, but now it is time for you to know your inner self."

Jason feared using a tonic to get inside of his mind. Howling Wolf fed the fire and stood up. He pointed to a mountain peak, "That ledge up there is where you fell to earth last night; it is your spot, and I must say Wandering Spirit, it is the perfect place for your vision quest."

Jason looked up to the peak; it seemed vaguely familiar. He nodded to Howling Wolf, "Yeah, not a bad spot at all."

The old man got comfortable and stated, "Very soon you are going up there, and once again, you will open yourself up, but this time it will be to yourself, and to the Great Being. Instead of outwardly sight, you will explore insight and take charge of yourself so that you can become one with your mind, body and spirit. I remember you saying earlier that you still had a longing. It is this longing you must meet and identify within yourself, because you cannot conquer it with external means. You could ride your iron horse as far as the great oceans looking outside for the answer, but you will not find it. You have an identity, a heritage to embrace; go find it. I know who you are, the Creator knows who you are, and now you must find out who you are." The old man slapped his shoulder saying, "Tag, you are it."

"Tag, you're it?" Jason repeated trying not to laugh at the slur. "So, what I'm trying to find out on my vision quest is who I am. What is the who that I am, and why is the who that I am here?"

Howling Wolf responded joyfully, "You continue to impress me, Wandering Spirit, for I could not have said it any better. Now that you know what to do, you had better get moving. The fire you started will continue to be fed until you return. It will anchor you if you need it."

*****

Thankful it didn't require the use of a tonic; Jason stood up, focused on his mountain ledge and without a word headed toward it. His hike started out easy crossing the meadow. Entering the forest, he'd periodically look back to see Howling Wolf sitting in the same spot. The higher he traveled the more he could see. Mile upon mile of canyons, valleys, and distant mountain ranges opened up to him. The view was breathtaking and he stopped often to enjoy it. The ledge stuck out on the side of the mountain. He carefully studied the face and mapped out a path of travel that looked the easiest. He called upon the mountain to accept him and support him on his quest. Beads of sweat formed on his forehead as his body embraced the rough, cool rock that nourished multicolored lichens. He climbed on; one foothold after another until he was able to pull his body onto his ledge. It was larger than he envisioned, allowing him to sprawl out. The heavens were alive with soaring birds, slithering clouds, and a light wind that caressed his body.

After a short rest he sat up and scanned the world around him. It was a perfect spot for his quest; the view of the valley was panoramic, he was sheltered from the elements by the overhang and he noticed it was also a place for other animals by the bird droppings at one end on the ledge, and a rather large bedding depression of some kind of animal at the other end. A steady breeze blew up the mountain. Wanting to feel more; he stripped his jacket and shirt, spread his arms out, and wished he could fly. He settled into the lotus position and began breathing slow and deep. The last rays of the sun warmed his core. He knew it would be a struggle to take the journey inside, because the elements he'd experienced earlier were so powerful they continued to pull on his senses. He blocked them out by using moss growing on the rocks as ear plugs, and his bandana served as a cover for his constantly wandering eyes. He continued his breathing exercise and started his inward journey by asking himself, "WHO AM I?"

He asked the question over and over, yet no answer came. The difficulty of looking in from the outside was posing a challenge. As he struggled for answers; childhood memories flooded his mind. He saw a little kid beating on pots on the kitchen floor while his mother cooked. Suddenly, a raspy voice interrupted his vision, 'Hey, we're not here to walk down memory lane, man. I'm thirsty; haven't had a cold beer in a long time, and I'm starving.'

A different voice sternly injected, 'Back off; that's all you think about, there's more to life than just eating and drinking. We have a cause going on here, so take a back seat pal, and shut up.'

The raspy voice chuckled, 'Yeah right, a quest for what? For parents that didn't love you enough to raise you? A reason for losing your wife, your unborn child, your job, and your home! You're broken down; just like your bike! Just face it; you're being tested just like Job was tested by God!'

"That's enough!" Jason yelled out. The voices scattered. "I'm only a man. I have faults, but why? Why Rose? She was innocent. If it was something I did then I should be punished not her, not our child. How could God do that to her?"

The raspy voice crawled back out. 'You have no faith, no foundation; like Richard said, you're a wandering soul, lost in your own pity; therefore you're subject to the dark side.'

"That's not fair." Jason yelled out.

'Life's not fair,' raspy laughed.

Jason shouted, "Screw you."

'Screw you too,' echoed back.

He became frustrated and wondered what kind of quest was this becoming; a duel with himself? He didn't want to deal with his inner turmoil. While he fended off the voices, he had a feeling that he was being watched. He removed his ear plugs and bandana. Looking across the moonlit valley, he saw the fire light from their camp. Wondering if it was Howling Wolf, he looked around the granite shelf. His eyes locked onto those of a cougar, sitting silently in the far corner of the ledge. Fear froze him like a winter snow storm. The look in the cat's eyes didn't show aggression, so he continued to look into the piercing brown. Eventually the cat lowered its head and appeared to sleep. He didn't know what to do. Should he try to slip out quietly or accept the cat as allowing him to share the space? He was physically and mentally drained and felt like doing the same. He curled into a ball and dozed off.

The sound of drums woke him. He sat up slowly, not wanting to startle the cougar. Slowly, he turned his head to where the cat was and to his relief, and regret, it was gone. Redirecting his attention to the drums, he looked down to the source and jumped to his feet. The vision was shimmering, like looking across the desert at high noon. Circled around a large bonfire were many Indians dancing and chanting loudly, dressed like braves in an old western movie with bows and spears in their hands. They were shaking them to the drum beat as they circled the fire. He watched intently and noticed one of them break from the loop and walk toward him. The brave stopped, raised his spear high, pumped it three times in the air and spoke to Jason in his native tongue. Jason couldn't understand what the man was saying. He tried to commit the words to memory, for he felt they were of great importance.

Behind the brave, a white woman broke from the loop and stood next to him. She looked at Jason and he instantly noticed her blond hair and deep blue penetrating eyes; they looked just like his. Tears snaked down her cheeks as she spoke, "Judge not my little one, for what was done had to be done. Carry your spirit high and know that you are always looked upon and dearly loved."

That was all she said. They both turned and walked back to the loop, where they disappeared into the circle. The vision also disappeared, leaving Jason standing on the ledge looking out into an empty space. "What the hell was that?" he yelled out to the night, only to hear it echo down the mountain. He paced the ledge, coming dangerously close to slipping over the edge. He'd had enough of the spirit world and wanted to leave, but it was too dark to do so safely. The mountain lion reappeared on a rock to the side of the ledge. Its tail stuck out and it shuffled its weight on all fours, as if ready to pounce. They locked eyes, blue against brown, testing wills. Her will was far superior to his; he looked away in submission. He walked to the corner of the ledge and sat down. The cat jumped onto the ledge and took its corner. Jason began talking to the cat until the moon took its leave and the sun began to lighten the valley.

It was time for Jason to leave the shelf. He ran his hand along the flakey granite wall as if offering his hand to someone who'd done him a great service. The cougar watched intently. When their eyes met again, chills ran through him. The cat stood, stretching its long sleek body. Sorrow filled Jason for he knew this would never happen again and to have this magnificent creature share its space with him almost brought tears to his eyes. "I must take my leave protector of the night. Thank you for accepting me into your world, I will never forget you!" He nodded to the cat and slowly climbed off the ledge and down the rocks. Looking up occasionally, he saw the cougar's head peering down at him. He carefully made his way from the crags, until the cougar was a little brown dot on the shelf. Fatigue and weakness had reduced him to a pair of wobbly legs. He entered camp to find Howling Wolf relaxing against a tree stitching beads to an animal hide. He put his project down, stood up, and welcomed Jason with a nod and a hug. "Welcome back, Nobel Spirit. I can see in your eyes that it was a revealing journey."

Jason faintly smiled and took a seat by the fire. Howling Wolf didn't initiate conversation; he'd wait until Jason was ready to talk. The silence continued as Jason began to fall asleep on the stump. He'd suddenly jerked his head to keep himself from falling into the fire. The old man quietly said, "Go lie down, you can relax now."

*****

After a few hours of deep, restful sleep, Jason emerged from the tepee feeling much better. The smell of food cooking made his stomach growl. Howling Wolf was tending a small cast iron pot hanging above the fire and the thought of eating had his mouth watering. He eagerly went over to Howling Wolf and stared at the pot. "You look as though you haven't eaten in a week," erupted from the old man as he stirred a mixture of maze, squash, and venison. Jason positioned himself so that he could inhale the scent. Wondering how it had gotten to the camp, he asked, "Where did you get this food, Howling Wolf?"

The old man chuckled, "Joseph brought it up here last night, thinking that you'd probably be chewing on pine cones by now."

"That was nice of him," Jason responded as he watched Howling Wolf spoon out a portion into one of the bowls they'd used earlier. Handing the bowl to Jason; he began shoveling food into his mouth.

Howling Wolf barked at Jason, "Slow down, hungry spirit, you're going to get a stomach ache from eating so fast. Try to enjoy it." The food created a burning sensation going down his throat, but he choked it down anyway. When he'd finished, he felt rejuvenated. He had a bounce to his step as he walked to the creek to wash up. Howling Wolf was still working on his meal when he returned. He put his bowl down, "Tell me Wandering Spirit, how did your quest go? You made big noise up there last night."

It took him some time to find the right words. "I have often asked myself the question, who am I? But it was always from the ancestral point; not from within my own self." He chuckled, "After some debate, I was able to strip away the outer layers and what I found underneath was not complete. I know I was on a good foundation, but everything else was in question. I was not disappointed, nor discouraged with it." He looked all around the camp, the meadow, the mountains, and then back to Howling Wolf. "I realized that this journey I'm on may have started out as a result of being abandoned. Abandoned by my birth parents; abandoned by God, left to suffer out the rest of my days not knowing the reasons why. I questioned the Great Creator, and he gave me hope." Howling Wolf stared at Jason. A vision quest, more times than not, raises more questions than it answers, and Jason was showing him the power of his resolve and maturity. The old man was speechless.

Jason mentioned, "A mountain lion was on the ledge with

me; it seemed to be protecting me, from what I can only guess, maybe from myself, I don't know."

Howling Wolf swallowed hard, "Your spirit has great power and potential, that which I have not seen in quite some time, Wandering Spirit. Your path has a heart the size of a buffalo."

Jason wasn't hearing him; he was focusing on the vision of the Indian and the white woman. "When I yelled out last night, it was after seeing a young brave and a white woman breaking out of a fire dance and talking to me. The brave raised his spear to me and said something in his native tongue, but the woman spoke to me in English. She said, 'Judge not my little one for what was done had to be done. Carry your spirit high and know that you are looked upon and dearly loved.' This freaked me out Howling Wolf, because we had the same eyes."

Howling Wolf leaned close to Jason. "Do you remember what the brave said?"

Jason recited the words the best he could and when he'd finished, the old man began muttering words in his native language, while staring into the flames. The Shaman took a deep breath and said, "First, Wandering Spirit, if your spirit aches over this, so does mine. There is a legend among the Sioux which involved the union of a young brave, who later became a powerful and respected medicine man within the Indian nations, and a white woman who had eyes the color of the sky. They birthed a son that carried Indian features, but his eyes also reflected the sky. He too became a powerful medicine man and produced one daughter and three sons, all with the sky in their eyes. These children were absorbed by the white man's world and that's where the legend had its end. I honestly don't know how to interpret your vision; it is too strong for me. Take it to heart, Wandering Spirit, there was a reason for you to see this."

Jason's mind raced, "Could they have been my ancestors? Is one of the three males my father? What happened to them?"

Howling Wolf tried to relieve Jason's distress, "I will send word out to our brothers and sisters and try to find out if anyone can help answer your questions."

Jason squirmed on the log, "I would really appreciate your help Howling Wolf. Maybe there is hope after all!"

The old man cautioned, "I will do what I can, but there are no guarantees, and if all fails Wandering Spirit, remember the woman's words."

Jason nodded, "I understand."

"Now about the cougar," awed the Shaman, "she is one of the most feared and respected hunters of all our four legged friends. For her to allow you to be in her presence is strong medicine indeed. Not only is the spirit of the eagle within you, you now have the puma as an ally. You must keep good thoughts in your mind, always, for if she senses that you are in danger, she will try to protect you."

While Jason mulled over his words, Howling Wolf went to the creek and gathered some water. He ceremoniously put the fire out and began securing the campsite by packing the eating utensils and tying the tepee flap snugly. Jason asked if he needed any help, but the old man said, "Not much clean up here, relax." When he'd finished, he looked at the sun and commented, "If we leave now, we can make our next destination by dusk."

Jason took one last look at the meadow and the rocky ledge on the face of the mountain and groaned, "I'm going to miss your place, Howling Wolf."

The medicine man replied, "I now feel that it is as much your place as it is mine; you can always come back if you want, my friend."

"I might take you up on that. This spot will always be sacred to me," Jason replied as he reached for the pack containing the gear. They headed out in a different direction than they had entered the meadow. The walk was at a leisurely pace, as Howling Wolf collected and showed Jason the numerous plants, roots, and leaf material he used in his medicine. He explained the particular use for each herb. The Shaman also recited the prayers he used in conjunction with the herbs. Jason had become so absorbed listening to, and learning about Howling Wolf's medicine ways that he didn't notice they'd entered another of Howling Wolf's camps.

CHAPTER 14

They settled in for the night around a campfire and the Shaman went into great detail showing Jason the proper use and care of the herbs he'd collected. Everything had a purpose and nothing went to waste. "As I said to you when we met," the old man told Jason, "everything one could possibly need to survive is all around us, not like in the cities where everything is dependent on others to provide. One can be totally independent out here; always remember that my friend, and never fear being in a position of self-reliance, for Mother Earth provides all that we could possibly need to survive."

"Do you ever go to the cities?" Jason asked.

The old man laughed. "What could they possibly give me that I need?"

Jason reflected for some time and said, "I've been brought up to depend on what they provide. I need food, shelter, companionship, a sense of belonging."

The old man laughed, "Do you feel the same way now?"

"Actually," Jason mused, "I'm learning your way. Maybe with time, I can say the same."

Howling Wolf answered sternly, "It is the only way. Joseph has kept me informed on how life outside the reservation is deteriorating. Look at what the cities have spawned; religious confrontations, racial unrest, political dysfunction, crime, and fear. What if the gasoline supply runs dry; how will food be distributed? How will you get around? What if the electrical grid goes down; how will the people survive without it? What if a global war erupts; where will the people hide? City people are too dependent on the cities and one day a force, an evil force, will decimate the cities and those who depend on them. Look how fragile their lives are. I'm not trying to be negative, Wandering Spirit, but look how things are going in this so called 'civilized' world they live in."

Jason nodded. "You're right Howling Wolf; the civilized

world is a step away from self-destruction and I'm glad you've shown me an alternative world."

"Keep your eyes on them and be prepared, Wandering Spirit, and also know that you have this world to come back to."

"It does bring me comfort knowing this. Thank you for opening my eyes."

Howling Wolf laughed, "Your eyes have been open, only now you can see." He got up and signaled Jason to follow as they collected tree branches. From the surrounding pine trees, they gathered pine needles and fashioned mattresses. Lying down on the needles, Howling Wolf pulled the branches over his body and said, "We must rest. Tomorrow will be a busy day. Sleep well, Wandering Spirit."

"Good night, Howling Wolf." Jason struggled to keep warm from the frigid night air. He woke often hearing animals scurrying about and wondered if it might be the cougar checking up on him. As the sun rose, it got even cooler, forcing him to get up. Howling Wolf's pad was empty and a small warming fire attracted him. As he fought off the cold, Howling Wolf returned. "Good morning, Wandering Spirit."

"Morning Howling Wolf. How long have you been up?"

"Quite some time," he said shaking his head. "You had a restless night, talked a lot of gibberish."

"Sorry, I've been told I talk in my sleep."

"Signs of a restless sub-mind, Wandering Spirit. It will get better with time and knowledge."

Howling Wolf stoked the fire and removed a plant root from his pouch. He took a bite and handed it to Jason. "Chew this; it will help with your hunger." A few minutes later, Jason's stomach pains disappeared. "Today," the old man said pointing to the ridge line, "we will hike."

*****

When the fire died down, Howling Wolf snuffed it out and dispersed the pine needles and branches. They then followed a game trail to the top of the ridge and followed it south. Howling Wolf showed and identified all the trees and shrubs to Jason, describing their medicinal uses. At one point, Jason found something totally out of place; a long yellow crape paper panel weighted at one end by a metal rod. He stared at it in wonderment. Howling Wolf picked it up and stuffed it in his pouch explaining, "This is our fire season time and that panel is one of many that are thrown from a plane."

Jason didn't understand, "Why are they thrown from a plane and what does it have to do with your fire season?"

"I've watched it many times over the years after thunderstorms passed over the mountains. In the old days we'd let the fires burn, but these days fires are put out quickly by government firefighters. These panels are used by the Smokejumpers."

"Smokejumpers," Jason hollered, "my best friend Scott is determined to become one of those guys."

The old man nodded saying, "That's a noble ambition indeed. Last month," he said pointing to the south, "I was hiking toward a lightning fire when a plane appeared overhead. It circled the area dropping these streamers. After a couple sets, two figures jumped out of the plane. After another pass, two more bailed out. I positioned myself so that I could see where they landed. One of them crashed into a big Ponderosa tree and had to use a rope to get to the ground. The plane made a very low pass and dropped two boxes with little parachutes attached to them. They scurried to the boxes removing hand tools. The four of them worked long into the day removing fuel from the fires edge with their tools. They didn't stop working until the fire was contained."

With awe, Jason yelled, "Wow, you got to see that!"

Howling Wolf nodded and started walking. "After they had the fire under control, I decided to give them a visit."

Entering the burned area, they followed the hand line around the fire. The old man let out a laugh, "I think I scared them when I came out of the forest, because they became frozen in place. After an awkward introduction, they warmed up to me. They said they seldom encounter people on fires."

"Where were they from?" Jason asked.

Howling Wolf laughed, "It was quite the encounter. They had nicknames of Vice, Pigpen, Ry-son, and Gramps, and they joked a lot. They offered me some of their food made from freeze dried meats and vegetables. I can't see how they could eat that stuff or get enough nourishment from it, but they seemed to enjoy it. They said they were a group of Smokejumpers from bases in Montana,

Oregon, Washington State, Idaho, and California. They man a spike base out of Silver City, not far from here during our fire season. When our season is over, they go back to their respective bases. I had a great time with them and I didn't stop laughing the whole time. When it was time for them to leave, the one who had landed in the tree had to climb it to get his parachute out with spurs and ropes dropped in a little box. While he was getting his chute out, the others packed their jumpsuits, parachutes, and the cargo into large packs; they looked as large as they were. We said our good-buys and they hiked out."

Jason added, "No wonder Scott wants to become a jumper. Sounds like a unique group of people."

"Yes," Howling Wolf nodded. "I plan on seeking them out next time." He looked up at the sun, "We must get going."

*****

They hiked until Jason noticed the village off in the distance. He thought of how out of place it appeared, symbols of civilization looking like blemishes on an untamed land.

Walking down the last ridge, Jason wished he was back at the holy place in the meadow, being consumed by Mother Earth. A bonfire threw sparks high into the darkening sky from behind the store. As they drew closer, the old men noticed them and stopped what they were doing. They began singing and chanting and bodies appeared from all around. The spirit travelers were accepted with much jubilation. Jason noticed the elders nod to him as he passed, while others gathered around Howling Wolf, intently listening to him explain the journey in their native tongue; gesturing with his body and arms. The atmosphere intensified as the last light of day transformed into darkness.

Joseph greeted them both with a strong hug. Turning to Jason, he proclaimed, "You have traveled far my friend, news of your return was signaled by the great eagle. We will now celebrate your initiation into the spirit world. Howling Wolf is proclaiming to the elders that you are now one of us."

Jason was speechless; it was he who owed them the respect and honor they were bestowing upon him. He humbly said to Joseph, "I'm not worthy of such an honor."

"Nonsense, Wandering Spirit, it is not often, even for our own people, to be embraced by the spirit world as you were and from what Howling Wolf has been saying, you are not only protected by one, but two strong spirits in the eagle and the cougar. Let's join Howling Wolf and the elders."

They took a place among the tribe and exchanged greetings. Jason was patted on the shoulder and congratulated by all of the old men. He continually looked over to Joseph for a translation, but he was too absorbed chatting himself. There was a beauty in the sound of their words. They flowed like the wind around the fire. As they began to sit, Running Pony sat next to Jason, "Howling Wolf had me research the meaning of your name. He feels that a person's name can tell a lot about the spirit of that person. So, I found that Jason comes from the Greek name, Lason. It means, 'To heal.' Did you know that Lason was the leader of the Argonauts in Greek legend?"

Jason shook his head, "No, I didn't know that."

"Well, he must have had an idea that you are a natural healer, or he would not have taken such an interest in you. He wants you to stay and learn the healing powers of the land, for they have worked through you and you have the ability to help others with their power."

Jason was curious. "Tell me, Running Pony, how did Howling Wolf get his name?"

Looking over to Howling Wolf, he said, "It is said that he was named by our last medicine man, who one night caught him answering the howl of a pack of wolves. He also saw in him the ability to sense danger at a great distance. He became an excellent tracker at an early age and he was a cunning hunter. His sense of smell was compared to that of the wolves. He had a strong sense of family and protected all around him. Being a teacher and mentor came naturally to him, but most significant of all, was his ability to show us how to hunt for meaning in all things. He named me. I remember the day he said to me, 'You are Running Pony; one day you will carry us on your back to the otherworld. You have the energy of the earth in you. You will be able to pass through the gateways of all the dimensions.' From that day forward, he has been teaching me and helping me discover my destiny. Just as your name means healer, he is guiding you to your destiny."

Destiny, Jason wondered. Maybe it wasn't a fouled carburetor that brought them together; maybe it was his destiny. "What about the eagle and cougar?" Jason asked Running Pony. "Is there a destiny in them too?"

Running Pony smiled. "The eagle brings the light of the soul. The moment Howling Wolf saw you, he saw your light, even though it was shaded by a vast emptiness. He saw flashes of intuition from your soul. The eagle lives in the realm of spirit and fire, of which both have come to surface in you. He is very proud of you, Jason the healer. As for the cougar, it teaches us how to be in harmony with our instincts. Wisdom is the way of the cat."

"I have much to learn, Joseph Running Pony."

"You have learned much, Jason the healer!"

One of the elders offered a long smoking pipe to Jason. It was decorated with a colorful arrangement of beads, feathers, and the bowl was made from a deer antler. Tobacco smoke swirled from the bowl. He accepted it graciously and took a drag, coughing from the bitterness. The elders laughed as he passed it to Running Pony. After his puff, he explained to Jason, "This is our sacred ceremonial pipe. It has been used for generations, and especially when meeting with the white man in older times. It was done so that the meeting could be witnessed by the Great Spirit. The smoke rises upward carrying with it the prayers of those who smoke it. It is a very symbolic medium that provides a witness to our prayers and thoughts."

When the pipe had completed the circle and in the hands of the original bearer, Howling Wolf stood and addressed the circle. After he had spoken and sat down, another elder stood and spoke. Under his breath, Joseph said to Jason, "Tribal business." Whatever they were discussing went on for almost an hour. When it appeared as though they had concluded, Howling Wolf stood up again and this time he spoke in English, "This young brave here was brought to me, or maybe I was brought to him, of that I am not sure of yet. What I do know is that he shall be known as Wandering Spirit, for he has embraced the spirit world as this world has embraced him. The medicine ways work through him and we shall treat him as one of our own."

Joseph slapped him on the shoulder, "Welcome to the tribe, brother."

The gathering went on well into the night. Jason mingled

with the elders, communicating with them as best he could until the group slowly thinned out. On the walk to Joseph's home he told Jason, "The part for your bike came in today. I hope you don't mind, but I took the liberty and installed it for you."

The status of his bike was the furthest thing on his mind. He smacked Joseph on the shoulder, "Thank you Running Pony, you didn't have to do that. Did you have any problems with it?"

"Nope," he smiled, "I've worked on many motorcycles before and this repair was a breeze."

"Would it be okay to check it out?" Jason asked looking back toward the garage.

"No problem," Joseph answered with a happy grin. They turned around and returned to the garage. A tarp covered his bike and as he removed it; he instantly noticed how clean and shiny it was, quite the opposite of how it had looked when he arrived. His reaction was that of a child opening a Christmas present. All he could say was, "Wow Joseph, she looks brand new," as he bobbed his head around the bike admiring it from different angles. His eyes were drawn to the cross bar; they lit up when he noticed an eagle feather attached to it with a piece of leather. On the shaft of the feather were the colored beads that represented the four directions. Seeing the gleam in his friend's eyes put a smile on Joseph's face. Jason wished he'd had something to give in return. All he could say was, "You're too much, man."

Joseph shrugged it off, "It was nothing; I was getting bored waiting for the two of you to return." He looked at the medicine pouch with uneasiness and said, "I didn't handle the pouch, for it is strong with spirits. I did not want to disturb them."

Jason's eyes clouded, "You are very perceptive, Running Pony. My wife and child are in there." Jason fired up his bike. It idled better than it did before arriving there. He shut it off and covered it. He smiled at Running Pony, thankful to know he wasn't stranded there, not that he felt stranded, anymore. As they left the garage, Jason had to ask, "What's that pile of lumber over there for?"

"I don't know if you noticed, but many of our homes are in need of repair."

Jason nodded his head, "Yes, I did notice. How about we form a work party and get it done. I'm a carpenter by trade and we could knock out the repairs in no time."

The offer delighted Joseph, "That would be such a help; I've been very concerned about it."

"Well then let's do it."

*****

Joseph set up a work party and Jason was able to do what he loved the most, pounding nails. He put the kids to work looking for bent nails, since new ones were in short supply, and he showed them how to straighten them out with a hammer and reuse them. The kids followed the adults to each home, running around searching for nails in between playing tag. One particular girl that he guessed to be around three years old with big black shinning eyes and long flowing ponytails stuck close to him. Whenever she had the opportunity, she'd hug him around the legs with a smile that spanned her entire face. He felt love coming from her and wished he'd had a child of his own to bath in such closeness. As the repairs went on, he looked forward to the little girl's greetings. He named her, Little One Who Smiles.

He also spent many days in the woods with Howling Wolf gathering Mother Earth's gifts. The old shaman taught Jason which herbs to use for relief from colds, colic, digestive disorders, headaches, influenza, inflammation, and an array of insect and bug bites. He learned to identify rag leaf, paintbrush, dogbane, mistletoe, antelope sage, and stone weed. Heart and circulatory problems were relieved with hemp. Sedatives could be found in wild black cherry, hops, and wild lettuce. The world he walked on was rich with cures. One day, curiosity forced Jason to ask Howling Wolf, "What happens if someone needs a hospital?"

The old man developed a frown; then looked sad. "The government sends out a doctor once a month to assess the health of the tribe. If someone needs advanced care, they're taken to a hospital. I don't like the doctors; they think our methods are barbaric. I avoid them when they're here. Most of our illnesses were brought to us by the white man, so putting trust in them is difficult for me." He seemed lost in thought. After an uneasy silence, he continued. "They sent out priests to convert us from our beliefs. The elders and I would have none of it. Our beliefs transcend any of those who have invaded our country. We have a God in Mother Earth. What more have we ever needed? She has sustained us both physically and spiritually. Who has the right to come to us and say we are savages? In your sleep talking, you shouted out the name, Job. Running Pony has read me the Bible. This Job was tested by God, just as we have been tested by the white man. He survived God's wrath, just as we have tried to survive the wrath of the white man." Howling Wolf grew angrier. "How can we trust a government that displaced entire tribes by forcing them to march hundreds of miles to a land they chose, resulting in the death of women, children and the elderly? Where is the godliness in that?"

Jason knew of the 'Trail of Tears'. It saddened him to know that the entire Cherokee nation was displaced by the whites. He didn't have an answer to Howling Wolf's question, for he had a similar question; where is the godliness in losing his wife and child?

That evening, Jason had nightmares about the plight of the Native American people, as well as his own plight. It continued to bother him and the day came when Howling Wolf noticed Jason's restlessness. On one of their herb gathering trips he sat Jason down under his tall standing brother and said, "You came here in darkness, Wandering Spirit, not knowing your linage, having lost your wife, your child, and your livelihood. It has been a difficult journey for you, but now, I see light in your soul. You are anxious for something. I knew this day would come, for it was meant to be. The spirits have counseled me by saying, 'when his soul shines with light, it is time for him to journey to his destiny.' You must follow your spirit, Jason the healer. We will meet again, that I know. There will be no sorrow in your leaving, for your prophesy is greater than ours. Your destiny awaits you, go find it with the knowledge that you have gained here."

Returning to the village, Running Pony knew his friend was ready to continue on his journey. He wheeled the bike out of the garage. "Your bike is fueled, tire pressure is good. It will get you to wherever you are going, my friend." Jason looked around for Howling Wolf. "He is not good with good-byes," Joseph said with a grin, "and neither am I for that matter. He will always be with you."

Jason hugged his friend tightly, saying, "Thank you for everything, my brother. You will always be in my thoughts." He straddled his bike, fired up the engine, and took one last look around the village, and then at Running Pony. They both nodded in respect. Jason throttled away. The wind dried his tears. He stopped at the entrance of the reservation, the same spot he'd shared water with the lizards. They received a last watering. His spirit protector screeched above him. He looked up and waved, knowing that Howling Wolf was watching him. A scan of the mountain range revealed a plane circling a small spiral of smoke rising from the ponderosa forest; the product of a lightning storm the night before. Two parachutes popped open. His thoughts centered on his friend Scott, and Howling Wolf's encounter with the Smokejumpers.

The eagle guided him to the edge of the desert. It swooped down in front of the bike and screeched its good-bye. He waved to his protector and opened the throttle. The road soon had him hypnotized. Power poles zipped by in a steady cadence, leading him back into his journey. He set the cruise control and motored all day until a thunderstorm reared its black ominous front at him.

THE WAY

CHAPTER 15

The sign ahead read, *WELCOME TO HENLEY, HOME OF THE COUNTY FAIR*. Jason rolled into town at dusk, exhausted from the long days ride. A motel sign flashing in the distance beckoned to him. He checked into a room and went straight to bed.

Restful sleep was difficult to come by. He tossed and turned most of the night, rolling in and out of disturbing dreams. He was experiencing the spirit world all over again, but this time it was without the guidance of Howling Wolf. He was in the water, his body spreading out endlessly over the vast oceans, rivers, and streams, and at the same time, he was in the air blanketing the deserts, mountains, valleys, and oceans. It wasn't the pure and refreshing sensation he'd felt earlier; instead there was pollution all around him and it blurred his vision and choked him. The water had disease and human garbage floating everywhere, killing the marine life and the microorganisms that gave life to the seas. The air was darkly tainted and smelled foul; he felt like he was being poisoned, slowly and deliberately.

He woke in a cold sweat. After a few moments, he was able to center himself; it was then that he remembered a saying Howling Wolf had quoted from another medicine man:

'The earth is our mother
She gives birth to all living things
We must honor her to be worthy
She is sacred, beautiful, strong, and vulnerable
She must be protected from her greatest enemy:
Her children of the human race.'

The room closed in on him. He bolted outside and inhaled deeply; the air was sweet to his lungs. He looked into the sky and saw bands of high cirrus clouds streaking across the horizon, pushing the storm away. A brilliant blue sky emerged. Relief rushed through him as he sat on a bench and enjoyed the sacredness of it all. He'd slept through the storm and guessed it to be mid-afternoon. Faintly in the distance, the distinctive rumbling of a big motorcycle caught his attention. He perked up and tuned in on it. It didn't have the familiar sound of a Harley, which he could pick out a mile away. It wasn't the sound of a rice burner, either. He was thinking maybe a Norton, or a Triumph. He got up from the bench and walked to the railing to get a better look at the street and parking lot ten-feet below.

When the bike came into view, he immediately noticed the full skirt fenders practically covering the wheels. He thought to himself, this is an old bike. It was red with a coating of road dust. The rider down shifted using his hand on the side of the bike, instead of his foot. He knew of one bike that shifted that way. The excitement of seeing an Indian brand motorcycle on the road overtook him. These were classic show bikes, rarely seen on the highway.

As the rider approached the motel, he glanced at Jason's Harley and pulled in next to it. He sat on his bike for a long while, looking up and down the street, at the buildings, and the people on the boardwalks. He noticed Jason leaning on the railing and nodded. Jason nodded back as the man got off his bike smacking the dust off his riding leathers. He removed his sunglasses and helmet exposing long brown hair that reached his shoulders. He sported a Fu Manchu mustache. He looked to be in his late thirties.

"Nice Harley," he directed toward Jason.

How did he know it was mine? Jason wondered. "Thanks," Jason said as he walked down the stairs to the bikes, "but your Indian deserves the praise. What year is it?"

"This baby rolled off the line in Springfield, Massachusetts in 1951. It's the Indian Chief; 80 cubic inches of power in that engine," he proudly replied.

"Do you mind if I check her out?" Jason asked as he looked at the man, instantly noticing gentle green eyes that radiated a feeling of warmth and friendliness.

"Be my guest," he said stretching.

"Thanks, by the way, I'm Jason."

"My friends call me Loner, nice to meet you." They shook hands and Jason began to look over the bike.

"Man, this is one fine machine," Jason gawked.

"She is a beauty," Loner replied with pride, "rides like a

dream, very little vibration. I can go all day long. The only problem is finding parts when I need them, so I keep her in top shape."

"I can see that," Jason said nodding his head. "This here Harley has given me some problems in the past. I'm no stranger to those down low Harley Davison blues." They both laughed, knowing the maintenance requirements of a cruising bike.

"So where did you ride in from, Loner?"

"I left Wyoming early this morning."

"Now that's a good day's ride," Jason answered.

"Yeah, I've been riding for months, years for that matter, I love the open road man, there's nothing like it. Where were you last?"

With a nervous chuckle Jason replied, "Physically, I was on an Indian reservation in New Mexico," he paused for a moment. "But mentally, I was on an incredible journey with an old Indian medicine man."

Loner looked sharply into Jason's eyes and emphatically said, "I'd like to hear that story," as he unpacked items from his saddlebags.

"You would?" Jason replied happy to be able to share his experience with another biker.

"There're so many adventures to experience on the road; but this one sounds pretty unique. How are the rooms here?"

"They're decent."

"I'm going to check in and get cleaned up. Any place to get a hot meal and a cold beer around here?"

"There's a bar a few doors down the street. They serve food also."

"Great, I'm starving. How about meeting there in an hour or so?"

"An hour it is," Jason said excited in meeting the Indian rider.

*****

Jason went back into his room and took a long, hot shower, then sat on the deck. The afternoon sun almost bathed him to sleep. Loner came out a few doors down and noticing Jason relaxing, joined him. Jason was amused with this man's name and felt there had to be a story behind it. He casually asked, "So what's with the name, Loner?"

He laughed, "It's a nickname, of course, but sometimes I wonder. There was a time in my life when I did drugs, raised hell, and hung with the wrong crowd. We all had nicknames to keep from incriminating ourselves." He winked at Jason adding, "If you know what I mean. Anyway, my bros' called me Stoner. When I decided to quit the drugs, they called me Boner, which I didn't allow for very long. As I started to split from them, they called me Loner. It fits, so I decided to keep it. Now, I ride alone, no direction home; like a rolling stone."

"It must be lonely," Jason added.

"If I do get a taste of it, I make up for it when the kickstand touches pavement. I've met so many good people on the road, far more than my other life offered. Hell, I got dozens of open ended invitations all over the country."

Jason asked, "How do you afford going wherever you want, for as long as you want?"

Loner leaned toward him, practically whispering, "When I was Stoner, I banked a lot of dough." The man looked to be a scrapper. He was lean, muscled, and was always scanning his surroundings. Jason stared at a well-healed scar running the length of his cheek and commented without thinking, "A product of the bank?"

Loner noticed and laughed, "You're an observant one, aren't you?"

Jason had a smirk when he said, "I've had a lot of practice lately." Loner was about to say something when Jason added, "So anyway, where are you from?"

He responded in a hollow tone, "I'm from the last town I was in and depending on how long I stay here, I will be from this town."

"No," Jason emphasized, "I mean where are you really from; your home town, your family?"

He looked at Jason defensively, "Like I said, man, I'm riding the wind; wherever I rode in from is my home. The people I meet are my family, simple as that! But if you really need to know, my childhood sucked. My parents were alcoholics and drug abusers. They beat on each other and when they got tired of that, they beat on me. They were losers, unable to keep jobs or a steady place to live. When I was 16, I couldn't take it anymore. I felt like they were going to kill me, or better yet, I was going to kill them. So instead of landing in prison, I ran away and never looked back."

Silence wrapped around Jason. Loner's confession surprised him; he didn't appear to be the kind of person with such childhood scars. He was confident, walked tall, and smiled a lot. Jason admired his bluntness and wanted to learn more about him. He said, "I'm ready for that beer now, how about you?"

"Let's do it," Loner replied.

*****

Fashioned like an old Western town, Henley's main street featured raised wooden plank walkways paralleling rustic storefronts. The boards creaked under their feet and the benches that dotted the walkway were occupied with tourists. Swinging doors cut in the Wild West fashion ushered them into the saloon. Huge rough sawn beams crisscrossed the room supporting a high vaulted ceiling. Cedar plank paneling rose from the wooden floor to the ceiling giving the place a sweet scent. Trophy deer mounts, bear skins, and stuffed animals decorated the walls, as did rusted long rifles. A smoky haze encircled the ceiling lamps. Rock music competed with laughter and clinking glasses. They found an empty table and settled in. The bar ran the length of one side of the room. It was made from solid oak with a thick layer of varnish encasing it. A waitress approached the table, "What can I get you boys?"

Loner looked her up and down and with a grin said, "How about a pitcher of your best micro-brew and three glasses."

She looked to the door asking, "Are you expecting someone else?"

"No," Loner replied, "The extra glass is for you."

She looked him over as he did her and giggled, "I still have four hours of work left; if you can stay sober long enough to pour me a drink, I might take you up on the offer."

Loner laughed, "I can definitely keep my part; shall I keep you to yours?"

She winked at Jason saying, "One pitcher of beer and three glasses coming up. Oh, by the way, I'll be your server; you can call me Katie."

As she walked to the bar, Loner said, "Man, what a babe." Jason nodded, although his concentration was on a stuffed mountain lion perched high on a beam.

"I thought they were protected," Jason said motioning to the cat.

Loner looked at it and replied, "Nothing's protected these days. Maybe it was taken before the ban."

Katie returned. "Here you go boys, a pitcher of our finest and three glasses." She poured Jason a glass, then turned to Loner. Their eyes locked as she poured his glass and she caught herself just as the foam slithered over the lip. Still fixated on Loner's eyes she said, "So who might you two be?"

Loner kept her gaze, "This is my friend Jason, and I'm Loner."

She looked at Jason, "Hi Jason," then returned her eyes to Loner saying, "Loner? That can't be your real name."

"It's a long story," he said.

Coyness saturated her words, "I'd be interested in hearing it sometime."

"That could be arranged," Loner offered.

She struggled to break away from him. Jason couldn't help but notice he had the power to attract people, making them feel at ease and engaging. After an awkward moment, she managed to say, "I have to get back to work."

They toasted to life on the road; to always having bugs on your windshield and feeling the wind on your face, not to mention meeting good people. Just before the pitcher was empty, Katie returned and asked, "Another one?"

Loner nodded and said, "Can we also get a menu, I'm starving."

"Right away," she said heading straight to the bar. She returned with a fresh pitcher and menus. "The steaks are our specialty. I guarantee you, you won't be disappointed."

Loner winked at her saying, "I bet I won't."

The steaks were still sizzling when the plates met the table. "Can I get you anything else?"

Loner looked at the plates, then Jason, and said with a Cheshire cat grin, "It looks too pretty to eat."

Jason nodded his head in agreement as Katie giggled, then took her leave. As Loner sprinkled pepper on his steak, he said, "So tell me the story about this Indian shaman you met."

In between bites, Jason recounted his journey. "I was in the high desert of New Mexico when my bike broke down. This old Indian showed up and towed me behind his pickup to his village. I was able to order parts from there and they allowed me to stay with them. When the grandson of the old man told me he was the tribe's medicine man and that my ending up there was not by chance, I didn't know what to make of it. They called the old man, Howling Wolf. He took me into the forest to his holy place where we took part in traditional ceremonies, traveling the spirit world with the aid of peyote, and a vision quest. It's hard to explain what I experienced; some of the visions seemed impossible to comprehend. I actually traveled through the elements and the spirit world."

A look of disbelief shrouded Loner's face, "Hold on a minute," he said putting his fork down, "you say you went on a journey through the elements?"

Jason leaned toward him, "Like I said, it's hard to explain. It was as if I was a physical part of it all. I felt, saw, smelled, touched and heard the elements; and saw spirits. It was freaky, man." Loner sat in silence, staring at Jason in wonderment.

Katie made her way back to their table breaking Loner's silence. He quickly said to Jason, "I want to hear more about this later," then turned his attention to Katie. "This is a unique place you have here."

"Yes it is," she said with pride. "It's been in the Barkley family for over 40 years; they hunted all these trophies on the walls themselves." She smiled broadly, "They also treat their employees very well. I love working here."

Jason noticed a stage cluttered with band equipment, "Is there going to be a band playing tonight?"

"There sure is," she replied, "we have a Blues band playing tonight."

Jason became excited, "Who?"

"Actually," she said, "the man calls himself Buddy Guy." She giggled, "He wears overalls, like a farmer, and his guitar has polka-dots all over it."

Jason almost fell out of his chair, shouting, "No way, you have to be kidding?" They both looked at him. "Buddy Guy is here? He's going to be playing here, tonight?"

"Yes he is," Katie said laughing, "I guess you've heard of him, huh?"

"Anybody who knows the Blues knows Buddy Guy. He's up there with the likes of B.B. King, Albert King, and Eric Clapton to name a few. The guy is totally awesome, you'll hear what I'm talking about, believe me."

Katie smiled and made a suggestion. "I was thinking, Jason, since I have a date with Loner here tonight," which took Loner by surprise, "I'm also meeting a girlfriend; maybe we all could party together. I think you two would like each other. What do you think guys?"

Loner looked at Jason with an expression that clearly indicated, you had better say yes. Jason nodded, "I'm up for it."

"Great," Katie said, "I'll give her a call and fill her in."

As she headed toward the bar, Loner raised his glass in a toast, "Looks like we're set for the night partner."

CHAPTER 16

They had a few hours to wait before the real action started. Jason wondered about the scar on the side of Loner's face, "How did you get that scar?"

Loner thought a moment before saying, "Anger is a very destructive emotion Jason; it almost destroyed me. I left the gang after a drug deal went very bad. One of my bros' was shot dead." Loner ran his hand along the scar; "I was cut by one of them. We popped a few rounds in them before the sirens had us all scrambling. We had to leave one of our brothers dead in the street. That haunts me to this day, man. It really sucked. Then this friend of mine, not a gang member but a guy I knew from my hood, had been studying Kung Fu for many years. He convinced me that if I studied the martial arts, my life would turn around and change for the better. I didn't have anything to loose, so I entered the dojo and as it turned out, it was the best damn thing to happen in my life."

The martial arts were foreign to Jason, except for what he had seen in the movies. People trying to hurt each other are all it represented to him. He couldn't make the connection between Kung Fu and Loner getting his life together. In a sarcastic tone, he said, "How could kicking ass help control anger?"

Loner took a swig of beer. "The study of Kung Fu is much more than meets the eye, Jason. Hollywood is responsible for that image. What you see in the movies is miles from the true essence of Kung Fu. Most people don't have a clue what it's really about."

"So, what is it all about?" Jason demanded.

"It's actually quite involved. I can't sit here and tell you everything in ten minutes."

Jason shrugged, "I'm not going anywhere."

"Okay, Jason, I'll tell you what I'm going to do. Whenever I can enlighten you, I will. There's so much to say about Kung Fu that needs time. I will try to give you a true picture of it, a little at a time, how's that?"

Jason was still picturing the fighting, man systematically trying to wipe out an entire Hollywood set, when Loner said, "The real and true essence of Kung Fu is not self-defense, it is about philosophy and preservation."

"Philosophy?" Jason questioned.

"That's right, philosophy. The fighting is a way to develop discipline and self-control, the least significant part of Kung Fu. It's a total way of life, where one can achieve happiness through inner peace and good mental health. There's also the benefits of self-confidence and self-awareness, which helps to free the mind to deal with the many outside forces we have to deal with. Kung Fu puts us in touch with our bodies. Stress occurs when the mind tries to dominate the body and pushes it beyond its limits. Strength and inner peace are found when the mind and body work as one. When you are one, harmony with the laws of nature and the universe are possible."

"Sounds a lot like what Howling Wolf taught me."

"The parallels are very similar," Loner added. "Native American culture stresses in becoming one with the universe; then you can become one with yourself."

"Yeah, I wish I was more at peace with myself."

"Don't worry about it, what you experienced with the Shaman will serve you well in the future, just be thankful for the experience," Loner said emphatically. He stood up, "I'm going to the head." As he walked away, Jason's eyes went back to the mountain lion and the other animals on the walls. He wondered if their spirits were honored and released in the Native American way. His guess was they were shot for sport rather than necessity, being dishonored in the process. Jason remembered Howling Wolf saying that reverence for all living things should be practiced and by doing so, harmony will fill one's life. He was beginning to see the similarities between the Native American ways and Loner's Kung Fu.

*****

Katie's laughter forced him to look toward the bar. Loner had her and the bartender in his spell. His self-confidence, gracefulness, and poise affected the people around him. Loner made his way back to their table, "Katie's friend, Jasmine, is looking forward to meeting you tonight."

Jason wondered aloud, "I hope I don't blow it."

Loner laughed, "Why would you say that?"

"It's a long story," Jason said.

Loner rolled up his sleeves, revealing another knife scar. Jason blurted out, "You look like a cutting board, man. You're not going to get me killed tonight...are you?"

"Don't worry, my scrapping days are over. This one almost did me in though. Just missed an artery; cut a lot of muscle and some nerves but with the help of an acupuncturist my teacher turned me on to, it's much better now."

"Acupuncture!" Jason marveled, "I've heard of it, but never met anyone who's actually had it done. Did the needles hurt?"

"Not at all; it actually felt good."

"No way, how could being stuck with needles feel good?"

"Acupuncture is a whole body form of medicine that taps into a person's Chi. Chi being inner strength and a vital force everyone has. It is in the mind, the spirit, and the body drawing energy from the universe through the subconscious. It's like an energy controlling thought and a thought controlling energy." Loner stated, "My acupuncturist explained to me that this energy is the basis of acupuncture science. Our bodies have another circulatory system, a network of energy fields. Blockage of the energy flow results in weakness, pain, and sickness. The needles release the blockage and congestion; they restore the energy flow. Chi is not psychic; it's measurable energy that flows through the body on pathways of high electrical conductivity. Anytime I hurt myself, that's the treatment I seek. The art has been around for centuries and it works. I have a sweet little Chinese girl doing the sticking."

Jason cringed, "Whatever you say, you can keep your needles."

"If you don't like needles there are herbs," Loner added.

Jason had been experiencing mild flashbacks ever since leaving the Reservation and confirmed, "I've had enough herbs for a while. Tell me about the Chinese gal."

"She's not only a skilled acupuncturist, she's also an herbalist," Loner said with a fond smile. "There aren't too many ailments she can't treat between the two methods. She also helped me to understand the realm of the Dragon."

Confused, Jason said, "What do you mean by that?"

Loner perked up, "Well, in the martial arts there are two basic realms. There's the Tiger realm, where a student learns power and tenacity. It took years of training for me to learn the self-defense techniques and condition my body to be ready to move beyond the physical. When I started my training I had too much anger, too many distractions. I needed to purge all the useless emotions I carried around with me in order to be a worthy student. I took my time putting myself in touch mentally with my physical self. A person finds true strength and inner peace when the mind and body work as one. Once that is attained, then there's the Dragon realm. This is what Kung Fu is all about, Jason. From the Dragon, we learn to ride the wind."

Jason spontaneously added, "Like riding our bikes with the wind in our face."

Loner smiled. "That could be a good vehicle to get a person closer to the larger reality, just like your bike took you to Howling Wolf. When we practice using our minds, we find ourselves sometimes breaking through to an expanded reality where we are able to perceive a new set of mysteries, previously invisible to us. What I learned from my China gal was that through devotion, faith, and choice, we can bring our world into harmony with the various truths we discover and with that comes enlightenment. I know this sounds involved, if nothing else, remember one thing."

"What's that?" Jason asked leaning close.

"Conquer your fear by facing it, get rid of the distractions by getting rid of the belief in them and you'll do alright."

Jason sat back pondering on what Loner had said. Kung Fu was a way of life that taught choice, to have the power to see all the alternatives, to act according to one's own will instead of on the whims of other people or events. Jason admired Loner's ability to convey these thoughts simply. Loner's acupuncturist so intrigued Jason; he had to ask, "How did the girl help you with the Dragon realm? What's her name?"

"HuiHui," Loner answered with a gleam in his eyes. "HuiHui knows herbs, acupuncture, and definitely massage; she also teaches martial arts. One day when she was treating me, I told her I was having difficulty concentrating during meditation. I felt restless, out of touch with my body. She said to me, 'Your perception is stuck in a bubble and in order to free yourself, we must pop that bubble to allow your senses to be in a fluid state.' I asked how that was done and she handed me a capsule saying, 'Take this; it's a mixture of herbs that will help to open your receptors.' And sure enough, it opened me up to some sensory experiences I'll never forget."

Thinking about Howling Wolf's peyote, Jason asked, "Did you trip on it?"

Loner laughed, "No, it wasn't like that; she said it would only help me to feel, taste, hear, smell, see, and sense what is already there."

Jason thought for a second, "I could use something like that, I feel bubbled in at times."

Loner pulled a pouch out of his pocket and slipped Jason a capsule saying, "Then try this!"

With the last of his beer, Jason washed it down. Noticing the empty pitcher from across the room, Katie rushed back to their table, "Can I get you boys another pitcher?"

Loner put a fifty-dollar bill on the table, "No thanks, not for me, I need to service my bike before it gets dark. How about you Jason?"

"I'll pass; I'm going to check out the fair."

"Okay boys, so I'll see you two later?" she asked with a head tilt.

"You can bet on it," Loner said, "and keep the change."

"Thanks guys, I'll save a table for us tonight."

Before going their separate ways, Loner looked at Jason with a knowing grin, "Just go with what your senses show you, I'll catch up with you later. Have fun."

"All righty, I will," Jason replied, wondering what was behind the grin.

CHAPTER 17

Jason walked down the boardwalk toward the fair, looking into the stores and watching the people as they passed. He could feel the slightest twist of the boards beneath the moccasins Running Pony had given him. Every footstep, every creak, radiated through his feet and traveled up his legs, turning into a symphony of sound reverberating in from every direction. The tones varied in range from heavy thuds to light taps. It sounded like a drum troupe, pounding out an endless rhythm. When the tones resembled a recognizable song, he'd stop to listen to this newfound experience conducted by people simply walking the boardwalk. As he neared the end of the walkway, he stopped one last time to savor the audio enhancement.

The transition from soft flexible fibers to a hard rigid surface changed his awareness. The cold, hard concrete pounded through his feet. He maneuvered off the sidewalk onto the soil to avoid the discomfort. Nearing the fairground, his ears were bombarded with screams, yells, and laughter from high pitched children to the baritones of adults. Mixed in with human noises the atmosphere seemed to be in utter chaos.

The light emanating from the fairground resembled a colorful orb hovering over the area like a spaceship filled with excitement and anticipation. At the gate, he especially noticed the children. Some waited calmly at the gates holding their parents' hands. Others jumped wildly anticipating a world of fun and games. What Jason noticed most was the children's eyes; they bulged with excitement, their broad smiles spanning the limits of their faces. They looked so happy. He wished he could look into his birth father's eyes, like these children did. Guilt ripped through him knowing he'd had fun times like this with his adopted family. He quickly diverted his attention back to the children.

The crowd funneled through the small openings, creating a vacuum of bodies ready to be catapulted into a world of fun. Once inside, they dispersed in all directions like butterflies being scattered by the wind. Emerging from the gauntlet, he walked aimlessly through the grounds. Smells instantly invaded his nose; popcorn, cotton candy, pizza, chicken, and hot dogs. Even though he'd just eaten, his stomach awoke and he fought off the feeling until the aroma of ribs, a dish he loved, beckoned him to a Texas style rib stand. The desire to indulge again had him ordering a basket of ribs with a side of barbecue beans, bread, and corn on the cob. Zesty meat peeled off the bones with ease making every bite feel like a decadent pleasure. His thoughts confirmed what his taste buds experienced; it doesn't get any better than this!

Finishing his feast he stretched out on a bench and concentrated on the crowd as it passed by. Another sensation gripped him; electricity emanated off the individuals as they passed, becoming stronger the closer a person came to him. The degree of intensity varied with each person. Jason wondered if this is what Loner called a person's chi. He craved more and ventured into the crowd. Maneuvering the sea of people washed him with energy. An extremely strong pulse caused him to turn and behind him stood a pretty woman smiling at him. His initial desire embarrassed him, causing him to look away. When he looked back, she had disappeared into the crowd. He ventured on often looking back to see if she would reappear.

A stronger force pulled him toward the back of the fairgrounds where the less popular exhibits were located. The crowd was thin enough to allow him to stop instantly without impeding the flow. Something on the bottom of his moccasin drove him crazy. He removed his moccasin to find a chunk of chewing gum plastered on the bottom. After removing it with a small stick, he looked up to see a sign on a rundown trailer. The caption read: *THE WORLDS ONLY LIVING REPTILE MAN, DARE TO COME INSIDE!* A blurry, hand painted picture of a half-lizard-half-human creature crawling through a swamp stretched across the side of the trailer. Curiosity pulled him inside. A dimly lit room featured a large mural spanning the entire back wall depicting a prehistoric scene. Dinosaurs fed on clump grasses surrounding a mucky swamp as slimy creatures in all phases of evolution wallowed in the ooze. Others made their way to dry land growing legs as they emerged. In a dark corner, a semblance of a figure caught his eye. He walked closer and noticed a person, or a mannequin, sitting motionless with scales tattooed all over its upper body. The head appeared deformed by an oblong shape and its facial features were blurred. He edged closer. Suddenly its eyelids opened revealing two squinting, bloodshot eyes hinging on him. Startled by the intensity of its eyes, he tried to look away but the figure shackled him in place. It leaned toward him spewing, "What the hell are you looking at?"

Paralyzed by shock, Jason looked about the room. He was alone with this Reptile Man. The man said louder, "I don't give a shit if people look at me, but you were looking inside me, and I don't like that!"

Jason had no idea what he was talking about. He lowered his head, averting his eyes, and said, "I didn't mean to upset you; I thought you were a mannequin."

"A mannequin?" it spewed. "You think I'm a mannequin? I'm for real boy, just like those idiots out there?"

Jason forced himself to engage its eyes. Sadness poured in; he knew that look, and allowed himself to be drawn in. A calming voice instructed him, "That's right boy, keep coming in; this is going to rock your world." Its eyes didn't blink; large black pupils narrowed to slits, squeezing Jason in. Movement escalated from the mural. Human figures appeared, slowly devolving into apes. The dinosaurs shrank into smaller mammals and every creature struggled to reenter the swamp.

"Oh my God," Jason cried. Vertigo kept pushing him deeper until all movement stopped and he found himself being submerged in the swamp. Fish turned into unrecognizable life forms, while single cell organisms painfully consumed his body. He yelled out, but his voice was powerless. Reptile man's burst of laughter whirled Jason back into the room. He toyed with Jason. "I know what you saw; do you know what I saw?"

Jason was too confused to answer. His sense of reality became distorted. He yelled out to the man, "Why are you doing this? I didn't do anything to you."

The creature ignored him and leaned closer, his eyes burning into Jason. "Do you believe in evolution?" he asked.

"Evolution?" Jason repeated. "I don't know. I never gave it much thought, until now."

The Reptile man then asked, "Do you believe in God?"

Confused, Jason answered from his gut. "I don't know, maybe. I was brought up around religion, but never felt spiritually connected to it."

Reptile man let out a haunting laugh, "I heard you say, 'Oh, my God,' just a little while ago. If you don't believe in God, you sure use the term freely."

"I believe in a higher power," Jason said.

"What's the purpose of life if you don't believe in something that you can identify with? What do you think I believe in?" The man yelled at him, "Look at me! Look at this place. Do you see any God protecting me from this hell hole of a life?"

Sadness overcame Jason; a God sadness. He wondered how God could allow someone to do this to another human being. The man came into the light, totally revealing himself. All the tattoos, piercings, and implants disturbed Jason. He was speechless and while trying to absorb it all, the man said, "What I saw in you is someone who is lost, going backwards in time looking for something that is gone." He leaned close, his eyes narrowed to slit's again, and his voice was so forceful, it scared Jason, "You're devolving boy; going backwards instead of going forward. Look at me; do you think I'm a product of a stinking swamp?" He pointed to the mural, "Hell no, I'm not! I'm a human being. I might look like a freak in everybody's eyes, but deep down inside, I have to accept who I am. The circumstance of my life sucks, for sure, but at least I'm looking forward even if it doesn't change my predicament." Tears formed in his eyes as he said, "I can't lose faith."

The back of Jason's neck tingled. Faith, he wondered. How could this man being stuck in a freak show trailer have faith? Reptile man broke in, "What's your name boy?"

"Jason."

"Jason! Good name." He laughed sarcastically, "Do you know what they call me? They call me Damian; the nice way of saying demon. I believe my parents named me that for the suffering I caused them. Do you think anyone cares how much suffering my looks have caused me all my life?" Tears slithered down his cheeks, "I've learned to be an adaptive mutation; a freak in a freak show. The only thing that bothers me is people like you."

"People like me?" Jason questioned.

Damian paced his display clearly agitated. "People come in here crying about shit they can't change, or they're looking for something that ain't there. I can read their looks; I can read your look! Dealing with children feeling sorry for me is easy. It's when adults come in here feeling sorry for their own lives that I draw the line." He jumped over the display and got into Jason's face, spittle spraying, "Go home boy, what you're looking for is what you left behind. Your time is up; now get the hell out of my home!"

Jason stumbled out of the trailer frightened and sad. How could a human be treated like that and still have faith in anything? The man's soul was chained to the trailer with no way to escape; no freedom, no future. Damian's last words settled hard on him. Maybe Reptile Man was right, maybe his search should take him back home.

*****

The intensity of his surroundings waned as he walked back down the boardwalk. He felt mentally exhausted as he passed the saloon and made his way up the motel steps. Loner was sitting on a bench looking relaxed and reading a book. Jason took a seat next to him and let out a deep sigh. Loner put his book down, "So, how was the fair?"

"It was quite an eye opener; thanks to you."

Loner smiled, "What makes you think there was anything in that capsule that made you experience what you did?"

Confused, Jason said, "I thought you said it would enhance my senses."

"Maybe it was a placebo," Loner replied, "Maybe I planted a seed in your mind and you responded all by yourself; popping the bubble surrounding your senses."

"You're messing with me, right?"

Loner grinned, "What did you experience that you think you needed help with?"

Jason stared into space, "Well, everything seemed so intense; I don't think I could've done it on my own."

"Think again!"

"No way," Jason said shaking his head, "there had to be something in that, I just know it."

"Trust in yourself, Jason. The power of the mind is staggering when it's unchained."

Jason went over his experiences riveted by the energy that was emitted by the people he came close to, especially the Reptile Man. "Tell me more about this chi stuff."

"So, you must've felt the energy."

"I felt something coming off people; it was barely detectable with some; very evident with others."

Loner explained, "In ancient China, Chi was referred to as the Dragon's breath. It's present in all things, yet it cannot be seen or measured. It's both matter and energy; it defines and comprises all life and all inanimate objects in the universe. Chi translated means energy or breath, and as I said earlier, it is the basis for acupuncture. People with a strong Chi look healthy, youthful, and have a strong immune system as well as abundant energy. It's the life force of the natural world. Chi is a difficult concept for Westerners to comprehend since our world is centered on working hard and playing hard; striving to be successful by being vigorous and aggressive. Chi is strongly tied to the Chinese concept of Yin and Yang, which I'll explain after you digest the power of Chi."

Jason wondered aloud, "Did your Chinese gal teach you this stuff?"

At the mention of her, his eyes lit up. "She's my friend, my lover, my teacher, and my mentor. Our hearts are bound forever, regardless of what I do, or what she does. For me, it's a perfect relationship." Loner smiled at the sky, "Have you ever had unconditional love?"

Jason felt an ache in his heart. He'd had unconditional love with Rose. At night before going to sleep, they'd talk about their future and he'd feel their son growing inside of her. He fought off the tears remembering the last night they'd bonded. He'd tried to convince Rose to take maternity leave because he was concerned about her flying around in a life flight helicopter, but she was so intent on helping people she dismissed his concerns saying she'd been cleared to fly by her doctor. How he wished he'd been more forceful, more demanding, but her passion was too strong. Sadness smothered his words as he simply answered, "Yes, I have."

Not noticing Jason's struggle, Loner continued on with flair.

"We went to China. I saw where she grew up; met her parents, siblings, and her childhood friends. Meeting her martial arts instructor was a gift I will never forget. He taught me so much while kicking my butt all over the Dojo. She took me to the original Shaolin Temple where the martial arts were born." His look became solemn, "And talk about sacred places; the Buddhists temples were the most spiritual places I've ever seen. Huge hand carved statues adorned the temples and they were painted so brilliantly, they sent chills up my spine."

Jason's thoughts were on Rose as he stared at the yellow hue following the sun over the distant mountains casting a soothing glow over the land. A lone band of clouds morphed from red to orange; then purple as they chased the sun. Jason saw Rose's face in the clouds and blurted out, "What would you do if it was suddenly ripped away from you?"

Loner jumped up swiftly. He paced the deck shaking his head, saying, "No way!" He stopped in front of Jason, clapped his hands hard, "Enough of this, okay? It's time to check out your Blues man."

CHAPTER 18

The swinging doors of the saloon greeted Loner and Jason with a wave of laughter and chatter. Loner stopped just inside scanning the room. Energy bounced off the walls from the packed crowd and jump style blues rang from the jute box. Jason's eyes moved to the mountain lion on the beam; he said a few words of respect before looking for Katie and Jasmine. On stage, musicians were setting up. Out of the corner of his eye, he saw Katie signaling to him, he waved back.

Sitting next to Katie was a pretty girl with long strawberry-blond hair that cascaded over a purple low-cut blouse. As their eyes met, she bit her lower lip. She was petite with a light touch of makeup that didn't distract from her alluring blue eyes, or pleasant features. Closing in on the table, Katie said, "Hi Jason, this is my friend Jasmine." Jason looked at her again; her eyes hadn't left him since he approached the table. Jason offered his hand saying, "It's nice to meet you," meaning every word of it.

Katie said, "Have a seat, Jason," while looking around. "Where's Loner?"

Jason looked back, "He was right behind me, maybe he went to the head."

Jasmine poured him a beer saying. "Katie said you went to the fair this afternoon, how was it?"

"Very interesting," Jason said accepting the beer. "It brought back childhood memories and created some new ones, too. That Reptile Man was a trip."

Jasmine's expression hardened, "I've heard he doesn't talk to anyone, just sits there and stares at people; way too creepy for me!"

Jason shrugged, "Well, he had a few choice words for me."

Jasmine raised an eyebrow, "Like what?"

"Oh, stuff about his life and mine."

"That's quite an accomplishment," she added. An awkward silence followed as he pondered the encounter.

She looked toward the stage saying, "Katie says you like blues music."

"Actually," Jason said perking up, "I love the Blues. It's the only music that touches me way down in my soul. Tonight's band can hammer out the Blues."

"Yeah, Katie says they're pretty good." Katie became excited as Loner approached. She introduced him to Jasmine and he took a seat next to Katie. The band was on stage casually finishing their sound checks when suddenly, they exploded into a hard driving tune that got everybody's attention. Heads bobbed and bodies began to rock to the beat on the dance floor. Jasmine looked at Jason slightly tilting her head toward the dance floor. He jokingly asked above the noise, "Are you asking me to dance?"

She stood up and grabbed his hand. As the dance floor crowded up, they edged closer. She moved effortlessly to the beat, swaying in front of him like an angle dancing on a cloud. The song ended to cries for more. A guitar ripped out a solo that sent shock waves to the ceiling, yet none of the band members were playing. Jason knew the chords; it was the man himself, but where was he? From back stage, a black man with coveralls emerged jamming on a black guitar with white polka-dots all over it. He walked into the crowd and stopped in front of Jasmine. He looked at her and nodded; she began strumming on the strings to Buddy's delight. He was all smiles as he moved through the crowd and out onto the boardwalk. He went into a staggering rift, bending the strings to their limit to the passerby's. When he returned, the band kicked in and the house began rocking. Jasmine didn't let up, she grooved to the beat brushing into Jason as if she was lost in the moment. He quickly abandoned his inhibitions and became lost with her.

When the song ended, they gazed at each other like puppies until Buddy laughed, "We're gonna slow this one down to give ya'll some close time." The song started out with a slow, crying guitar. They embraced as the music worked through them. Her firm body sent waves of desire through him. Guilt riddled him as he became aroused by her touch. She noticed, and the look in her eyes put him somewhat at ease. When the song ended, she grabbed his hands from behind, pulled his body in close, and escorted him to the table.

Safely seated, Jason calmed down and whispered to her,

"Thanks."

She bit her lip in the way that drove him crazy and said, "The night's not over yet."

Loner and Katie were deep in conservation. When the music started again, they made their way to the floor. The four of them talked and danced the night away. Toward the end of the last set, Katie suggested they go to the river for a dip. They hopped on the motorcycles and headed out of town. The deserted, winding road glowed in the moonlight. Following Loner from a distance, Jason noticed he'd turned his headlight off. All he could see was a dim reflection of the bike. Feeling adventurist, Jason followed suit. After a couple seconds of adjusting to the moonlight, he found he could see the road rather well. Jasmine tightened her grip around him. Driving took on a new perspective. Loner's brake light glared, Jason slowed. They turned off the pavement onto a dirt road that led them to the river. Getting off his bike, Jason said to Jasmine, "That was a different experience."

Loner overheard and shrugged it off, "Got to use your night vision whenever you can."

"This way to the water," Katie said nudging Loner. They paired up and headed down the path. Jasmine brushed into Jason often playing a game of body tag. Katie whispered to Jasmine, "We're going to my spot, see you later."

Jasmine said to Jason, "Follow me, I have a spot also."

*****

A small sandy beach appeared by the water's edge with large boulders nestled in the current. While Jason absorbed the serenity of her sanctuary, she stripped off her clothes behind him. When he turned around, her naked body glistened in the moonlight. She allowed him to wander over her body before wading into the gentle current.

Jason slowly stripped as she watched his every move. He felt embarrassed, but her look reassured him as he waded out to her open arms. Her embrace petrified him; she shuddered, and then pulled him into the water to thaw his reaction. The coolness slithered between them. She quietly revealed, "I've been coming to this very spot ever since I was a little girl. My father used to bring me here to fish and relax. This was the only place where we could talk about things that were on our minds. He listened to my problems, gave me advice, and made me feel special here."

Looking around, Jason replied, "I can see why, this is a nice place you have here."

"Whenever I need to chill or think about things, this is where you'll find me; a little heaven in a big hell." She breathed in the light breeze that skipped over the twinkling water then turned to Jason saying, "Have you ever wondered why certain things happen to people?"

Jason didn't have to think long, "All the time; I've been wondering that all my life. Why do you ask?"

"I don't know, sometimes I think my life is all messed up. I know my heart is in a good place yet the more I try to please people, the more I seem to get hurt. I was born and raised here; got married and divorced here. I feel like a stationary recipient of life's injustices." Sadness poured out of her eyes. Jason embraced her thinking he was a moving recipient of life's injustices also. She softly cried, "When bad things happen to me, I come here in the hope that the current will carry it away. I've been coming here a lot lately, but it doesn't always work. If it weren't for my family and friends, I'd be a total mess."

Jason couldn't make the connection. He'd left his family and friends to find answers to his dilemma. He thought of Sarah and how she'd accepted his decision to leave. He could see in her eyes that she would always be there for him and he felt bad for abandoning her and Scott. Jasmine admissions confused him. She looked like an angel, showing no outward signs of her life's torment. His heart ached for her. "I'm no expert in dealing with life," he confessed. "I've been searching for answers to ease my mind, but I keep coming up with more questions than results."

A groan escaped her as she stood up and said, "I'll be right back." Jason watched her glistening body wade to shore, where she picked up a boulder and returned. She placed the boulder in between them, sat down and said, "My father said that by moving a rock or putting a new one in the river, it changes the current forever. This rock is you, Jason. The riverbed is me. I'm putting you into me. It could be a big change or a subtle one, but regardless, it is change. When you ride out of here, your rock will stay in me, pretty corny, huh?"

Jason wondered aloud, "What have I done to change your

life?"

She snuggled into him. "You have awakened desire in me. You've come out of nowhere and landed in my bed here. I haven't put a rock in this current since my father died. I can't predict what change it will bring. I just need change even if it's for a little while. Time is like this water, Jason, you can't touch it twice. That's all, I'm not asking you to do anything; you've already done it."

Her confession stirred him. He cradled her in his arms and she clung to him like hope clings to uncertainty. She quivered as he carried her to shore. While they dressed, she suddenly stopped and plopped onto the sand.

"Are you okay?" he asked.

"Yeah, kind of," she said running her hands through the sand. She looked up to him, "This has been on my mind lately...don't get me wrong, I don't have a death wish or anything like that, but I can't shake it."

"What is it," he asked sitting next to her.

With tears forming, she replied. "I had a cat; I called her Mama Cat because when I found her, she was pregnant. She had three male kittens. We played together and went for walks. It was so cool watching them grow up. Over time, we lost two of them, probably to the coyotes or bobcats. She got old and was on the decline. One day before going to work, I got a strong feeling that she didn't want me to go, but I had to, so I told her I'd be home soon." She wiped tears from her eyes. "When I got home, she was on her favorite spot on the couch and that feeling I got from her in the morning...well she was dying and she waited for me Jason, so I cradled her. She purred and purred in my arms while her heart raced and then slowed down and raced again, but she never stopped purring even with her last breath." She stood up and while finishing dressing asked Jason, "What does it mean when a cat purrs? Are they happy? Are they content? Do they not feel pain?"

Jason shrugged, "I don't know, probably so?"

"Well," she said, "It'll probably never happen, but you know Jason, when it's my time, I want to be held and I want to purr during my last breaths. It seemed so peaceful being cradled, being loved in such a way at the end." She walked to the bike saying, "Sorry for that, but like I said, it was on my mind."

"No need to apologize, Jasmine, I'm sure Mama Cat will be waiting for you on the other side.

"Yes," she giggled, "on the other side. Shall we go?"

"Should we wait for Katie and Loner?" he asked.

"No, Katie has plans for Loner tonight. Can you take me home?" Her grip around him brought closeness back into his life. Before throttling away, she whispered in his ear, "This is a dream Jason. I'm not looking to extend it. I'm looking to wake up in it." He pulled into her driveway letting the bike idle as she got off. After a few hesitant paces, she turned to him biting her lower lip. The rumbling stopped.

CHAPTER 19

"To attain knowledge one must add something every day," Loner explained. "You've been doing that ever since we've met, right?" Jason nodded. "To attain wisdom one must remove something every day."

Jason didn't understand, "What have you been removing?"

"Preconceptions, rigid plans, and assumptions. I strive to be in a state of nothingness. Yin is the most difficult to attain; its represents emptiness and nothingness. Yang on the other hand, is movement and action. Our society encourages movement, like climbing up the ladder of success using vigor and aggressiveness. Right now, I'm an empty vessel, Jason. I'm doing without doing. I'm allowing things to unfold in their own way, in their own time."

Jason had difficulty grasping the concept. Loner noticed. "Acting at the appropriate time with the appropriate amount of energy is the key, my friend. For example, I appreciate what you brought to me."

Now totally confounded, Jason pointed to himself saying, "Me? What did I do?"

Loner put his hand on Jason's shoulder, "You caused my spontaneity. I'm just acting to the demands of the situation you put into my emptiness."

Jason shook his head in discernment, "I used to be a pretty good chess player, but I'm not following your move at all. Could you take the Checkers approach...please?"

They both laughed. "Okay," Loner said. "When you asked about my Chinese girlfriend, I realized how much I love her. The thought of her has filled my emptiness. Now, I'm going with the flow of those demands. I'm going back to her, thanks to you."

"What about Katie?"

"Katie? She knew we were traveling through nothingness. Acting out of spontaneity rather than preconceptions, she has no problem with it. I still have an open invitation from her. How about you? What pretense did you have with Jasmine?"

Jason took an aggressive step toward Loner. "What makes you think there was any pretense? We didn't pretend there was nothingness between us. We added something to our lives. I'd rather have knowledge than wisdom when it comes to people's feelings."

Loner stepped back. The weight of Jason's words hit him hard. "I didn't mean to offend you, Jason. Everyone deals with their insecurities in their own way. I thought I didn't have any until I met you. I now realize I have been riding around the country running from myself, from my fear of commitment. You have been riding toward something. There's a big difference between the two. Today, I will be riding forward; no more looking back at a shadow trying to catch up with me. I knew there was something about you the minute we met. What I didn't know was that you would open a door for me. For that, I can't thank you enough." He handed Jason a book. "This is the Tao Te Ching; it has some good stuff in it. I think you're more in tune with these teachings than I am."

Jason accepted the book graciously; he knew Loner was preparing to leave. He concealed his sadness as best he could. "Thank you, Loner; I learned a lot from you too. Tell your China doll I said hi."

"I definitely will and here's my address, if you're ever in the area, I'd be honored to hook up with you again. I know HuiHui would be very interested in talking with you. One more thing, I'm not going by Loner anymore, I think it's time to be called Jia, which means family and home in Chinese. I have a new name for you too. From now on, I'll know you as Xiaodan, meaning little helper." He embraced Jason saying, "Thanks bro'." He released himself to his bike and his journey home. Jason watched him disappear out of town just as he had witnessed him ride into town. He felt very alone standing there. All the things Loner had said and taught him flooded his memory. His smile was one of sadness and joy.

*****

Jasmine heard the Indian motorcycle thunder past her home. Her stomach instantly curdled. She became weak as if a part of her soul had been pulled away by the sound. Her breath became shallow, her ears strained, praying not to hear another rumbling motorcycle pass by. Seconds passed, tormenting her as if she were falling helplessly in a dream. Her whole body braced for the impact that never came. The road was silent. A deep breath escaped her; she knew she was still in the dream, yet knew her time with Jason was nearing an end. She felt his restlessness and anxiety. There seemed to be an underlying need in him not yet satisfied. She accepted her role in his life and his in hers. A new love for life awakened in her; she'd been clinging onto the love of the deceased until meeting Jason. The love for her father and her cat continually preyed on her.

Knowing their time together was coming to an end also caused Jason's heart to ache. He'd never met such an innocent soul, except for Rose. A soul so deserving of love and so easy to love, he wished he had his act together enough to let it consume him, but something was tugging on him, forcing him to continue his journey alone.

She melted into his arms saying, "This is not a goodbye Jason; this is a see you later, okay? You've awakened desire in me. My life has been missing that; I believe I can love again thanks to you. You will be my first new love, even though you will not be with me. No good thing ever dies, does it Jason?"

He didn't want to let go of her. He whispered, "You're so right. Good things never die and our bond will never die."

Her tears penetrated his cheek. She stepped back holding onto his hands. A flush of cold air stung the wetness. Her voice trembled as she released him, "Be safe, my knight," and turned toward her house. Jason froze in place; his thoughts wrestling with him. A strong voice echoed in his mind, 'follow her in now, or get the hell out of there.' He wanted both. A louder voice screamed out, 'don't leave her hanging!' He fired up his bike. It shook him to his core as he eased out of her driveway and disappeared down the highway.

THE CROSSROADS

CHAPTER 20

Riding down the eastern slope of the Continental Divide humbled Jason to his core. He dropped thousands of feet through sweeping canyons that offered miles of granite peaks rising out of the dense forests as if he were a bird soaring through an endless time. The scent of pines filled the air and touched his lungs until the divide transformed into the Great Plains. He didn't know why the road was pulling him southeast, but a gut feeling filled him with excitement and anticipation. Kansas hypnotized him from mile after mile of unrelenting cornfields where insects hovered like clouds over the top of a sea of glistening green.

Two dirt bikes racing to keep up with him on a frontage road broke his corn maze trance. He slowed to wave at them. Seeing the dust trail erupting from their tires took him back to a time when he and Scott rode recklessly through the mountain trails around Shasta Lake until the sun set. He missed his riding buddy a lot.

More memories crawled through his cluttered mind. A smile broke on his hardened, wind burned face at the memory of him carrying Rose across the threshold of the home they'd built together into a foreign world of sheer happiness, and when her big brown eyes glowed like the sun when she purred of being pregnant, his heart thundered and lightning flashed in his eyes. Even Sarah, his old flame, was happy for them. She and Rose got on well in spite of that fact, showing how open and loving her heart was. They were a tight family always looking out for each other. He laughed at the time when Sarah had brought him a joint for his birthday. Laughter echoed off the deck and through the forest until their cheeks ached. He wondered if those days would ever return.

He set the cruise control and tracked a hawk that'd swooped in beside him and they rode together sharing the freedom. The wind carried ever-changing temperatures, from cold pockets of shaded areas to the warm thermals of the farmlands. Wild flowers followed the road for miles, filling the air with nature's sweet cocktail. Even the scent of a dead animal couldn't override the sweetness. The hawk kept his company until he had to slow down for a small town.

White picket fences surrounded cozy homes. Children played in yards with their dogs. Old pickup trucks chugged through town carrying farm supplies. He pulled into a gas station and sat on his bike absorbing the small town feel. He saw himself walking lazily down the street with Rose and their son in a stroller greeting friends and showing off their child. Tears began to form when an attendant's voice grounded him, "Fill her up?"

"Yeah, okay if I do it?"

"Sure, you can pay inside when you're done."

He filled his bike and parked beside the store. After buying a soda and a candy bar to mask his hunger, he sat against the building enjoying the sugar rush. The people who passed had looks that reflected what he was; a stranger in their town. The sun beating down on his leathers warmed him into a comfortable, sleepy feeling. He got up to fight the urge and walked to a park next to the store. Parched leaves on a stately oak across the street rattled like sabers in the dry wind. A raven landed near the top and began squawking. The sound vibrated painfully in his head, taking him back in time once again.

The pastor recited, "Dearly beloved, we are gathered here not to mourn the untimely passing of one of God's children. We are here to celebrate the life she lived, the love she shared. The Lord works in mysterious ways. Yea, though I walk through the valley of the shadow of death, I will fear no evil, for you are with me, your rod and your staff, they comfort me."

There was no comfort in those words; no justification for such a beautiful soul being taken away at such a young age. As he mourned her passing, he welcomed the valley of the shadow of death. In fact, he wanted to meet the keeper of the valley so that he could unleash his rage on him; to beat him to a bloody pulp. The sound of the raven's wings streaking past him broke his trance. His jaw muscles tightened as he said, "I love you Rose, and I'll make someone pay for this!"

He sprawled out on a bench and watched the people stroll by. An elderly lady approached with a little Pug on a leash in one hand and a cane in the other; she moved slowly with her eyes fixed on the ground as if she had to watch her every step. When she was in front of him, she froze looking at his boots. The dog barked at him. He sat up moving his feet in thinking he was impeding her. She kept staring at his boots. He cleared his throat, "Good afternoon."

Still fixed on his footwear, she said, "I hate boots."

He didn't know what to say as her small blue eyes met his. "I'm sorry," he said, "But they do serve a purpose. May I ask why you hate boots?"

"Yes you may," she said as she nimbly took a seat. Her Pug settled in between her feet. She remained silent as she looked out at the stately oaks in the park and a family barbequing.

He gathered she might have forgotten his question, so he asked her again, "So, why is it you hate boots?"

"Russians," she blurted out.

"Russians," he questioned.

"Yes Russians."

"I'm not following you, what do my boots have to do with Russians?"

She looked at him sadly and said, "When I was a young girl, my sisters and I had to hide under the bed when the Russians invaded our little village. All we could see was their boots as they searched our home. It was the most terrifying thing I've ever experienced."

Confused, he asked, "Why were they searching your home."

She practically yelled, "They hated us."

"Why," he said leaning closer to her, "why did they hate you?"

"They hated the Nazi's, Hitler, and even us poor innocent civilians." He shook his head realizing what she was talking about. World War II. "First," she continued, "American and British pilots bombed our region. We could see the glow of the fire bombs they dropped on Dresden day and night from our village." Her eyes teared up. "I remember seeing fighter planes strafing our town. I could even see the faces of the pilots as they shot at anything that moved. Then the Russians came. They raped the girls they found and murdered anyone they felt like making an example out of. It was so horrible."

"I'm very sorry," he said touching her shoulder; her dog

growled at him. He pulled his arm back saying, "But you obviously survived."

She shook her finger at the dog saying, "Be nice Fritz, he's a nice man." She looked at Jason saying, "He's very protective," and pulled a treat out of her pocket dropping it to him. She continued, "Yes, fear kept me alive, but our family was splintered. I managed to flee to Berlin where the American, British, and French soldiers protected the fleeing children from the Russians. My sisters and parents didn't make it to Berlin and spent their lives in East Germany under communist control until the Berlin Wall came down."

Jason felt sad for her and asked, "How did you manage to get to the U.S.?"

She formed a slight smile. "Have you heard of the Berlin Airlift?"

He shook his head, "Can't say I know much about that."

Her smile broadened, "Well, let me tell you about it. When the war ended, the Allied forces divided Berlin into four districts with each ally country getting a section. The Russians turned on the other Allies and built a wall around their section of the city creating East Berlin. They wouldn't allow anyone to enter or leave their section. As the Cold War developed, the Russians became more threatening and eventually shut down traffic into West Berlin. We were stranded with no food, fuel, or medicine. That's when the Allies decided to transport everything we needed to survive by way of airplanes. They landed every few minutes, day and night, for months bringing in supplies. The Russians were furious over this."

She became quiet. "Are you okay? Jason asked.

"Oh, yes. Just remembering things like it happened yesterday. I was adopted by a couple. The husband worked for the Americans. One day, he brought home a young American airman from their shop. I was seventeen and over time we became good friends and eventually lovers." Her smile beamed when she said, "We wanted to get married, but the Americans frowned on such arrangements, but it didn't stop our resolve and eventually they gave in and allowed us to get married. My life changed forever that day."

Jason matched her smile, "Sounds like a good ending to a

fearful life." Then guilt riddled him for leaving his family behind voluntarily, while she had to flee. He had to ask, "What happened to your family?"

She sighed deeply, "While I had six children and traveled the world as a military dependent, my family suffered under the communist regime. I had very limited contact with them. When my husband was able to get a tour of duty in Berlin, he was able to arrange a meeting with my parents in East Berlin." She wiped a tear and then became bitter. "My husband had to wear his uniform during the visit, which attracted many Russian soldiers. At one point they were able to separate us and they had the nerve to pressure me into becoming a spy for them in exchange for more visits with my family. What nerve," she cried. "It's no wonder I hate the Russians so much."

Jason looked at her frail body with pity. "I'm sorry you had to endure such injustices; I've often wondered why bad things happen to good people."

She patted him on the leg saying, "Bad things happen all the time, young man. I've survived many hardships and I've realized it's how a person deals with such adversity that really matters. You're young and have your life ahead of you. My life is about over and having survived so much the only thing I long for now is to be with my husband again. Love never dies, only people do."

He felt her pain. "I'm sorry for your loss."

She stood up saying, "It's only temporary." She fumbled with her cane and looked back to the family in the park and quietly said, "It was nice talking to you," and walked away. He watched her struggle with the leash and cane until she was out of sight. He mounted his bike and left the small town thinking getting old and being lonely didn't look very appealing.

CHAPTER 21

The Arkansas River merged with the highway. He set the cruise control and settled in for the ride. The river led him into the northern part of Oklahoma and the Ozark Plateau. He knew this country from old western movies he and Scott used to watch as youngsters. This was Indian country, home to the war for the Great Plains. He pictured himself being chased by a Calvary patrol along the river. What they didn't know was that he was leading them into an ambush. His motorcycle was a lean stallion painted for war. He smiled at the prospect that maybe Howling Wolf would smile upon him for exacting this kind of revenge when a turn in the road suddenly appeared. The bike veered onto the shoulder fishtailing in the gravel. Adrenalin flooded through him as he braked to a skidding stop, almost dropping the bike. He set the kickstand, jumped off, and cursed the Calvary while looking at the front tire sitting on the edge of a cliff that jetted down to the river. He cursed at himself for allowing his imagination to put him in danger.

After gathering his wits, he continued, concentrating on the road. Arkansas soon greeted him with the Ozark's and a road weary body. He decided it was time to stop riding for the day. When he found out his motel room had a Jacuzzi style bathtub, he almost hugged the clerk. He soaked himself until his skin wrinkled. After a good night's sleep followed by a hearty breakfast, he was ready for another day of riding. He hadn't looked at a map since leaving Wyoming and after some internal debate, he decided to let the road take him wherever it wanted. He remembered Bob Dylan's words; 'No direction known; like a rolling stone.'

The broadleaf forest of the Ozark's stretched beyond his vision. An early morning mist hovered over and coated the brilliant colored leaves giving the land a surrealistic look. The river continued to guide him through Arkansas. Soon, thick forests gave way to a fertile valley. A Delta influence became more evident the further south he traveled. A light humid sweat coated his skin. Relief came from the wind. Cotton fields stretched for miles in all directions sprouting puffy white crowns. His fantasy of being an Indian galloping across the plains changed dramatically. Now he was an observer of yet another human tragedy. He saw black people bent over cotton fields singing their songs of repression. All of a sudden, something clicked in his mind; the road was taking him home, not a physical home, or his ancestral home, it was taking him to a home that lurked deep within his soul - the home of the Blues.

His heart pumped with excitement as the road guided him north, then east to the muddy waters of the mighty Mississippi River. At Helena, he stopped to feel the power of this iconic river. Visions of Huckleberry Finn lazily fishing the banks eased him into the pace of the Deep South. Steamboats chugged by carrying with them the melody of, '*Ol' Man River*.' He remembered from history class the outcome of the Civil War was determined by the decisive battle of Vicksburg. The river was as much a barrier to the explorers as was the Continental Divide. The phrase, '*you won't find this or that east or west of the Mississippi River*', rang true because of this daunting barrier.

An emotional spike rippled through him knowing that what lie ahead could provide some of the salvation he so desperately needed. The bridge beckoned him to cross over to a past that was now represented in song. Songs of the slaves; songs that reflected the pain and misery of being oppressed, of lost love and broken hearts. He'd first met the Blues with Sarah. Their little town was blessed with having the King of the Blues on their very own stage. Mr. B.B. King touched his soul. He remembered how his facial expressions practically mirrored his notes. He wasn't playing the Blues; he was the Blues, and Jason bought a harmonica and a guitar right after that show. He learned to play by ear and Sarah supported him, often singing while he played.

He toyed with the harmonica in his pocket and crossed over onto Highway 49, which soon merged with old Highway 61. This place is known to all Blues players; the place where Robert Johnson was said to have sold his soul to the devil to be able to play the guitar with feeling. He was at '*The Crossroads,*' a mournful drifter roaming the Delta looking to pour his desolation into salvation.

Sitting on the dirt shoulder of The Crossroads, he felt Robert Johnson's spirit merge with his. Robert Johnson was a dangerous musician. He contested the very idea of America by exposing its dark undercurrents with a sound that was complicated, dangerous, and alive. His life was short-lived, mysteriously poisoned into a violent death at the age of 27. The twenty-nine songs he recorded has inspired every blues player ever since, throwing them into a world without salvation, rest, or redemption. The images of doom he portrayed in his music were so powerful it is said that it made his doom an eventual fact.

Doom or salvation! Jason felt the Delta would deliver one or the other. Maybe he could accept the loss of Rose and his son, rekindle his passion for life, create new aspirations, deal with the anxieties, the deferred dreams, and hopefully transcend his despair through the power that lurked in the Delta, and his own soul.

Old Highway 61 led him into the past. Outside of Lula, he stopped at the remains of a wooden railroad bridge partially submerged in a swamp. Decaying vegetation in murky water enveloped the air with a sticky, fetid smell. Dark, stagnant water stretched into the distance seemingly untouched by time. Jason knew this land was 90% swampland prior to the slave trade era. Unlike his ancestors, who were pushed from their lands by the settlers and the Army, the slaves were forced to this land by plantation owners to drain the swamps and plant cotton. The sense of repression was as fetid as the air that surrounded this place. It mirrored the struggles his ancestors endured at the hands of the white man.

Promise filled his heart as he took one last look at the old bridge. Entering Clarksdale, his bike took him to an old train depot. The main building was converted into a museum, a place that held the secrets of the Delta Blues. His excitement was so intense he almost forgot to set the kickstand on his bike. A heavy presence cloaked him as he entered the museum, like he was entering a holy place. His soul was creeping out of its hiding place. Old guitars decorated the walls. A guitar Muddy Waters had made from a salvaged plank of wood from his cabin captivated him. It bore the name, 'Muddywood.'

Posters of Robert Johnson, John Lee Hooker, B.B. King, Son House, Mamie Smith, Charley Patton, Willie Brown, and many other blues legends brought faces to the history of the Blues. Original scores of sheet music had Jason memorizing the notes for later exploration. He spent hours revisiting every display, memorizing the pictures and their histories, visualizing old black men expressing the mournful universe of the human soul in seductively primitive, sublime voices that could reach peaks of emotion no other race could duplicate. He felt akin to these men and knew there was a role for him being there.

An unexplained urgency forced him from the museum onto Highway 49. He headed south from Clarksdale following the call to a small, deteriorating hamlet called Tutwiler. On the side of the road, two wooden planks formed a railroad depot sign. One plank bore a large replica of a harmonica, on the other, an outsized guitar. An inscription announced, *'Tutwiler, Where Blues was born.'* Old wooden buildings lined the main street with a few of them boarded up giving evidence to the changing times. Jason walked through town absorbing the humid, stale air. He noticed a glimmer of sun radiating from a brass plaque mounted on a stone pillar alongside the railroad tracks. It read:

A LANDMARK OF AMERICAN MUSIC

In his autobiography Father of the Blues, W. C. Handy stated that he first heard the blues. A native Negro ballad form, in the railroad station of Tutwiler in 1895.

A mural in the form of a triptych was painted on a long brick building not far from the plaque. Jason walked in front of it in awe. On the left panel, a steam locomotive was entering the station; on the right, a bluesman and native Sonny Boy Williamson filled the panel. The middle panel showed two black men sitting on a bench, one in ragged jeans, a work shirt and holding a guitar. The other man was sitting stiff and rigid in a dark suit. Between the murals was a painted sign that read:

In 1903, while touring the Delta and playing musical engagements, W. C. Handy was waiting for a train in Tutwiler. At the train depot, an unknown musician was singing while sliding a knife blade down the strings of his guitar. The sound and effect were unforgettable to Handy and became the music known worldwide as "The Blues."

As he absorbed the murals, a spine tingling, religious feeling consumed him. He reached in his pocket, felt the warm steel of his harmonica, and nodded at them in appreciation before returning to his bike. The sun thickened the air into a boiling mass of humid air. The breeze merely pushed it around like a blanket dipped in hot glue. It was draining his energy. Dehydration sent him searching for liquids. Cruising through town revealed how the local people coped with the humidity. Store front benches accommodated women fanning themselves while eyeing him curiously. Children ran around seemingly unaffected by the stagnant air. Not much adult foot traffic was visible at this time of day. At the far end of Tutwiler, he found a store and parked.

The wooden planks creaked under his weight. His momentum froze at the sight of a guitar leaning against an empty bench. This was no ordinary guitar; it was a very old Dobro Resonator. Jason guessed it to be a vintage model from the 1930s. He entered the store wondering who would leave such a treasure unattended. An old black man with white hair was at the counter talking with the young clerk. The rough scratchiness of his voice reminded Jason of the old recordings of the original Bluesmen of the Delta. He listened intently as he rummaged through a bucket of ice filled with unfamiliar soft drinks. The clerk said, "Here's your Wild Irish Rose, Mr. Lowe."

An uncontrolled laugh erupted from Jason. Hearing, "Wild Irish," reminded him of the Grand Canyon, where he'd met the Irishman. They both looked at him with suspicion. He mumbled, "Sorry," loud enough for them to hear and continued to search the bucket. A label reading Sassafras caught his attention. He pulled it out of the bucket and stepped to the counter as the old man went outside with a eurhythmic stoop. The clerk eyed him carefully before saying, "That be seventy-five cent, Sir."

Jason handed him a dollar bill and feeling he had offended the men, said, "I wasn't laughing at you. When you said, 'Wild Irish' it made me think of an Irishman I'd met recently. I couldn't control myself."

"No offense taken, Mister; here's your change."

"Keep it," Jason said looking for a bottle opener.

The clerk noticed. "There's one outside the door hanging on the wall."

"Thanks," Jason said, and stepped outside. The old man was checking out his bike. He heard Jason and turned, "California? You rode dis thing here from California?"

"Yes sir." Jason said, "Been traveling around the country."

The old man's face took on a sad look. He said with homage, "My ole' friend John Lee Hooker moved out there. He had a Juke Joint in California, but heaven's been callin' a lot of old Blues players back home. Him passin' on was a sad day, indeed." He fell silent and looked at Jason in wonderment. After a moment he shook his head and said, "What in God's name brought you here, son? Dis ain't notin' but a small poor town off the beaten track."

Jason's heart raced; he remembered Rose treating him to a night at Hooker's juke joint down on Fillmore Street in San François. He declared with sadness and pride, "I've been to the Boom Boom Room in Frisco. John Lee's son is keeping his memory alive." Jason moved closer to the old man and barely able to contain himself, asked, "You knew John Lee Hooker?"

"Dis was his home. We played together many, many times."

Jason looked to the guitar, "How old is your Dobro?"

The old man raised an eyebrow, "How you know dat's a Dobro?"

"I know a little about music," Jason declared with pride. "Play it sometimes, too."

"Well, well," the man declared walking to the bench, "what kinda music you be playin' son...rock 'n' roll?" He looked to the sky, saying, "You know Elvis came through here when my hair was black as night. He was just a pup like you, searching for some soul, 'n' you know what, he found it right here in little Tutwiler."

Jason's eyes widened, "You met Elvis Presley?"

"Met him?" the old man declared loudly, slapping his knee. "Hell, I taught him a few chords 'n' a few steps. He done left here a baby of the Blues."

"A baby?" Jason questioned.

"Dat's right, son. Da Blues had a baby 'n' the name of dat baby was Rock 'n' Roll." He let out a deep rolling laugh. "You lookin' to be a baby too, son?"

"No sir." Jason pointed out proudly, "Nothing but the Blues for me!"

"The Blues?" he declared deeply, "What you know 'bout the

155

Blues?"

Without hesitation, Jason said, "I got 'em bad, sir."

The old man cocked his head, "Don't be callin' me sir. My name's Curtis, and who might you be, son?"

He offered his hand saying, "I'm Jason, pleasure to meet you, Curtis." His hand shake was firm and his long, calloused fingers dwarfed Jason's hand. Curtis searched his light eyes; he shuttered and then looked away, saying, "You got it bad, huh? Its one thing having the Blues 'n' I seen dat in your eyes, but it's another thing playin' the Blues. You know what I mean, son?"

"Yes sir, I mean Curtis. I can play the 12 bar scale; got my harp right here in my pocket."

Curtis moaned, "Got your harp in your pocket, do ya'? Can't be playin' no Blues havin' it there." He picked up his guitar, "What key you carryin'?"

"D," Jason answered as his heart raced. His hand slipped into his pocket clutching his harmonica. Curtis nestled his guitar on his lap, the varnish on the neck and body well worn. The silver cover plate glistened in his eyes. "When was your Resonator made?" Jason asked wanting to hold it.

Curtis stroked the neck, said as a matter of fact, "Nineteen-thirty four, last year for the model 36. No other sound like it." He strummed on the strings sending a rich tone through the air instantly drawing Jason in. He stopped strumming and stated, "I be playin' in A."

Jason pulled out his harp saying, "Just happen to have my D right here."

"OK," Curtis said nodding his head, "You got's the right key, let's see how you feel today." His guitar came to life. Pressing on the strings, Curtis began crooning a story of the plight of his people in a way Jason had never heard before. A submerged history of suffering rang from Curtis's voice and guitar. Jason felt the truths of the past coming from Curtis's wild, untamed longing. The ballad froze Jason. Its emotional intensity reached out to him. Curtis finished his song and started strumming a basic chord pattern. His look was one of invitation. Jason closed his eyes, raised the harp to his mouth, and started to follow Curtis's lead. The emotions peaked and subsided, guiding Jason into his sublime world of pain and suffering. His harp wailed as Curtis's guitar was drawing on Jason's soul.

The clerk came out of the store clapping his hands. Children gathered and started dancing to the music, kicking up a cloud of dust in the parking lot. The old women Jason had seen fanning themselves earlier slowly migrated to the rhythm. Their bodies rocked, hands clapped, and their voices rang out, "Lord have mercy!"

Curtis pushed Jason to the edge, running through the E, A, and B7 key turnaround. When he realized he couldn't lose the youngin'; he let Jason lead. Curtis smiled, laughed, and stomped his feet. He stopped playing long enough to take a swig of his Wild Irish wine and grabbed his metal slide. His Resonator twanged out howling blues rifts as Jason pushed on; living his blues through his harp. Curtis stopped, dripping with sweat, yet Jason kept playing. His harp howled through town, over the cotton fields, and through rundown plantations. The crowd watched in awe. Curtis cocked his head in amazement; disbelief resonated in his eyes. When Jason realized the guitar had stopped, he lowered his harp. The clerk tossed him a towel to dry his sweat.

Curtis tapped the bench for Jason to sit. He looked suspiciously into Jason's piercing eyes and shuttered. He looked away shaking his head. "When I was a youngin' my momma told me; 'There's only two kinds of music, son. There's the lords music 'n' there's the devils music.' I spent my days in the cotton fields listenin' to the women singin' the lord's music. At night, I'd sneak out to the Juke Joint 'n' listen to the men singin' the devil's music. I know the devil's music." He shook his head, "You didn't by chance stop at The Crossroads comin' here, did you, son?"

Jason wondered why he'd asked such a question, and replied from his heart, "My life has been nothing but a crossroad."

Curtis took a swig of wine, cradled the bottle, and said, "You know Robert Johnson sold his soul to the devil down at The Crossroads to play like you just did. I've heard a lot of harp players in my life, but notin' like what I just heard. Sonny Boy 'n' Little Walter would be wantin' to hear you play." He paused, looked around, and leaned in close to Jason so nobody could hear him, "You sure you didn't sell your soul to the devil, son?"

Jason searched Curtis's face to see if he was serious; he noticed a scared look on the man's face. Jason lowered his head thinking of Rose. After his silence pooled, he looked at Curtis, "Sometimes I think the devil GAVE me this soul to torment me. I didn't have to sell it to him."

He slapped Jason's knee saying, "Your soul is crying out your harp, son. Dat's good; if you don't get it out, it'll eat you up for sure. Dat's what da Blues is all 'bout 'n' we gonna get you right, son." He took a moment to enjoy the last of his wine and looked at Jason with sympathy. "Where you stayin'?"

Jason shrugged his shoulders. Curtis pointed down the road, "There's a motel over there. How 'bout you get a room 'n' come on down to da Juke Joint tonight. There be some people there you need to meet, you know, to get you back on track. Hell, I believe you gonna show them a thing or two 'bout the Blues." He moved close and whispered, "You ever smelled da Blues?"

Jason laughed, "Can't say that I have."

"Then come on down, son. You gonna see, smell, hear, taste 'n' feel the Delta Blues. It's gonna cure your demons." He stood up and patted Jason on the shoulder, "I got's to get going; hope to see you there."

Jason watched him limp down the road with his guitar slung low. When Curtis turned the corner, Jason went into the store. The clerks smile brightened the room as his eyes followed Jason. He returned to the counter with a six-pack of beer. "Mister," the clerk confessed. "I ain't heard no sound like that in a long time. The Blues needs you as much as you need the Blues. I'm buying your drinks here Mister and if you go down to the Juke Joint tonight...you won't regret it!"

Jason thanked him and rode to the hotel wondering what lie ahead. He felt like he was on another vision quest. The fan swirled musty air over his showered skin as humidity returned in the form of a light glistening sweat. Haunting visions of the Delta filled his nap. Plantation workers stripped down to the essence of elemental despair bred by the Jim Crow movement and slavery had him tossing and turning. The Blues sprung from this alienation, transmitting history through guitar strings and the rough, spontaneous, and crudely emotional voices of the lonesome drifters that echoed the pain of an older generation's cries for justice. Jason woke to his own cries and those of his past generation's. He felt a similar loss to these Delta dwellers.

CHAPTER 22

A piano rift echoed from the Juke Joint. Jason stood outside hesitant to enter; he was the only light skinned person he saw. The sound made him feel at ease although the surroundings intimated him. He took a deep breath and swung the door open. A cloud of sweet smelling smoke hovered at the ceiling. The air was sticky with body heat. No one seemed to care about his color; smiles greeted him like he belonged there. His name echoing through the crowd got his attention. At the end of the bar, the store clerk waved him over. He greeted Willie with a handshake. The bartender slid a beer in front of him. Willie introduced him to the bartender and a couple of lady friends he was sitting with. The music was so loud, he found himself shouting at one of the girls who took an interest in him and asked where he was from. She was slender and had a low cut top revealing firm olive skin glistening with a touch of humidity. Her smile was broad and infectious. As he answered, "I'm from California," the music had stopped.

Curtis made his way to the bar and greeted Jason with his customary warm hug. He returned to the stage announcing to the crowd, "Ya'll, we got's us a special guest here from California." Embarrassment petrified Jason; his face flushed as he tried to conceal himself behind the girl named Brianna, yet he felt everyone's eyes on him. Curtis continued, "He got's the Blues, too. I done heard it. Ya'll want to hear him play?"

Clapping and hoots filled the room. Willie nudged him as Brianna looked on in surprise. She winked at him saying, "Go on up there California boy; show us what Curtis is crowing 'bout."

Before he reached the stage, Curtis had the piano player hammer out a Muddy Waters song, '*Got My Mojo Working.*' They waited for Jason to start playing his harp before bringing it all together. Curtis's raspy voice rang out the lyrics, stopping between choruses to encourage Jason. Each band member introduced themselves through their instruments. They created momentum to his harp playing. Keyboard and harmonica notes soon meshed seamlessly as the piano player guided him through the twisting progressions. Jason wailed his heart out, keeping up with the bands increasing rhythm, until everyone in the joint was on the dance floor.

Brianna was at front stage swinging her body to Jason's rhythm. He fed off her movement and the band's encouragement. The song reached such frenzy and all the musicians spotlighted their instruments with wild enthusiasm. Jason never felt such intensity before. Curtis took control of the tempo; he slid into the song, 'I Can't Quit You Baby', by Otis Rush. His guitar screamed with the notes being stretched beyond the conventional. Curtis and his band played from a world only they knew. Jason watched his facial expressions stretch with every note. He escorted Jason through time, into his world. Curtis exhausted himself and with a slight gesture to the band and they broke into Sonny Boy Williamson's song, 'Bring it on Home.' Jason led the band through crying harp rifts, as if he were Sonny Boy himself.

The bass player moved in on Jason, thundering the beat through him. Curtis moved in, ripping out guitar riffs, half bent over. The rhythm guitar player followed suit; they pushed in, squeezing the blues out of him. When Curtis brought them back down, Jason felt reborn. He smiled at the piano player to acknowledge their connection, but the man had no reaction. He just rocked his head almost throwing his sunglasses off, while running the scales. Curtis brought the band down slowly until all that could be heard was clapping and hooting. Jason was all smiles. Brianna stood before him hypnotized. Curtis raised Jason's hand to the crowd and they erupted again. The bass player escorted the piano player to Jason's side; he reached out to Jason finding his shoulder and in admiration said, "Man, am I happy to hear you. You remind me of days gone by." He turned his head toward Curtis and said, "Lord have mercy Curtis, where'd you find this man?"

Curtis grabbed his arm and whispered, "At The Crossroads. This here is Jason from California. Jason," he said guiding his hand to the piano players, "this here is Blind Boy Williams from Tutwiler, Mississippi."

Jason tried to shake his hand, but Blind Boy grabbed him in a bear hug, "I can believe Curtis found you at The Crossroads, but California? You's a long ways from home, man."

"Mr. Williams," Jason said with deep respect, "I believe I am home."

"It's Blind Boy to you," he laughed. "And I do declare...you done took me home with your crying harp. Don't be going too far, I ain't done with you yet."

The scent of alcohol, marijuana, tobacco, body sweat, and humidity saturated the joint. Jason breathed in deeply, savoring the scent of the Blues. Before Brianna could pull him from the stage, Curtis whispered, "The face of love can be hypnotizin,' son. Ain't notin' better to cure the Blues than some good 'ole pussy 'n' if you don't smoke...leave 'em smokin'." His deep laugh followed him off stage as he escorted Blind Boy to the bar.

Brianna grabbed Jason's hand and escorted him to a table. She couldn't take her eyes off him. He felt like she was looking into his soul. "I ain't never seen a stranger come in here 'n' play like you did. Most people try 'n' keep up with Curtis; you had him following you all over the stage. You sure you ain't got some black in you?"

Jason laughed while sensing her desire. It ignited a flood of emotions in him that swung from guilt to desire. His eyes bore into her, "I have red blood flowing in me, but I sure was feeling the black."

"Damn sure," she wailed. "Whatever you got's flowin' in you nobody can say you ain't got's the Blues. I ain't totally black either, but that don't mind nobody round here. If you can feel the Blues, you're welcome here."

Jason wondered about her statement. She continued, "My grandmama worked the plantation just down the road. Her master was doing her all the time on the sly. She says he was like a rabbit on her, pounding her every chance he could." She laughed at the thought. "Anyhow, my mama came out lookin' like me. A different kinda Blues, if you can imagine. Maybe like yours; don't know, for sure. I'll take you to the plantation tomorrow, if you'd like. Then you be seein' my roots." Her big brown eyes signaled an agenda all her own.

Curtis made his way to their table and took a seat. Looking at Brianna's googling eyes, he said to Jason, "I got's some reeds 'n' horns passin' through tomorrow night from Chicago. They gonna want to talk to you, if you knows what I mean." As he got up from the table, he made the comment, "I saw you lookin' at that Stratocaster on stage; you wanna give it a try tomorrow?"

"Hell ya," Jason yelled leaping from his seat. Curtis walked away with his soulful laugh. He took the stage whispering into the microphone, "Don't know what I'd do without this here guitar," and started playing. Brianna and Jason took to the dance floor, bumping and grinding to Curtis's Blues. All inhibitions slipped away in the sea of hot bodies. Brianna ran a finger down his moistened chest and licked it; sending shivers down his spine. They toyed with desire until Curtis's last screaming note left the Juke Joint ringing in silence.

CHAPTER 23

The knocking on his room door in the morning startled him. He cracked the door open enough to see Brianna's smiling face. "Give me a minute," he said, "I'm not dressed."

Her smile broadened as she gently pushed herself inside. She let out an, "Oh, my!" as Jason quickly slipped on his pants, blushing from embarrassment. He noticed the morning humidity had lightly blanketed her skin with a light sheen. It glistened down her low-cut top, accenting her cleavage. Her hair was in rope like braids that fell below her shoulders, and her shorts revealed long, slim legs. "Good morning, Brianna," he said, eyeing her also.

She giggled, still checking him out as he finished dressing, "I do believe it will be!"

As the bike warmed, he lowered the passenger foot pegs and told her, "Hop on." She swung her leg over the seat and settled in declaring, "I'm glad you agreed to take me for a ride," and pointed down the road, "Head that way."

The plantation house and slave quarters where Brianna's mother and grandmother grew up was in disrepair from years of neglect. It appeared as an eerie testament to the past. She guided him through history, telling him how life was for her relatives during the Jim Crow days. "My grandma sang all the time. I remember the words to her songs; they were sad words, but the rhythm lifted me." She laughed softly as she added, "I used to play around here imagining I was a little slave girl." She guided him by the hand to the slave quarters and stopped at the door. With a yearning in her eyes, she rubbed her leg against his and said, "Do you want to be my master?"

"Master?" he answered. "I'm nobody's master; not even my own, and definitely not yours."

"Wouldn't you at least like to pretend? It could be fun," she purred. As he wondered about it, she opened the door and guided him in. An hour later, they emerged drenched in sweat. She took him to a small pond, stripped and jumped in. Watching him deliberate, she said, "Come on Blues Boy, the water is refreshing!" He stripped and joined her. While they bobbed in the water stuck together like glue, she said, "I still can't figure out what brought you here. Of all the places in Mississippi, you happened to end up in our little town. What gives?"

Her eyes drew him out. "Can't say for sure," he said shaking his head. "Got on my bike some time ago and here I am; must be a calling of sorts."

She laughed. "The only calling card Tutwiler has is the Blues. We get white musicians come through here from time to time to search out the origin of da Blues, but I ain't never seen a half-breed like you play the Blues as if you was black."

"Maybe it's not a totally black thing, anymore," he said. "Half-breeds get the Blues, too."

She eyed him suspiciously before asking, "Did you stop at The Crossroads coming here?"

"Yes, I did. Curtis asked me the same thing; what's up with that?"

"What did you find?"

His eyes grew big and he shuttered, "The devil!"

She splashed him with water. "There ain't no devil there, just echoes from the past."

He wiped the water from his face, "Found that, too."

She grabbed him low, "Oh my, look what I found." With a big smile she added, "Ain't no devil there!" He blushed as she giggled, "Don't you know the Blues originated from what us girls do to you men? We can make you or break you and the Blues is a testament to that!"

"I think it goes deeper than that," he answered.

"You got the Blues, right?"

"Damn right, I got the Blues."

Conviction laced her words, "Well then, I'll bet there's a woman involved." Guilt shot through him like a lightning bolt, killing the moment. She noticed, saying, "Water too cold for you?"

He clammed up. She looked into the sky, "Damn, it's getting late. I have a special date tonight; can you give me a ride home?" They dressed and left the plantation in silence.

CHAPTER 24

Curtis was setting the stage when Jason entered the joint. He noticed the beaming smile on Jason's face and when they greeted Jason winkled and said, "I left her smokin'."

Curtis laughed, "You be gettin' all kinds of cures round here, ain't you? Come on up here 'n' help me set up, will ya?" While shuffling amps around to make room for the horns, Curtis asked, "Did she take you to the plantation?"

"Yeah, she gave me the tour."

"That girl," he said shaking his head. "She done got's a fascination with dat place. All it means to us old folk is bad times and misery. Why she be drawn there is beyond me. Hells, I can't even look at the place, let alone goin' there."

"I guess if it weren't for that place, there wouldn't be any Delta Blues," Jason wondered aloud as he shuffled an amp in place.

Curtis stopped moving equipment. He cornered Jason, "Well, you got's the Blues 'n' you done never slaved on a cotton farm!"

Jason mulled over his words. Here he was, a half-breed in the Deep South being acknowledged by a master of the Blues. He firmly believed there was no other form of expression that captured the essence of the soul like the Blues. The emotional intensity he felt while playing with those people came from a place so deep inside him; he couldn't begin to explain it. With reverence he said, "I'm honored to be accepted by you."

"It's not a matter of being accepted," Curtis explained. "You done made your mark by your playing, son. Lots of peoples use all kind of words tryin' to explain a feeling they done never had. They don't know the Blues like you 'n' me knows it. As long as people live, there's always gonna' be the Blues 'n' like you's showed me, it just ain't the black man's music anymore!"

Jason picked up the Stratocaster and strummed it; he felt magic in the strings. "I'll tell you something Curtis, I can't see playing the Blues with any other people. When I listen to the great masters like Robert Johnson, Son House, Muddy Waters, John Lee Hooker, and Howlin' Wolf to name a few, I'm taken to a place I recognize in my soul. Now, I'm actually in the place where it all started."

"Maybe so," Curtis laughed, "but I dun think your soul brought you here for some fixin'. When you said your wife and child was taken from you, I had a dream dat the only thing dat's gonna' save you," he cleared his throat, "is the devils music...dat's why you's here; to get him out of you."

Jason cradled the guitar, looked to Curtis and softly said, "To tell you the truth, I haven't felt this good in a long time."

Slapping Jason on the shoulder, Curtis replied, "Well, you see now son, it be workin' for all of us cause we ain't heard the devil playin' in a long time 'n' the guys can't stop talkin' about the harp playing half breed; especially the way you be talkin' to Ole Blind Boy. He done thinks you's his soul brother."

"Soul brother?" Jason laughed, "He said that?"

"Plenty more, too. Him bein' blind was a gift for expressin' his Blues. Best damn piano player I ever heard 'n' he done found a brother in you."

"Wow," Jason said taking the seat at the piano. "I'm honored. I can't wait to talk to him with that Strat, if that's still in the plan."

"We be countin' on dat. You can talk to all of us tonight, cause we gonna be talkin' to you son, real serious like."

Jason's skin tingled. He eyed the Stratocaster with a reverence he'd never felt before. They finished setting the stage and sat at the bar to loosen up. Curtis mentioned Brianna, "Why dat girl always be goin' to dat place is a mystery to me. Don't she knows our cotton pickin' days is over?"

Jason smiled, knowing she wasn't thinking of picking cotton. Curtis went on, "Dat girl has had a rough life. Her daddy died when she was thirteen 'n' her momma passed two years later. Her aunt raised her. Poor girl never had a sense of belongin'. Dat's why I think she likes the ole' plantation house so much. It connects her to somethin'. I been tryin' to cure her of it, but damn, she done got's it in her head dat she got's roots there."

Jason declared, "Nothing wrong with wanting roots!"

"Well," Curtis said proudly, "you done got roots here."

*****

The juke joint doors swung open to a trio of sharply dressed men in suits of maroon, orange, and bright green satin toting instrument cases. All conversation ceased as Curtis jumped up and greeted them with handshakes and hugs. He directed them to the bar and introduced them to Jason. One of them commented, "We done heard ya'll got's a half-white, half-red man playing the Blues like he's a black man. So, this be the dude, huh?"

Jason looked away embarrassed as Curtis put his hand on his shoulder like hugging a son and said with a laugh, "Can't you see he's a brother?"

"We'll see," said one of the horn players as he signaled to the stage.

"Well then, let's do some confessing," Curtis said leading them to the stage. Curtis pointed to the Stratocaster and Jason strapped it on and waited while the horns did their sound checks.

Blind Boy talked it up with the horn players, "You boys ready for a treat, tonight?"

The trumpet player laughed, "What you gonna' do Blind Boy, play the piano backwards?"

"Man," he said, "you's already knows I can do dat. I be talking about my Blues brother, over there."

Curtis reigned them in, "Okay, boys, let's start with a warm up." He led them into Muddy Waters', 'Key to the Highway.' Jason followed his lead, playing rhythm, while the musicians took turns featuring their instruments. When Curtis didn't signal him out for a solo, Jason was relieved. By the end of the song they were all on the same page and Curtis took to the mike, "Good evenin' ya'll; you's ready for some Blues?" The house erupted. He smiled and announced, "At this time I'd like to introduce you to our soulful sister, Miss Brianna."

Jason swallowed hard. He thought she was on a date but when he saw her walking through the crowd toward the stage in a tight, low cut red dress, he lit up with a smile that could make the whole world smile back. She took to the stage amid applause and greeted him with a bump. He whispered to her, "I had no idea."

She whispered back, "This is what I do," and turned to the microphone and began belting out Etta James's song, 'Something Got a Hold On.' Her rich sultry voice saturated the joint and when she started rubbing up against him while singing, he lost all concentration. Curtis had to step in between them to keep it from getting too hot. He signaled to Jason to get a rift on and Jason began playing to her singing. He became absorbed in her, the notes ripped out of the guitar like he'd been doing it all his life. The band got behind him and the more he bent the strings, the more his life's heartaches poured out of the amps. His eyes clouded over and the guitar cried with him to the point where Brianna stopped singing; she looked at him in astonishment. The demons that had been tormenting him were slipping out through the guitar. He didn't want to stop.

When Curtis brought the band back down, Jason kept on purging to the encore of the rest of the band. Blind Boy was hooting and running the scales to encourage him to keep going. The horns joined in and the Juke Joint exploded. When Curtis was able to bring it down, the crowd screamed for more, so they took off again.

At the end of the set, the band paced the stage as if lost. They patted Jason, hugged him, and shook their heads in disbelief. Brianna grabbed his hand and led him outside. She pushed him against the wall and said, "What in God's name was that?"

Jason couldn't believe it either. He grabbed her tight and said, "I don't know, it just happened. Maybe you brought it out of me."

She hugged him tight tasting the sweat on his neck and softly said, "That's not something someone brings out of a person. You got's the Blues for sure...for damn sure!"

"I guess I got caught up in the moment."

"Caught up," she yelled. "You were the moment 'n' you got's my juices flowing. I can't believe it!"

"What about you," he countered. "You never mentioned being a singer. You blew my socks off."

She gave him a seductive look and said, "When we's on the road, I'm center stage but in Tutwiler, Curtis is the man."

Curtis came out and looked at the pair. He kept shaking his head while pacing in front of them. "You's got the crowd all pumped up 'n' wantin' more. How bout's we go inside 'n' heat it up again?"

Brianna grabbed Jason's hand and followed Curtis inside. By 4:00 AM, the crowd and the band were drained. The roof had been blown off the place and as the horns packed up, an open invitation was extended to Jason to play with them anytime, anywhere. Jason led Brianna to his motel room where they blew the roof off the motel until the sun came up. While cuddling in bed, Brianna asked Jason, "Have you been on the Blues Trail?"

He perked up saying, "Girl, if what I'm experiencing here isn't the Blues Trail, I don't know what is."

"Okay," she cooed, "You's been blazing your own trail here 'n' I'm half-baked on you. I should ask Curtis if we can take you on the road with us so you can feel how it all got started, but in the meantime you need's to check it out."

While she ran her fingers through his hair, he said, "I'd love that. Let's grab some breakfast before heading out."

CHAPTER 25

They rumbled out of Tutwiler toward Vance and within half an hour, they were in John Lee Hooker's stomping grounds. At the marker Brianna said, "John Lee was one of the most famous and successful of all Blues singers. He worked in the cotton fields with his family until he migrated to Detroit in the '40's to sharpen his trademarked, "Boogie" style blues. His daddy was a preacher who frowned on the Blues, which probably sent him north. In the '60's he moved to California."

"Yeah," Jason added with excitement, "the Boom Boom Room in Frisco; been there. It was a sad day, him passing. His son is carrying on for him now."

"Him 'n' Curtis was good friends."

From Vance, they motored south to Indianola, home to Albert King. He was known for his powerful string-bending style and his soulful, smoky vocals. Albert was also known as the 'King of the Blues Guitar' and one of Jason's idols; not just because they were both south paws, but after he saw Albert and Stevie Ray Vaughn in a televised jam session, he did everything he could to emulate the man. While Brianna walked Jason around the house peeking in the windows she said, "Albert made his first guitar out of a cigar box, a piece of bush, 'n' strands of broom wire. When he bought his first guitar, he had to play it upside down, being a lefty like you. How you can do dat is a mystery to me," she said, and then added with a laugh, "but I guess you's in your right mind, huh?"

Jason laughed, "He influenced Jimi Hendricks, too, another lefty, and let's not forget about Eddie "The Chief" Clearwater."

Brianna rubbed her stomach saying, "You done wore me out last night. I'm starving again. How 'bout's we grab some lunch before going to Rolling Fork; it's only forty miles south of here?"

"I'm feeling the same way," he said with a grin. Over fried catfish, sweet potatoes, summer squash, and onions fried in butter and garlic, Jason wanted to discover more about this girl. "So, why aren't you married?" he asked staring into her big brown eyes.

She cleared her throat, "Tried it once, but it wasn't for me."

"Why not?"

"Jason," she said putting her fork down. "I's a woman of the Blues. If your heart ain't breakin'...you ain't got's da Blues and if you's ain't got da Blues, you's can't rightly be singing 'bout it, now can you?"

That uneasy feeling crept into his gut. He didn't like the feeling and sensed impending doom. She slid her hand across the table and took his, "This is my life, baby; I'm not cut out for domestication. You 'n' I's just passin' through."

The door slammed on his budding feelings. He composed himself and said, "The Blues ain't notin' but a bitch!"

She smiled, "Now you be gettin' it."

"Already had it," he said pulling his hand back. "Just don't know how to shake it."

"By your playin', Jason. You be channelin' it through the guitar. If you can't get it out, it'll eat you alive."

"Then I need to get more of it out."

"Come play with us in Clarksdale. We can pull it out of each other. I'd like dat."

"If Curtis is okay with it, count me in."

She smiled big and said, "He'll insist on it. Let's go down to Muddy's place."

*****

Riding down Highway 61, the air became sticky with a heavy scent of wildflowers and rotting water. Brianna's arms were out like a bird's wings. Jason saw her brightest smile yet. She yelled, "Now dis is what I call freedom." As they neared town, corn, cotton, and soy bean fields stretched out for miles. Rolling Fork was a small town with brick homes that sprouted lush lawns. They found Muddy Waters' old wooden shack behind the courthouse. Brianna walked on the rickety porch and while peeking in the window, said, "His grandmamma nicknamed him 'Muddy,' because he liked to play in the mud. His playmates added 'Waters' a few years later. He emulated da powerful influences of Son House and Robert Johnson, and eventually transformed the traditional Delta Blues into da electric Chicago style blues that paved the road to rock 'n' roll. He coined the phrase, 'Da Blues had a baby 'n' da name of dat baby was rock 'n' roll." She put her hand on the door and said, "Bless his soul."

From Rolling Fork they headed north and joined the Yazoo River to Greenwood, Robert Johnson's resting place. Steel framed bridges spanned the Yazoo with steamboats lining both banks. As they headed downtown, hundreds of heritage oaks lined the streets providing much needed shade. Greenwood was smaller than Rolling Fork and Jason instantly liked the place. The people were friendly and the downtown area was sharply restored to its legendary past. At Johnson's gravesite, Brianna seemed sad; she kept looking at his picture. In a hollow voice, she said, "What a shame! He's such a good-looking man. Dat's probably what did him in though, poking around with a married woman. Poor man was poisoned at the age of twenty-seven 'n' only recorded twenty-nine songs. He should've stayed traveling the Delta from one juke to another." She looked at Jason, "I know you's been to The Crossroads. Famous place 'round here. He done learned to play from Willie Brown, Charley Patton, and Son House, but most folks believe it was trading his soul to the devil at The Crossroad's that made his guitar come alive." She shook her head, "Damn shame losing dat man before his time."

A documentary flashed in Jason's head of Eric 'Slowhand' Clapton, detailing how he tried to emulate Johnson's songs on a tribute album. He said it took him quite a few takes on Johnson's songs just to get the flavor and the notes down right. He was amazed at the man's musical prowess. Jason touched the headstone; electricity shot up his arm and blew out the top of his head. He went into a trance and returned to Howling Wolf's spirit world and there the man was; strumming on his guitar in the presence of all the lost blues players. Jason nodded to him. Robert Johnson nodded back.

Brianna touched his arm, "You okay?"

He saw Brianna from afar; her touch shot him back into his body where a huge smile formed. He stared into her eyes, saying, "He sends his regards!"

She tried to keep his look, but his piercing blues made her shudder. As she looked away, she mumbled, "You's scaring me!" His sinister laugh followed her to the bike. With a quiver in her voice, she asked, "What's dat all 'bout?"

He saw fear in her eyes and said, "It's complicated."

"Try me," she demanded.

Still feeling the out-of-body sensation, he concentrated on her soothing eyes. When he felt centered, he said, "I was on an Indian reservation not long ago...a shaman took me under his wing...we traveled the spirit world."

She looked around nervous like and whispered, "We's in the bible belt, Jason!"

He laughed, "I know; even though I'm still pissed at God, I was in heaven. Mr. Johnson may have sold his soul to the devil, but he ended up in heaven...along with my Rose."

"Rose?"

"My wife."

"You's married?"

"Was...till she died and went to heaven!"

She walked around the bike, "I had no idea. I'm so sorry; so dat's why you got's the Blues so bad?" His eyes clouded over. She took his hand and led him to a bench. "Sit down, baby. You needs to talk about it...get it out or it'll eat you up."

He slumped his head into his hands; tears rolled down his cheeks. "We were about to have a baby. I insisted on her taking maternity leave, but she would have none of that. She was a nurse on a Life Flight helicopter. They went on a call and she never came back. It's my fault. I should've demanded her to stop working. I could've prevented it!"

She put her arm around his shoulder, "We can't prevent destiny, Jason. Dat's why there's the Blues; to accept it 'n' pay tribute to the people we love through the music. Dat's our souls reaching out baby, 'n' you's soul is talking to her like I's never heard before. She be hearing you, dat's for sure."

"I missed her so bad, I wanted to die."

She kneeled in front of him and said, "Write her a song."

He lifted his head, "Yeah, a song; her song." He jumped up, "She loved the piano. I wish I could play it for her."

"Blind Boy is tapped into you. He done said he'd never heard such an aching soul like yours 'n' he knows people's souls. I bet's he'd be honored to play through you."

"You sure?"

"I'm sure; dat man 'n' you got's a connection. How's about we work on a song on our way to our last stop. Tunica is under a couple hours' drive, enough time to work it out."

"Let's go!" Jason said eager to the idea.

*****

They motored out of Greenwood heading north. They yelled back and forth the whole ride, working on a fitting song. When a sign welcomed them to Tunica, Brianna guided him to the marker of Son House. She turned emotional at the site and Jason asked, "Are you okay?"

She fought back tears as she said, "Before my daddy passed, Son House would come by when the women were off at church 'n' they'd pull out their guitars 'n' play the Blues. I'd sit on the porch and hum along; then before I knew it, I was singing to their music. From then on, Ole Son insisted on me being there; they taught me the meaning of the Blues." She chuckled, "It's funny though, them both being religious men. By day, they'd preach the gospel 'n' when the spirit called at night, they'd be preachin' the Blues. They was torn between the two, for sure, 'n' in the early days, they influenced Mr. Johnson and Muddy Waters."

Jason wondered who this lady was; who was her father? He was about to ask her when she perked up and said, "There's a juke down the road, let's go finish your song."

The joint came to life when she entered; everyone greeted her with reverence. An old patron with salt and pepper hair trained his eyes on Jason and jokingly said, "So, dis is your blue-eyed, wrong handed, blues haunted half-breed we's been hearing about, huh?"

She put her arm around Jason and added, "Good news travels fast. He be teaching us somethin' bout da Blues."

Embarrassment flushed across Jason's face. The patron offered his hand to him saying, "No diss intended, son, but we's all curious 'bout you's coming to da Crossroads."

The man's grip was crushing. Jason applied as much back pressure as he could while bluntly saying, "So am I!"

Brianna laughed and winked at Jason. She said to the man, "Charlie, we be playin' in Clarksdale tomorrow. Come on down 'n' see for yourself."

He nodded, "Damn right then, I's be there."

Over a couple beers and numerous interruptions, they were able to hammer out a song. Jason was so excited on the ride back to Tutwiler he felt like he was out of his body again ready to take flight.

CHAPTER 26

Blind Boy, Brianna, and Jason took to the back seat of Curtis's Cadillac. The air conditioner blasted away, putting a freeze on. The Caddy filled the whole lane, occasionally drifting onto the shoulder when Curtis animatedly gestured to his bass player in the front seat, who was sipping on a bottle of Gin and smoking a reefer. Blind Boy leaned over Brianna and quietly said to Jason, "He can even scare a blind man with his driving!"

With a twinge of nervousness Brianna nodded, "Good thing we's only going to Clarksdale." When the sign for the Ground Zero Blues Club came into sight, Brianna's sigh echoed throughout the car. As soon as the Caddy came to a stop they scrambled out as if it were on fire. The joint was packed. Blind Boy had his hand on Jason's shoulder as they made their way to the stage. He sniffed the air and said to Jason, "Do you smell it, son? Can you feel it? There's Blues in the air!" Jason felt it and the smell was the same as it was in the car. The horn players were on stage in their flashy dress to impress suits and seeing them approach, they helped Blind Boy up the stairs to the piano.

Curtis gathered the band together, "I'm feeling the crowd tonight, let's give 'em what they came for, boys. We's gonna do a special song for Mr. Jason here a little later on so when the time comes, just follow my lead."

Curtis set the tone by opening with a stinging, string bending solo that had the crowd hooting and goose bumps running up Jason's spine. The band joined in one at a time matching his intensity. When Blind Boy started hammering away at the keys, he turned his head toward Jason and said, "Come on son, talk to me!" Jason closed his eyes and followed Blind Boy on a journey into both of their souls. He felt the man's pain as well as his own and the deeper they traveled, the more they bonded. They were so absorbed they hadn't noticed the rest of the band idly looking on in wonderment.

Brianna yelled into the mike, "Lord have mercy!" and joined

the fray. Jason turned to her and began to follow her with stinging guitar notes. Curtis looked at the band and nodded; it was time. Brianna cried out, "My babies are in heaven 'n' I'm crying the Blues. Lord knows, I've paid my dues. I'm here at the crossroads looking for you, to tell my babies, how much I love you." Tears dripped onto Jason's guitar strings. He looked to Blind Boy; he also had a trickle running from behind his sunglasses onto his crying Hammond. Brianna was bent over further crying, "And when my days are done 'n' the Lord comes a callin', I'm leaving these crossroads behind 'n' I'm coming home to you."

Jason shivered. He looked up and saw Rose and his son smiling down on him. He felt relief from the pain. A smile formed on his face; he looked at the band and brought them out of the sadness into a ripping finale. The ovation seemed to last forever.

When they returned to Tutwiler the next morning, the motel girl said to Jason, "You's got a call from a girl named Sarah."

"Sarah!" he said scratching his head. "Are you sure?"

"Yes sir, she seemed very worried. Wanted to know what's you be doing here."

"What did you tell her?"

"Nothin' just said I's let you know she called."

He muttered, "Thank you," and went to his room wondering how she'd found him. Dozing off into a waking-type dream, he saw himself riding his bicycle past her house like he'd done a hundred times before. Being too naive to know what was on her mind he remembered how her eyes followed him until he was out of sight. In school, she'd sneak looks at him and when he'd catch her; she'd blush and shy away. They became the best of friends and the fact that she was a Tomboy; loving to ride bikes, fish, and hike, drew them ever closer. They'd share their deepest secrets. She'd comfort him when the anxiety over his closed adoption filled him with doubt and insecurity. He'd tell her if her stepdad ever came into her room again to sneak out the window and come to his house. She was his first kiss.

The ring tone jolted him. He cleared his head wondering if it was her. Adrenalin coursed through him as he lifted the receiver and sheepishly said, "Hello."

A flash of disappointment blanketed him as Brianna said, "Hey baby, what you doin'?"

He looked around the bleak room and wondered the same. "Just chillin'."

"Curtis has invited us to dinner at his pad tonight. Are you up for it?"

He scanned the room again and said, "Are you kidding? I'd love to."

"Great," she cooed, "I'll see you there around six."

*****

Curtis's home was aged; it needed fresh paint and carpentry work yet inside, it looked like an old museum with memorabilia from decades past. Pictures of legendary Blues masters posing with Curtis decorated the walls and his vintage guitar collection was stunning from crudely made ones from household items to gleaming Fender's and Gibson's. His pad was truly a guitar heaven. Curtis handed Brianna and him a gin 'n' tonic, and said, "Let's sit on the porch." The old swing creaked as they rocked to the riveting boogie woogie piano of Pinetop Perkins on the stereo. Curtis took a swig and said, "Now that boy could play the piano. He's Blind Boy's idol."

'Idol,' Jason thought. 'I'm talking, playing, and living amongst idols.' Never in his wildest dreams did he see himself with the very people who so influenced his life and the fact that they helped pull him out of his darkness; he knew he'd be forever grateful. He slammed down another drink thinking of how he could possibly thank these people for giving him hope, but now knowing that Sarah was reaching out to him while he was blindly reaching out to others brought him hope.

Brianna noticed his distraction. When Curtis went inside to fix more drinks she faced him, took his hand in hers and asked, "It's the call from California, isn't it?"

He felt like she was in his head. He looked deep into her big brown eyes and said, "When I left home, I thought I was leaving everything and nothing behind; never to go back again. But now I realize there's something that's pulling on me."

She smiled knowingly and squeezed his hand, "What's her name?"

Looking away, he blushed and said, "Sarah."

She brought his eyes around and said, "Remember when I said to you's da Blues is the product of love gained and love lost?"

He nodded. "And dat you's 'n' me is just passing through?" He nodded again. "Well, baby, I could tell you's got a flicker growing in your heart; much deeper than this gal here could ever match. Let it grow; feed it Jason. You's done gave your wife and child your soul 'n' I know's they'd want you to move on with your life."

His eyes clouded; he squeezed her hand. She hugged him tight letting his tears flow. Tears of sadness, tears of longing, and tears of hope all wrapped together. He was about to say, 'I love you,' when she put her finger on his lips and whispered, "I know!"

Curtis came out with the drinks and noticing the exchange, asked, "What's dis, should I take a walk?"

Brianna's look silenced him. She stood up and paced the porch. After a disturbing silence she said to Curtis, "Our prodigy is about to move on down the road."

Curtis's head perked up; he looked at Jason for clarification, but he too was taken aback by the comment and didn't know how to respond. Jason looked to Brianna; she smiled, but there was sadness in her eyes. She sat down in between the men and slapped Jason on the knee saying, "But you's not getting outta here without another gig."

'Well that's it,' Jason thought, 'I guess I am moving on down the road.'

Curtis's housekeeper poked her head out the door and said with authority, "Supper is ready."

Curtis jumped up, "When she say's supper's ready, we better be getting in there." They feasted on fried catfish, turnip greens, okra, black-eyed peas, cornbread, and sweet tea. It was the first home cooked meal Jason had had in quite some time and he relished every bite complementing the chef to the point where he had her blushing.

After their meal they went back to the porch where Curtis broke out a couple cigars. While puffing on southern tobacco, Curtis asked Brianna to get him his Dobro and Jason a guitar. While she was away he leaned to Jason, "I's not much a man of the heart these days, but you's got one big enough for da both of us. I's can't thank you's enough for putting you's heart 'n' passion into your playin', son. It's changed the way my band be playin' 'n' dat's sayin' a lot! You done touched Blind Boy likes I's never seen before."

Jason put his hand on Curtis's shoulder, "If it weren't for you, Brianna, and your band, I'd still be roaming aimlessly across this country looking for God knows what."

Curtis smiled, "Well, I's so happy you's stopped here cause dis place ain't never gonna be the same."

Brianna came out with the guitars. She handed Curtis his Dobro and Jason an old Martin. Curtis started strumming, Jason eased in, and Brianna began humming. They settled into an acoustic rendition of the Delta Blues. Brianna's soulful voice sent chills through the night air and Jason. He wondered, '*who wouldn't fall in love with this girl*,' while his guitar gently wept.

*****

Blind Boy insisted that Jason set up next to him. Throughout the jam he'd smile toward Jason to egg him on, but Jason didn't want to steal the show; he felt like he'd been purged of his sadness through these people and wanted to be a part of the band, not a guest that was spotlighted. Brianna's singing is what they'd come to hear and her voice reflected what was in her heart; she had the Blues real bad and let everyone in the Juke know. After the last note rang out, Jason knew his time was at hand. The band gathered at a table; glasses clinked as the toasts went around.

Before they piled into Curtis's Caddy for Tutwiler, Blind Boy hugged Jason. It was the most sincere one he'd ever felt. The man's heart thundered into his. He whispered to Jason, "I ain't never felt a soul as overpowering as you's. Thank you for sharing it with us, you's won't be forgotten."

The bass player passed a bottle and a reefer around the car. They kept the mood upbeat. When Curtis pulled in front of the motel, he leaned back and said, "We be comin' by in the mornin'."

Brianna gave him a light hug; he knew she was pulling back. He reached over her and grabbed Blind Boy's hand, "You'll always be a brother to me," and quickly exited the car.

After packing his saddle bags, he paced the room feeling like he was in a dream. He was sad, yet excited. Howling Wolf's blue-eyed Sioux legend crept into his mind. He wanted closure on his adoption and decided to head north into Sioux country before heading back to California.

*****

In the morning, before he took one last walk through Tutwiler, he asked the girl at the desk to use the phone. She smiled while she put it on the counter and gave him space. When Sarah answered the phone, he froze. Her voice was so soothing. After the third, "Hello!" he said, "Sarah, it's me, Jason."

She practically yelled, "My God, Jason, why haven't you called? It's been months; everyone is worried to death about you."

He swallowed hard, "I'm sorry! You knew I had to do this."

"I know, baby, but you should've checked in. We've been calling every hospital and law enforcement agency in the country looking for you. If Scott hadn't opened your credit card statement and noticed this motel charge, we'd still be calling." She cried, "I haven't had a peaceful night since you took off...please come home!"

'Home,' he thought. 'Home wasn't a house or a job anymore, home was in her voice.' He held the phone close and said, "I have one more stop; then I'm coming home."

"Thank God!" she yelled. "Should I tell everyone? They need to know, Jason."

Feeling guilty for his indiscretions, he said, "Yeah, tell them."

She sobbed, "Please be safe. I love you, Jason."

He said, "I'll see you soon," and hung up.

He took that last stroll through town, touching the brick buildings and breathing in the heavy air. When he returned, Curtis and Brianna were on the motel's porch swing. Curtis stood and put his arm around Jason's shoulder and guided him to the street. He pulled a CD from his pocket and handing it to Jason, said, "We recorded all of our sessions 'n' you's be hearing this on the airwaves, soon."

Jason was shocked. He cradled the CD and said, "You're too much, Curtis. I owe you big time. I came here dazed and confused and I'm leaving with a new outlook on life. I'm indebted to you for that."

Curtis chuckled, "Well, son, you done brought life to dis sleepy little town you's self 'n' for dat, we's indebted to you." His eyes glassed over, "I's not good at good-byes so be safe son, and don't be a stranger." He hugged Jason and walked away. Jason followed his image as he did the first time they'd met, while tears clouded the image.

When Curtis was out of sight he turned to the motel. Brianna was sitting as stoic as a statue, her eyes fixed on him. He walked to the bench, sat down, and let out a sigh. She put her hand on his knee and tried to smile, but her tears distorted it. She handed him a piece of paper, "This is my address; you write me 'n' let me know how you's doing. Curtis also wants to send you somethin', so please keep in touch."

He put it in his pocket and stood up. She pulled him back down saying, "Give me one more minute, please." They sat in silence, hand in hand until she seemed satisfied. She stood on wobbly legs and said, "I'll walk you to your bike."

Before he mounted, they hugged long and tight. She whispered, "Thank you baby for showing me da Blues again. We's both going on a new journey now 'n' for dat I's always love you, 'n' take care of your Sarah cause I knows she loves you too." He squeezed her one more time, nodded and fired the bike up. It took all of his will to shift it into gear. He rode out of Tutwiler with Brianna in the rearview mirror, thinking, '*Loneliness is such a drag.*'

HOMEWARD BOUND

CHAPTER 27

Jason returned to The Crossroads and paced the desolate intersection, remembering how he'd feared the devil and the unknown for so long. Now, with a direction known and feeling the devil's presence, he yelled, "Thought you'd get my soul, huh. Well, think again, you bastard!" He fired his bike up and headed north toward Memphis feeling liberated. The joy of being on his bike returned. He looked at Rose's pouch, patted it and said, "I'm coming home, baby."

The Mississippi Delta's influence faded as he headed west from Memphis to Little Rock, Arkansas, then up to Kansas City, Missouri, where the prairie states opened up to a vastness that allowed his thoughts to roam. He reached Sioux Falls, South Dakota by nightfall and got a room. In the morning he found the county courthouse and researched the local Indian tribes. The information he gathered pointed him to the Pine Ridge Indian Reservation in the southwest corner of the state.

As he sat at the crossroads of Interstate 299 and State Highway 42, a steady stream of motorcycles passed by, heading north. He wondered if there was a poker run going on, but then noticed a sign on the back of a three-wheeler. It read: *Sturgis or Bust*.

The famous Sturgis rally, he thought, and then he remembered Rose's only condition when she surprised him on his birthday with the Harley. As they sat on the bike in the garage pretending to be traveling the country, she said, "Jason, baby, there's one place I want to go with you on the bike."

He turned to her, "Where's that?"

He remembered her giggling as she said, "The Sturgis rally." He promised her he would take her. He stroked the pouch saying, "We're going to Sturgis after all, baby," and joined the procession.

He followed the bikes north to Interstate 90 where they turned west. Bikes of all makes and models rumbled down the freeway. Custom choppers with brilliant paint jobs to factory models kept him entertained as they crossed the Badlands. Rolling hills covered with tan grass stretched as far as the eye could see with mountains looming in the distance. At every town he passed, bikes cluttered the parking lots of gas stations, restaurants, and bars. By Rapid City, the traffic became crazy. Signs sprung up for Mt. Rushmore, Custer, and Wounded Knee. Instead of heading northwest to Sturgis, he turned southwest toward the Pine Ridge Reservation. He smiled at the Wounded Knee signs knowing that Sitting Bull and Crazy Horse had at least won one battle for the Badlands by defeating General Custer.

A sign to the reservation appeared and he entered. The reservation was modern compared to Howling Wolf's home. A church steeple shone above brilliant red, orange, and purple streaked strata snaking into mesas that stretched for miles. Many buildings dotted the area; worn down trailers and deteriorating homes sprawled from the center and water towers stood out like sore thumbs. He found the Tribal Center and parked. A wave of apprehension kept him on his bike as he wondered what it would prove to go in there to find who knows what. Would it change him at this point of his journey?

The girl at the counter had shiny black hair that fell to her slim waist. She eyed him long before saying, "Can I help you?"

He cleared his throat, "I hope so. I'm looking for any documentation on a legend about a blue-eyed family that belonged to this tribe."

She kept a serious look on him and said with distain, "You looking for Indian money?"

Her comment took him by surprise. "No!" he said with the same tone. "I'm looking for my parents."

Her attitude instantly changed. "I'm sorry. We get a lot of people coming in here claiming to be distant relatives of the tribe. Most are looking for money since all the casinos have popped up." She locked onto his eyes. "There is a legend concerning a blue-eyed Sioux family, but as far as I can tell it's a legend. I haven't seen any documentation detailing such a family history in our archives and I've been over them quite a few times. What makes you think you could be related to this family?"

With searching eyes, he said, "I was on a reservation in New Mexico and their chief, Howling Wolf, told me of the legend. I was adopted as a baby and since my adoption was a closed one, I have no information on my linage. Having blue eyes, I was hoping I could find something here."

"I could bring it up when the elders meet, see if any of them know of a blue-eyed family, but they don't meet until next week. Are you a local?"

"No, I'm on my way home to California."

She slid a pad and pen toward him. "If you give me your contact information, I could do some research and let you know what I find."

As he wrote Sarah's information down she asked, "Did this Howling Wolf give you any names I could use?"

He shook his head, "No, just that he'd heard of the family many years ago."

As she looked at his information she said, "As soon as I find something, I'll definitely contact you. It will take some time though."

He sighed, "I've searched all my life. A little more time won't kill me. Thanks for your time."

A smile formed on her face that revealed how pretty she was. She closely followed him out the door to the parking lot. As he mounted his bike she walked around it, her big black eyes beaming. "It's beautiful. I've never been on a motorcycle before. I could see myself on this one."

He thought a moment and said, "Hop on."

She blushed, "I wish I could, but I can't leave now. How about coming back at five?"

He looked into her soothing eyes, "Five huh, maybe I will."

"Where are you staying?" she asked softly.

"I was going to check out the rally in Sturgis, probably get a room there."

She laughed, "Good luck with that, they've been booked up for months."

"Maybe I'll stay at the Buffalo Chip campground."

She suddenly said, "Oh, my name is Dancing Feather," as she ran her hand down the handlebar to the eagle feather by the pouch. She couldn't take her eyes off it and added, "You could be in big trouble for displaying a bald eagle feather."

He smirked, "I don't care. It was a gift from Howling Wolf's grandson. It's very special to me."

Dancing Feather locked onto the pouch, "And the pouch?"

"Even more special to me," he added.

"How so?"

"My wife and child are in there."

She stepped back embarrassed, "I'm sorry."

"It's okay, Dancing Feather. It happened quite some time ago."

After an awkward silence she said, "You look like you could use a place to relax. There's a couch and a shower in the back room. If you're serious about giving me a ride you can clean up and get a nap before I get off work."

Her bright smile had him instantly dismounting. Moving to a saddle bag he removed clean clothes and winked at her saying, "I'd love to."

CHAPTER 28

After a long hot shower he settled on the couch and quickly fell asleep. An unsettling dream awoke him. He was falling in a dark space that had no end. He looked around the room and his stare settled on pictures of an old time. Proud chiefs in full headdresses stood shoulder to shoulder holding rifles across their chests. Their dark eyes bored into him. Could they be his ancestors? Was this his elusive home?

Dancing Feather poked her head into the room and noticing Jason's trance-like stare, asked, "Did you get some rest?"

He rubbed his eyes, "Enough for today." He stood up and stretched. Pointing to the pictures he asked, "Who are the men in the pictures?"

"Our elders during the invasion of the settlers; they put up a good fight I've been told, but for what? Look at our people now. We've been corralled to a small piece of land a fraction of our original home. I feel like a prisoner here and the values of the white man have been forced upon us including their drugs and alcohol. No bright futures around here! Maybe you're better off still searching, because I know my heritage and it doesn't bring me much comfort."

Her hopelessness disturbed him. "Why don't you leave then?"

She laughed, "And do what, travel around aimlessly? Why don't they leave and give us back our land and our traditional ways. Let's take a ride through the Res.; then you'll see what I'm talking about."

Jason didn't like what he saw. They decided to leave the Res. and joined the procession of bikes heading toward Sturgis. Dancing Feather had a smile that reminded Jason of how Rose looked when they rode together. She looked so happy being on his bike he couldn't help but smile too.

They entered Sturgis to rows of bikes parked on either side of the road and in the center divider. They cruised through town admiring the fancy paint jobs and sparkling chrome. Jason found a spot to squeeze his bike into and they proceeded to explore the town on foot. Every imaginable type of bike and biker lined the sidewalks from rubs (rich urban bikers), to hard core club types. Girls dressed in skimpy clothes posed for pictures and occasionally bared their breasts to the delight of the crowd, and music blared from the bars. Jason stopped dead in his tracks at the sight of an old Indian motorcycle parked in front of a bar playing Blues music. Dancing Feather bumped into him saying, "What's wrong?"

He pointed to the Indian, "I know this bike." He grabbed her hand and rushed into the bar. Searching the crowd, he found Loner with a Chinese girl sitting at the bar. They shuffled through the joint until they were standing behind Loner. Jason forcefully slapped Loner's shoulder and in a flash he found himself in a hand lock, catching the attention of a bouncer. When their eyes locked, Loner released his grip and shouted, "My God, it's you." They embraced tightly as Dancing Feather awkwardly nodded to Loner's friend. Loner gripped Jason's shoulders and turned him to his girlfriend saying to her, "This is my bro, Jason." As she offered her hand to him, Loner said proudly, "This is my wife, HuiHui."

Jason smiled at Loner and said to her, "I'm honored to meet you. I've heard a lot about you."

She returned the smile, "And you, too."

Pulling Dancing Feather into the circle Jason said, "Loner, HuiHui, this is Dancing Feather." While they exchanged hugs, Jason became infatuated with HuiHui. She was petite with a solid body and strikingly beautiful with her long black hair and eyes.

Loner hugged Jason again, "I've been thinking a lot about you, man. How the hell have you been?"

"Spent some time in the Mississippi Delta with my Blues brothers, now I'm working my way home."

They had to yell over the crowd noise when Loner said, "We're camped out at Buffalo Chip. Let's head over there and catch up on things. We got lots of beer."

Jason looked at Dancing Feather; she nodded in agreement. "Okay, let's do it."

"Where are you parked?" Loner asked.

"At the north edge of town."

"We'll meet you there."

*****

They teamed up and headed to the Buffalo Chip campground. Hundreds of bikes, tents, and motorhomes were sprawled all over the place. A large stage had music blaring and everyone looked to be having a good time. Loner parked in front of a tent situated in between a van and a motorhome. When the bikes went silent, Loner pointed to the vehicles, "Great neighbors, they've set us up with chairs and an ice chest." He handed out beers and motioned them to sit. Loner's smile beamed as he looked at Jason. "When we parted ways in Henley, I rode back home and married my sweetheart here and it wouldn't have happened if it weren't for you my friend. You opened my eyes."

Jason blushed, "If you hadn't, I'm sure someone else would've. She's gorgeous."

"Yeah, we're really happy and I'm so glad you two have finally met. So, tell me about your travels."

As Jason began to describe his time in the delta, the girls were deep into their own conversation. "So, I sat at the infamous Crossroads where Robert Johnson supposedly sold his soul to the devil. I felt a strong calling that led me to a little town called Tutwiler, known for being the home of the Blues. I jammed with some the best Blues players in the land."

Loner laughed, "You're full of surprises, man."

"I used some of what you taught me about the martial arts, about finding my Chi and using it to release my demons. My spirit felt totally alive and free with those people, a real healing time for me."

From the other side of the van, a girl's voice shouted, "Bullshit!"

They all stopped talking and looked at each other. Loner shrugged his shoulder as Jason said, "Bullshit back to you."

A tall, blond-haired girl edged into their site and stared at Jason with alluring green eyes. "There aren't any spirits. Everything you believe in has been created by man," putting a strong emphasis on the word, 'man.'

The girls looked at Jason waiting for his response. He studied her face before saying, "Sounds like you've had 'man' issues."

"So," she said sarcastically. "It doesn't change the fact that there are no spirits. No soul, no religion, no God, no heaven, no hell; we're just forging through life only to suffer and end up ashes to ashes and dust to dust."

"That's a religious connotation you used," Jason said forcefully. "How can you quote something you don't believe in?"

"I'm just trying to make it easier for you to understand what I'm saying."

"What! Are you a Darwin fan? Do you think we came from a swamp?"

"It's a lot more believable than being created by a God that nobody's ever seen. Like I said, man created God. God didn't create man! Do you believe in what you can't see, or hear, or touch?"

"I've felt the spirits of the living and the dead," Jason countered. "I've felt the spirit of the earth through our Native American beliefs and practices, and at one point in my life I felt the Holy Spirit. I've connected with my own spirit through Eastern mysticism and I definitely felt the spiritual power of the black man's music." Loner, HuiHui, and Dancing Feather smiled and nodded Jason on. "I've traveled through the land, water, and air as a spirit."

She laughed loudly, "Oh yeah, on what kind of drugs?"

He answered as best he could. "Some drugs can be a medium which allows the spirit to transcend into different worlds."

"Like I said earlier, it's all bullshit. We're here in the now, living in the moment until that moment is gone and when that happens, everything is gone unless you can show me differently."

"It's hard to show someone who doesn't believe in the first place," Jason said standing up. He approached her saying, "How did you ever come to believe this way?"

"Have you ever lost someone?" She asked.

He looked into her sad eyes and answered, "Yes, I have."

"And how do you justify it?"

With trepanation, he answered, "We have to believe in something otherwise there's nothing."

"Exactly my point," she contended.

He started pacing, and then stopped in front of her again. "I'm not following you."

"Doesn't believing in nothing mean you believe in

something?" She smartly answered.

Jason became frustrated and looked to his friends for support. HuiHui motioned for the girl to sit beside her and she accepted. As she sat, HuiHui introduced herself and the girl said her name was Rebecca. She then introduced Rebecca to the rest of them. In a voice that sent calm through everyone, HuiHui said to Rebecca, "You may be wiser than we know. There's an ancient Chinese proverb that states, *'To attain knowledge add something every day, to attain wisdom remove something every day.'* In Chinese art the space in the picture is as important as the painted area and in meditation and the martial arts, an empty mind is viewed as the ultimate attainment. This is a logical application of the theory of yin and yang, where the yin side of emptiness and nothingness is just as important as the yang side of movement and action. Those following the Taoist path are advised to empty out our minds until nothing remains. You are in the yin side, which may eventually open you up to the yang side. A mind that has no preconceptions like I'm hearing from you or rigid plans is far more flexible." HuiHui gave Jason a quick glance before continuing, "A person who constantly labels, analyses and ponders can become stuffed up with intellectual ideas that stop them from seeing what's really there. The empty vessel of Taoist writings can act spontaneously as the situation demands because they are not tied to any particular set of actions. Are you following me?"

Rebecca seemed deep in thought and nodded.

HuiHui placed her hand gently on Rebecca's knee. "As well as emptiness the Tao teaches the benefit of nothingness. It's when we practice doing nothing, or in your case believing nothing, that our body and mind should relax and feel at peace. You are so close to attaining this state, but I believe there are some things that have happened to you that have closed off the flow for you."

Tears formed in Rebecca's eyes. Jason looked at Loner; he cocked his head. They both stood up, Loner said, "We're gonna grab us some food."

HuiHui winked at him and Dancing Feather glanced at Jason as if saying, 'Thank you.' On the way to the concession stands Loner grabbed Jason around the shoulder and pulled him close, "Man, I can't believe you're here. It's great to see you again.

What's with your Dancing Feather gal?"

"I met her at the reservation while looking for a clue to my linage."

"Any luck with that?"

Jason pondered on Dancing Feathers comments about his search. After some internal debate he said, "I believe my mother was a descendant of a white woman captured by the Sioux during the settler wars. There's some documentation about it, but very vague so I think I've gotten as close as I can. At least now I have some closure."

"That's good. I know it was tormenting you before we spilt ways in Henley. Dancing Feather is a beautiful girl; you plan on hanging with her?"

"I don't know, Loner. I'm pretty road weary. I'm looking forward to getting home. It actually feels like I'm being called home. How about you? You look happy these days."

"It's nice to settle down for a change. We've opened a martial arts studio with HuiHui offering acupuncture, acupressure and herbal treatments. We're going to get it into full swing once we return home. She wanted to go on a road trip, so here we are."

"That's great, I'm happy for you. Your Indian still looks good."

Loner laughed and jabbed Jason, "So does yours. You need to settle down, get married; make some babies."

"I tried that once and look what happened."

"You need to let go of the past, Jason. HuiHui and I have talked about it many times; your relentless search for answers. We think it's time for you to allow what's in front of you to unfold. You've been drawn to this place. It could hold your answers, be your new home, your original home. Start new, my friend. That's what I need to see from you so I can have peace also."

"You're a good friend, Loner. I've met a lot of good people on my journey and I think I've turned the corner on dealing with the things that have happened to me."

Loner smiled and smacked him on the shoulder. "That's what I needed to hear from you, bro. Let's get some food before we start the party. Guess who's playing on stage tonight?"

Jason looked at him with bright eyes, "No way!"

"Yep, it seems the man is following us around the country."

*****

They arrived at their site with arms full of ribs and fixings. Dancing Feather was focused on Rebecca saying, "Life is suffering and coping with suffering gives meaning to life; it's what gives us our strength. The trick is to turn negative situations into positive ones. Each day we're able to walk this earth is a loan, we must learn to use it wisely."

Loner placed the food down and asked, "So, how are you girls doing?"

Dancing Feather looked up with a smile, "All's good here."

HuiHui winked at Loner, "Girl talk."

Rebecca managed to form a faint smile as she stood up. She hugged Dancing Feather, then HuiHui, "Thanks for the talk, I'd better get going." She faced Jason, "Sorry if I came across as a jerk."

"Stay and eat with us," Jason offered.

She hesitated. The girls nodded in agreement. "Okay," she said and then added, "I promise to behave myself."

Jason laughed while dishing out the food. "What would life be without a little attitude? I do like your spunk."

They all laughed and devoured their meals. A sound check from the stage set the campground in frenzy. Like a magnet, a crowd gathered at center stage as guitar notes ripped out a stinging blues rift. From behind a large speaker, Buddy Guy emerged and the crowd went wild. Jason soon learned why Dancing Feather was named that. She moved to the groove as if the music was coursing through her body and the rest of them joined in. A cloud of dust soon orbed over the crowd as the sun dipped over the Black Hills, illuminating the clouds in an array of deep purple, orange and reds.

The party lasted late into the night. During an intermission, Rebecca turned to Jason and said in a soft voice, "I know you've been through a lot in your life and like you, I've been confused as to why bad things happen to good people. Why is there so much suffering in life?"

Jason said, "I set out on my journey to answer that very question."

She moved in closer to him, "And what did you find?"

He looked into her pained eyes. "I didn't find an answer to

that question, but I did find a number of belief systems that seemed to console those that suffered from loss. Most of these belief systems centered on subjective religions."

She looked confused, "I'm not following you."

"Just like you don't believe in contrived beliefs, I've found people that put all their faith in these beliefs. Are they any better off than me and you? I would say so, because their beliefs gave them strength that nothing else could. I met an old fisherman who lost his son to the sea. He put his faith in God, which gave him peace. Personally, I couldn't find my answer in blind faith."

She smiled and nodded, "Where did you find peace, or have you not found it yet?"

"I started to find peace when I first met Loner. He exposed me to Eastern mysticism, where I journeyed inside of myself first to put my mental and physical selves in touch with harmony. In doing so, I turned from seeking the answer to understanding the question. My questions centered on the why of it all. Excuse my expression, but mankind has been asking that question since the beginning of time. Has anyone found the answer to it yet?"

She shook her head, "I sure haven't."

"I gave up on finding the answer. After leaving Loner, I concentrated on achieving harmony with the laws of nature and the universe, which took a wild turn when I ended up on an Indian reservation and was mentored by a Shaman. He showed me many things. I reconnected to my heritage and learned the power of nature and the spirit world, which brings peace and comfort to my people."

"Your people...but not you?"

Jason looked over to Dancing Feather while answering, "My people didn't grow up like I did. We've had different hardships, different beliefs systems to cope with life. I hold some of my traditions dear to my heart but when it comes to dealing with loss, I've branched off. I've found music to be a tremendous form of healing. Look up on stage; there's a Blues legend up there using music to share the healing process." He remembered his time in the Delta and sighed, "Maybe, maybe there's only peace in death, I don't know."

She smacked him on the shoulder, "That's what I've been saying all along. When you're ashes, there's no more thought, no more pain, just silent peace."

He shook his head in protest, "I can't believe that. There's got to be more."

"Well," she said, "my system works for me."

Loner joined them handing out beers, "You two need to lighten up. It's party time, not a philosophical debate."

Jason put his arm around Loner's shoulder squeezing tight, "You're right man, let's party."

CHAPTER 29

Jason woke to the sound of girls giggling. He looked around and realized he was on the couch of a motorhome. He stood up to a spinning head and sat back down. Whispers filtered from the back of the home, "Come here Jason, we want to talk."

He rubbed his eyes whispering back, "I'm sure you do."

"Please."

He stood slowly and opened the slider to see Dancing Feather and Rebecca cuddled under a blanket. They lifted the blanket to two beautiful naked bodies and made room for him in between them. Rebecca cooed, "You only live once, come join us."

The whiskey still swirling in his head forced him to the bathroom. He emerged wiping his mouth, "Sorry ladies, I don't think I'd be much good to you," and made his way outside for some air. Loner and HuiHui were up and didn't look much better either. Jason mumbled, "I need some coffee."

"I'll go with you to the concession," HuiHui said standing up. On the way she started giggling. Jason's quizzical look had her saying, "You got pretty wild last night!"

"Oh no, what did I do?"

She kept giggling, "You and the girls were bumping and grinding to the music all night. I thought you were going to have an orgy right there in the crowd."

He shook his head, "Where did that damn whiskey come from?"

"Rebecca!"

He smirked, "I should've known. Haven't gotten that lit in quite some time."

She eyed him cautiously, "It was like you were out of your mind; not in the crazy sense; in a metaphysical way. You were saying some strange things!"

"For me," he said trying to remember, "it's better being out of my mind. Being inside is a lonesome sound."

She giggled, "Dancing Feather sure connected to you. She

kept calling you Wandering Spirit and asked you quite a few times what it's like being 'out there.' I swear she believed you were a spirit."

He stopped suddenly and turned to her. "She called me Wandering Spirit?" He'd never mentioned that title to anyone except Loner. How could she have known?

"Yes, she also went on about a local tribal legend. I didn't understand a lot of it, but she insisted that you were a part of it."

He shook his head, "Must've been the whisky talking."

"Whisky or not," HuiHui said staring him down, "she had me believing. I must admit, I don't know a lot about Native American culture, but she drew some distinctive parallels in the way us Asians think about life and death." They ordered up their coffee and while stirring in some sugar she bluntly added, "Legends are the dead coming back to life in spirit form."

Walking back to camp, that statement consumed him. He began wondering how he could've traveled to the spirit world with Howling Wolf being a human and why was Dancing Feather calling him Wandering Spirit. It was becoming too confusing for him; he wanted back out of his mind.

Loner graciously accepted the coffee from his wife. He cradled the cup with both hands taking little sips. When HuiHui went in the trailer, he looked up to Jason, "Man, what a night!"

Jason nodded to giggles coming from the camper, "It was pretty wild from what I hear."

"Very wild," Loner corrected. "I haven't let loose like that in quite a while and you my friend showed me a side of yourself I'd never seen before."

"Like how?"

"Like a man disconnected from himself," Loner said scratching his head. "You made references to the oriental philosophies that even had HuiHui doing a double take. Hell, you just learned a little of that from me not long ago and to ramble on about it like you did last night, I was feeling like the student. And Dancing Feather, now she put a light on you that had goose bumps running up my spine."

Loner's expression and words had Jason wondering again. He felt sick; not from the alcohol, but from something he couldn't understand. Maybe he was homesick. He edged closer to Loner,

"I'm in a predicament and could use your help."

"Anything bro, what's up?"

Embarrassment laced his words, "I've found that my credit cards have been canceled. Haven't made any payments and I maxed them out. I'm a few tanks of gas away from getting home."

Loner silenced him while pulling out his wallet. He slipped Jason a $100 dollar bill saying, "Is this enough? Are you leaving soon?"

"That's plenty, thanks," Jason said; then chuckled, "I'll reimburse you when I get back on my feet."

"Don't worry about it, what else are friends for?"

"Thanks again. I'm planning on leaving in the morning. Home's been calling on me for quite some time now."

"Yeah, we're probably going to head out soon too. It sure was nice running into you again. I've been wondering about you ever since Henley."

Jason shook his head, "It's been a long road trip, Loner. I've met some awesome people along the way."

"That's what I loved about the open road, but I can't say I miss it much ever since hooking back up with HuiHui."

Jason smiled, "She's a gem and you're one lucky man. I'm happy for you two." His thoughts turned to Rose and he added, "Cherish every moment you spend together for nobody knows how much time we have in this life."

The grief on Jason's face had Loner clearing his throat. "I'm sorry for your loss, Jason. It eats away at me sensing that you haven't found your peace yet. I wish there was something I could do."

Jason slapped him on the shoulder, "You've been a rock for me, bro. Some battles are never won. Maybe it's time to surrender."

"Surrender to what?" Loner asked with concern.

Before Jason could answer, the girls filed out of the camper giggling. When Dancing Feather locked eyes with Jason, she stopped giggling and quickly looked away. He shrugged it off and asked, "Do you need a ride back to the Res.?"

She still couldn't look him in the eyes, but answered, "No thanks, Rebecca's wants to check it out. She'll take me back."

"Okay," Jason said wondering why she was acting so strange.

Loner noticed the awkward exchange and shrugged his shoulder in response when Jason looked at him.

Rebecca and Dancing Feather took off in the RV. Loner, HuiHui, and Jason lounged around the rest of the day until evening when they rode into town for a meal. Jason had his favorite dish of BBQ ribs and the conversation was light. Inwardly, he was anxious to move on.

In the morning, he quietly packed his bike before getting a cup of coffee. When he returned Loner was up. "Ready to head home?"

"Yep, once I make it over the Great Divide, I'll be close."

"It should be a nice ride. The weather looks good." He handed Jason his personal information saying, "Give me a call when you get there, okay."

Jason put the paper in his pocket saying, "Okay, and thanks for everything bro. It was a pleasant surprise meeting up with you again and finally meeting HuiHui. It was the last thing I would've expected on this trip. I had a great time and you have a great girl there."

Loner smiled wide and nodded in acknowledgement. He pulled out a medallion and handed it to Jason. "This is a Chinese symbol of protection and good luck. May it keep you safe on the rest of your journey and life!"

Jason grasped it tightly and gave Loner a hug. "I think I'll take up the martial arts when I get settled in. I still remember all that you taught me. I could use a meaningful outlet." He stood back feeling his emotions welling up inside of him and moved to his bike. When he fired it up, HuiHui scrambled out of their tent and ran up to Jason. "You weren't going to slip away without saying goodbye were you?"

Jason tried to laugh, "No, I wouldn't do that. It was such a pleasure meeting you. Now I know why Loner couldn't stop talking about you. He's one lucky man."

She hugged him saying, "We'll all meet again someday and the pleasure was all mine."

HOME

CHAPTER 30

Jason settled into the seat, took one last look at his friends, and shifted into gear. They stood together in his rearview mirror until they were out of sight. The autumn dusted land of the Black Hills merged into Wyoming and the Big Horn Mountains brought on a familiar sight. He loved the mountains and as he motored into Montana and along the winding Yellowstone River, he cherished the towering peaks and the lush, fragrant forests. Only stopping for gas and a quick bite to eat, he crossed Montana until darkness and fatigue forced him to stop outside of Missoula where he camped on the Bitterroot River. The night air was cool signaling autumn was at hand.

He set his sleeping bag at the base of a tree and made a small fire to ward off the chill. The brightly lit constellations streaked across the heavens taking him back to the experiences he'd had with Howling Wolf. This was home. He inhaled the sweet scent of the pines as the river filled his ears with a rhythmic cadence. Late into the evening he suddenly awoke to the feeling that something was watching him. His head lifted slightly only to see a mountain lion sitting across from the fire. It just looked at him for a long while. "How's my spirit protector doing tonight," he asked. It lowered its head as if sad. He pulled out his harmonica and played a blues rift for the cat until it seemed to doze off. He crawled deeper into his sleeping bag as the cadence of the river carried him away.

By morning, the cat was gone and a layer of bone chilling fog blanketed him. He quickly rekindled the fire, hovering over it as the dampness shimmered off his cloths into a misty cloud. As the radiant heat continued to warm him, he layered on his riding clothes and danced around the fire rubbing his hands together. He figured it was early enough to make it home before dark so he quickly packed his bike and warmed it up as he doused the fire. He took a slow ride out of the basin until the fog cleared, which in turn revealed the towering granite gate to the Great Divide. Motoring up the mountain, he felt relaxed knowing home was close, but as the sweeping turns intensified he focused on the road.

His nose detected the familiar smell of burning brakes, not a good sign on a steep mountain road. He braced for the unknown. As he rounded a sharp turn, a logging truck was barreling toward him crossing over into his lane. He frantically looked left for an escape only to see the cut bank being cut off by the truck. He looked right to a sheer drop off. Dead ahead was the grill of the truck filling his vision. A second later, without knowing how it happened, he was floating through the air. His bike cartwheeled below him as if in slow motion and exploded into a ball of flames when it hit the ground.

The earth slowly swallowed his vision. He closed his eyes and yelled, "I love you mom and dad," but the crushing impact never came. He opened his eyes to find that he'd landed on the back of an eagle; Howling Wolf's eagle, his eagle. Its screech echoed down the divide as it circled his bike, flames shooting into the air. He gasped and yelled, "Holy shit!" as the eagle soared toward the heavens.

Howling Wolf then appeared in front of him like an apparition. He strained at the shaman, not believing his eyes. He looked down at the fire spreading through the forest then back to his mentor, gasping, "What are you doing here? Are we on another spirit quest?"

The old man smiled. "Don't worry Wandering Spirit; they'll put the fire out. As for me, I'm on the quest with Joseph Running Pony anchoring me from the meadow. It could be dangerous traveling alone. As for you, you are now in the spirit world. The path you have been traveling is over. You are finally home, where you always wanted to be. Now, journey with me for a while, if you will."

The tightening around Jason's mouth gasped, "Maybe I've changed my mind. Maybe I want to go home." He shook his head in disbelief, "Am I really dead, Howling Wolf?"

"As you have surely discovered on your journey, Wandering Spirit, home has eluded you from the beginning and death is just a word for skeptics."

Looking down, Jason shook his head again, "I don't get it Howling Wolf. This feels just like our trip to the spirit world. Can't we just go back and start over, please?"

Howling Wolf sighed, "What's done is done; you are on a new journey, a journey that will be different for you from now on. Now you must see how your journey has affected all those who wanted to help you."

As they ascended further away from the spiraling smoke, Jason yelled, "Wait! Howling Wolf, I need to see this." A plane began to circle the fire. A man appeared in the door. Jason looked at Howling Wolf. The old man knew what he was thinking and nodded. Jason soared to the plane and hovered in front of the man. Tears formed as he locked onto a familiar set of eyes; the eyes of his best friend Scott. He'd finally realized his dream of becoming a Smokejumper. A man behind him yelled over the slipstream, "Are you ready?"

Scott nodded. The man slapped him on the shoulder and as he pushed himself away from the plane, he looked into Jason's eyes and cried, "This one's for you bro." He floated down and landed next to the fire. When he recognized the remains of Jason's motorcycle, he fell to his knees sobbing. His face so distorted from despair it became too painful for Jason to see his best friend suffering like this. He couldn't take it anymore and pushed away.

Howling Wolf grabbed his shoulder and whisked him through a series of thick, moisture-laden clouds that cloaked their bodies until a hole opened up and Jason was staring down on his parents' house. His mother and father were sitting at the kitchen table; cold, half-filled cups of coffee in between them as they lifelessly gazed out the window with drawn faces and glazed eyes. Gray hairs and stress stained wrinkles made them look ghostly. His body tensed when his mother cried, "Did we do something wrong?"

His father's hands slid to hers, grasping them tightly; "I don't know, dear. We all loved him so much. I wish he would've given us a chance to help. I hope he's found peace now."

"Oh God," Jason cried, "What have I done to them!"

Howling Wolf's chest thundered, "You may have left the very people that could've answered the questions you so dearly sought after." He grabbed Jason's shoulders and pushed him violently. The tears streamed to his temples until he stopped over the house

Rose and he had built. Howling Wolf pushed him down into the living room where he saw Sarah sitting on the same futon he'd sat on prior to his journey. She was staring into the fireplace with a journal on her lap. He read her tear splattered ink:

Jason my love, I never stopped loving you, even when you married Rose. I came to love her also and losing her killed something in all of us. I knew you had to search for some kind of answers even though they were right in front of you. You were always a bit stubborn and I came to accept that. Please come home safely, for I have saved your home from foreclosure and I hope you will allow me to continue to be a part of your life. Love you always, Sarah.

Jason looked up to Howling Wolf crying, "Put me back Howling Wolf, please put me back."

The old man threw his arms up, "I can't undo what's been done, Wandering Spirit. You should've thought of this before you took off."

Anger boiled from Jason, "If I'd only known this would've happened, I would've stayed."

"It's too late for that, Wandering Spirit, we must move on." They flew East over the Sierra Mountains into Nevada's Black Rock Desert. They saw thousands of people milling around in custom fabricated costumes. Some had their bodies painted, while others were totally naked. They rode around on decorated bicycles, in mutant vehicles made to resemble ships, sharks, Trojan horses, insects, animals, street cars, and on and on. Sculptures of space ships, temples, churches, towers, people, and dragons dotted the desert. It was so bizarre; Howling Wolf looked on in disbelief.

Jason zeroed in on a dragon that looked familiar and sure enough, standing next to it was Burning Man Dave, the guy he helped with his stranded truck. He was with Gabe, the builder of the dragon, and they were testing the dragon's fire breath. Dave was on a radio. Jason heard him say, "Did the guy on the motorcycle show up yet?" The gate person replied with a hint of irritation, "No, Dave, not yet. How about I call you as soon as he does!"

He looked to Gabe, concern shrouding his face, "I sure hope

everything is alright with him and that he shows up. You'll really like the guy."

Jason finally had a reason to smile. "Can we check it out, Howling Wolf?"

Howling Wolf shook his head, smirking, "We have more important things to do."

In the distance, Jason saw an old man with a young adult. As they drew closer, the man sprouted a wide smile. Jason looked at the shaman in disbelief and quietly said, "That's Captain Cain. What's he doing here?"

"He's been waiting for you."

Coming face to face, Captain Cain hugged him tightly and with exuberance declared, "Jason, my lad, it's great to see you again! I wasn't sure if you'd ever make it up here."

"Up here?" Jason questioned.

"Yes, my lad, a lot has changed since we last met. He put his arm around the young man, smiling broadly as he said; "This is my son, Thor."

Jason looked at Thor and offered his hand, "Your father said you'd be together again. I don't know why I ever doubted him." Thor's beaming face said it all.

Howling Wolf tapped Jason's shoulder. "Someone else wants to see you," as he pointed in the distance. Jason strained and saw the outline of a familiar figure. Excitement forced him to yell, "Curtis!"

As they embraced like long lost friends, Curtis bellowed, "More blues player being sent home and they be dying to play with you. We be jammin' when you's get settled in. I's heard the man up here likes our digs." With a broad smile he added, "Oh, n' Brianna sends her love."

Euphoria washed over Jason like it felt when he was playing the blues with Curtis. He embraced Curtis again and looking over his mentor's shoulder, he saw Loner and HuiHui. He released with such furry, Curtis spun away. Jason soared toward them with outstretched arms and a pounding heart, but they descended out of sight as he drew closer. He followed them to their dojo, but was only able to hover above them. Loner and HuiHui appeared to be in deep meditation when HuiHui suddenly cried out, "No...no!"

Loner gently grabbed her, "What's wrong babe?"

Her voice ached, "I had a terrible vision. I saw Jason falling into a different realm and when he noticed me nearby he said to me, "Thank you HuiHui and Loner, I've found the dragon and will be riding the wind from now on." Her body trembled, "I'm scared for him."

Loner sprung to his feet and paced the dojo like a man who couldn't gather his thoughts. He stopped in front of her confessing, "We don't know how to get ahold of him. What can we do?"

HuiHui shuttered, "I don't know!"

Jason tried to yell out to them to not worry, but his words drifted away on the wind. Howling Wolf swooped in next to him, "You've left a trail of broken hearts, Wandering Spirit. They will learn what they need to in due time, but now we must get back to your journey."

They ascended to a peaceful place. Howling Wolf pointed Jason to a distant figure coming his way. As the figure became recognizable, Jason saw it was Rose and he lunged toward her. They melted into each other's bodies squeezing so tight air exploded from their lungs. Jason shuttered, "Oh God, baby, I missed you so much I couldn't take it anymore."

She squeezed him saying, "I know honey, I know what you've been through. I missed you too."

Howling Wolf appeared with a bundle in his hands. Jason gasped as tears fell like rain. The old man held out his arms, "I'd like you to meet your son!"

Trembling hands accepted the little bundle. He clutched the baby sobbing. Howling Wolf smiled at Rose and she acknowledged with a huge smile. He said to Jason, "Wandering Spirit, what you have discovered on your long difficult journey is that love never dies. The love of and for your wife and child is what you sought after all along, and now you will forever be in that love. The loves you left behind will be yearning to meet up with you again, when it's their time."

As Jason's tears dried, he asked, "Why? Howling Wolf, why is life so hard?"

The old man laughed, "You'll have to ask the man that yourself, but does it matter now?"

Cuddling his wife and baby, Jason cried, "I guess it doesn't Howling Wolf; I'm home and that's all I ever wanted."

ABOUT THE AUTHOR

Ralph Ryan grew up a military brat with his four brothers and his sister. He lived in six different states and spent fifteen years collectively in Europe. After attending high school for four years at the Berlin American High School, he returned stateside and acquired an AA degree in Natural Resources Management and began his fourteen-year wild land firefighting career. Ralph served on Engines, Initial Attack Helishot crews and ultimately, ten years as a California BLM Smoke Jumper.

After reluctantly leaving Smokejumping, he gained employment with the City of Redding and spent twenty-five years in the Parks and Water Departments. He acquired an AA degree in Horticulture at Shasta College and fathered two sons, Eric and Sean. He built a home on a mountain top overlooking Shasta Lake and recently relocated to the city of Redding.

The written word always fascinated Ralph and he began writing short stories and attended Creative Writing classes at Shasta College. One of his instructors, journalist and author Tony D'Souza, saw promise is his work and became Ralph's mentor as he turned a short story into a novel. Wildfire is Ralph's first self-published work and The Crossroads: A Journey of Discovery completes his second. His third novel, Freedom, is currently in the works.

Ralph retired from the City of Redding in 2013 and is now focused on writing, riding his motorcycle and bringing back life to an old house.

www.RalphRyan.com